THE MESSIAH OF THE CYLINDER

I put my feet inside and squeezed down to the bottom

[Page 28]

The Messiah of the Cylinder

by
Victor Rousseau

Illustrated by
Joseph Clement Coll

With a new introduction by
Lester Del Rey

HYPERION PRESS, INC.
WESTPORT, CONNECTICUT

Library of Congress Cataloging in Publication Data

Emanuel, Victor Rousseau, 1879-
    The messiah of the cylinder.

    I.   Title.
PZ3.E526M4 [PS3509.M17]   813'.5'2   73-13264
ISBN 0-88355-118-7
ISBN 0-88355-147-0 (pbk.)

Published in 1917
by A. C. McClurg & Co., Chicago
Copyright 1917
by A. C. McClurg & Co.

Copyright © 1974 by Hyperion Press, Inc.

Hyperion reprint edition 1974

Library of Congress Catalogue Number 73-13264

ISBN 0-88355-118-7 (cloth ed.)
ISBN 0-88355-147-0 (paper ed.)

Printed in the United States of America

A NEGLECTED MASTERPIECE

By Lester Del Rey

Victor Rousseau's *Messiah of the Cylinder* may be one of the most important seminal works in the field of speculative fiction. Yet it has been almost totally neglected by critics and historians of the field. Perhaps that is because it is emotionally less simplistic than its successors. It is an anti-utopia (or *dystopia*) that does not pursue despair remorselessly from beginning to end.

The anti-utopia is, of course, the opposite of the far older utopia. Some trace the beginnings of utopian literature as far back as Plato's *Republic*, others to 1516 when Sir Thomas More's *Utopia* was published and gave its name to a distinctly new genre of imaginative writing. For centuries, the literary utopia was a major part of all speculative or futuristic fiction. It reached its peak in Bellamy's *Looking Backwards* and some of the writing of H.G. Wells. Essentially, it was sugar-coated propaganda, usually designed to sell some single idea that would make the world perfect; and the story content was generally minimal — since how can you have conflict in a perfect world? There has been little utopian literature written in the twentieth century, and most of it has been unsuccessful.

Though the anti-utopia has been a comparatively recent development, two books with anti-utopian themes have achieved major importance in this century: Huxley's *Brave New World* and Orwell's *1984*. Both works are concerned with political power, unlike the earlier anti-utopias of Wells (*When the Sleeper Wakes*) and E.M. Forster (*When the Machine Stops*).

And it is the anti-utopia of political power without moral controls that we find in the pioneering novel of Victor Rousseau. So far as I can determine, *Messiah of the Cylinder* is the first book of this type, the true ancestor of Huxley and Orwell. It is curious, therefore, that the major study of the field — *The Future as Nightmare* by Mark R. Hillegas — should totally neglect Rousseau. In it, I cannot find one line or footnote referring to Rousseau!

Obviously, the republication of this important pioneer work is long overdue.

Rousseau's novel is also seminal in another, though lesser, field. One type of science fiction that has long been popular is the revolution against some all-controlling dictatorship by a small band of rebels — often led by a hero who has somehow come out of the past to save the future. This is the basic plot structure of Rousseau's novel.

In many ways, however, *Messiah of the Cylinder* is actually more logical than many later science fiction works constructed around this theme. Most depict a hero who almost single-handedly conquers some world power; Rousseau's Arnold is a human being, with doubts and indecisions, who must depend on elements within the future world he finds. We also know from history that most revolutions aren't the end of things — that the fanaticism of such revolutions produces an aftermath of turmoil and horror. Again, Rousseau is more logical; his revolution is led from within and from without, leaving an outside control factor that can prevent such later excesses.

Another yardstick by which we measure an early work of science fiction that deals with the future world is the prophetic light it casts on the real future. (I consider this unfair, however. Science fiction isn't intended to predict *the* future, but rather to depict *a* future consistently and interestingly.) In this area, Rousseau comes off extremely well, if we'll grant him the simple courtesy of not demanding full explanations for all his inventions and developments.

For example, in his future we find the widespread use of frozen foods — something that seems common now but was neglected in most early novels about the future. Rousseau also anticipated talking movies, and even added 3-D effects. Picture images are transmitted over the public telephone system, though there was no sign of television when he wrote his novel. Its prescient author also described aircraft that perform like helicopters — his air fleets are able to hover over a fixed area. And most surprising and startling are his descriptions of rays of energy that behave exactly like laser beams — in fact, his weapons of the future utilizing these rays have all the powers and limitations of today's ultra-powerful lasers.

Rousseau also carries his adventures into the future by means of suspended animation through freezing — the only method that currently offers any hope for success in this area. And his future world is ahead of ours in its use of solar energy (a surprising innovation at a time when the internal combustion engine seemed the key to the future, before pollution became a danger). Immortality is also developed in theory, though never put into practice as a medical treatment.

When it comes to predictions about the world's political future, however, Rousseau is off the mark. Though his hero rants against the Marxist state, it is America and Britain that are depicted as Marxist nations. Russia, on the other hand, is held up as the prime example of a true Catholic, anti-Marxist country.

When this novel was written (it was first published as a magazine serial almost sixty years ago), those assumptions seemed more logical than what really happened later. The United States and Britain were then the world's most highly industrialized nations, where the political organizations of the emerging working classes seemed likely to gain power and establish some form of socialism. Autocratic, conservative Russia, by contrast, appeared the least likely place in the world to go Marxist — that is, until the unexpected outbreak of the Russian Revolution. The unforeseen in the political fortunes and destinies of nations has constantly ruined the predictions of even the wisest of political seers, and Rousseau is no more in error here than most of his contemporaries. For that matter, from his position on the political spectrum, modern England would probably be viewed as a Marxist-socialist state, so there is some question as to whether he'd think of himself in error for having chosen it as the site of his conflict.

The important question for most readers, however, is how well the novel stands up as a story, disregarding its prophecies of the future and its importance in the development of anti-utopian literature. And the answer is that it stands up very well indeed.

The story evolves around the conflict of ideologies

and ideas, as personified by the humanistic-centered Arnold and the mechanistic pragmatism of Lazaroff. The conflict is well developed in early discussions. Then it is carried to the active level in another time frame when Lazaroff, by means of suspended animation, projects Arnold and himself into the future. Arnold wakes up after about a century to find that Lazaroff (now known as Sanson) has awakened thirty-five years earlier and has shaped that future with his ideas. And there they are plunged into conflict again, this time in a war between Sanson's controlled state dictatorship and those who cling to the old values of man, personified by the revived Arnold who becomes a symbol, or a so-called Messiah, around whom the anti-Sanson forces rally.

But the clash is not presented in oversimplified terms. Rousseau has portrayed a complex world driven by global political divisions as well as by power struggles within future England. Arnold is still limited by his doubts — and even Sanson has moments when he doubts himself, or when power alone isn't enough. There's a love-hate relationship between the two men from the common past that gives an emotional depth to the story beyond that found in many later novels that appear outwardly similar.

There's also a love story, in which the two men both seek to win Esther, another character sent into the future with Arnold and Sanson. The romantic elements tend to be Victorian and are the weakest parts of the story. Esther is endowed with little personality or character — she's simply the beloved female.

Yet there's probably a valid symbological reason for her presence. Sanson is a symbol of the present — a man who demands everything in his *now*; Arnold represents the morality of the past — tradition, culture, all that man has learned of good in thousands of years; and, in a way, Esther is the future — the promise of fulfillment and good that leads men to strive.

We can't accept love today as so unalloyed, so sacred, so pure — but perhaps that is because we've lost something Rousseau was fighting to save; perhaps we've come too far toward the world stripped of ideals as things to be cherished for themselves. He would almost certainly think so.

In essence, this is a novel about good and evil, as all important fiction is. Rousseau's concepts of good and evil are defined in a way that may seem hard for many readers to accept; the values of Catholic Christianity are equated with good; those of Marxist statism as set forth by his *bete noir*, "the prophet Wells", are considered evil. But these are only his symbols for something much deeper. His words are parochial, his message universal. He is fighting for the good to be found in individual human dignity and the spiritual search for a richer internal life; he is opposing imposed regulations that may promote order in the state but curb other freedoms, and he is against all kinds of pragmatism without idealism, He is, in essence, asking for a triumph of morality over self-interest.

In this sense, Rousseau's novel is as relevant today as when it was first written — perhaps even more so. Today's newspapers are filled with stories of that same conflict between morality and narrow self-interest at the highest level of government. Our young people are protesting against the incursion of narrow pragmatism into our entire culture, at the expense of morality. Perhaps we cannot define the battle of beliefs and ideas as narrowly as seemed possible to Rousseau. But we still view the issues posed in his book as being of central importance; and this was as true of societies of the past as it will be in those yet unrealized futures we continue to speculate about.

In the history of science fiction, Victor Rousseau's *Messiah of the Cylinder* occupies a special niche. It has been too long out of print. I hope this new edition wins it a new legion of readers and the recognition in deserves.

CONTENTS

Contents

ILLUSTRATIONS

Illustrations

THE MESSIAH OF THE CYLINDER

The Messiah of the Cylinder

CHAPTER I

OVER THE COFFEE CUPS

IF I recall the conversation of that evening so minutely as to appear tedious, I must plead that this was the last occasion on which I saw Sir Spofforth alive. In such a case, one naturally remembers incidents and recalls words that otherwise might have been forgotten; besides, here were the two opposed opinions of life, as old as Christianity, confronting each other starkly. And, as will be seen, the test was to come in such manner as only one of us could have imagined.

I picture old Sir Spofforth as on that evening: courteous, restrained, yet with the heat of conviction burning in his measured phrases; and Esther listening with quaint seriousness, turning from her father to Lazaroff and back, and sometimes to me, as each of us spoke. Outside, in the moonlight, the shadow of the Institute lay black across the garden of Sir Spofforth's house. The dining-room was fragrant with the scent of the tea-roses that grew beneath the windows.

1

The Biological Institute was less than five years old, but the London smoke, which drifted beyond Croydon, already had darkened the bright-red bricks to a tolerable terra cotta. The ivy had grown a good way up the walls. The Institute was accommodating itself to the landscape, as English buildings had the knack of doing. Lazaroff and I had been there under Sir Spofforth since the foundation, and there never had been any others upon the staff, the Institute being organized for specialized work of narrow scope, though of immense perspective.

It was devoted to private research into the nature of life, in the application of the Mendelian law to vertebrates. The millionaire who had endowed it for this purpose and then died opportunely, had not had time to hamper us with restrictions. Next to endowing us, his death was, perhaps, the most imaginative thing that he had ever accomplished. The Government concerned itself only about our vivisection certificates. But our animal experimentation was too innocuous for these to be much more than a safeguard. Carrel's investigations in New York, a year or two before, had shown the world that cell and tissue can not only survive the extinction of the general vital quantity, but, under proper conditions, proliferate indefinitely. We were investigating tissue life, and our proceedings were quite innocuous.

It will be seen that we already had gotten away from Mendel, though we did breed Belgian hares, whose disappearance always caused Esther distress, and we made fanciful annotations inside ruled margins about "agoutis" and "allelomorphs."

I am conscious now that we worked constantly under a sense of constraint; there was an unnecessary secrecy in all our plans and actions. Why? I think, when I look back, that it was not because of what we were doing, but rather of what it might become necessary some day to do. The work was so near to sacrilege — I mean, we viewed the animal structure as a mechanism rather than as a temple. That, of course, was then the way of all biologists; but that, I think, was the cause of our rather furtive methods. We were hot on the trail of the mystery of life, and never knew upon what intimacies we might stumble. We sought to discover how and where consciousness is born out of unconscious tissue vitality. Lazaroff had the intuition of genius, and his inductions were amazing. Still, that problem baffled him.

"Pennell," I hear him say, "at a certain period of growth, when millions of cells, working cooperatively, have grouped themselves in certain patterns, completing the design, consciousness comes into play. Why? Is it a by-product, the creak that accompanies the wheel? But Nature produces nothing in vain. Then why should we know that we exist? Why?"

Lazaroff was a Prussian Pole, I believe, though he spoke half a dozen languages fluently. Keen and fanatical, daring, inflexible, he seemed to me the sort of man who would welcome the chance to proclaim a Holy War for Science and die in the front rank. He had the strange old German faith that was called monism, and his hope for the human race was as strong as his contempt for the man of our day.

"The race is all, Pennell," I hear him say again. "We of this age, who pride ourselves on our accomplishments, are only emerging from the dawn of civilization. We are still encumbered with all the ghostly fears that obsessed our ancestors of the Stone Age. But others will build the Temple of Truth upon the foundations that we are rearing. Oh, if I could have been born a hundred years ahead! For the change is coming fast, Pennell!"

And, when I professed to doubt the nearness of that change: "If your frontal area varied by only five centimeters, Pennell, you would believe. That is your tragedy, to fall short of the human norm by five centimeters of missing forehead."

I can see his well-proportioned figure, and the mane of black hair thrown back; the flashing eyes. Animated by religious impulse, Lazaroff would have gone to the stake as unconcernedly as he would cer-

tainly have burned others. He had invented a system of craniometry by which he professed to discover the mentality of his subject, and I was his
first.

Certainly the conditions were ideal for our work.
We were both young men, enthusiasts; and Sir Spofforth Moore, our chief, was nearing eighty. The
Trustees had picked him for the post because of his
great name in the medical world. He was an ideal
chief. He interfered with us no more than the
Trustees did. He asked for no results. The Institute existed only for patient research. Yes, the
millionaire had certainly displayed imagination for
a millionaire, and it was fortunate that he died before his hobby, whose inception came to him, I
believe, from reading sensational newspaper articles,
grew into an obsession.

The Trustees refused to accept Sir Spofforth's
resignation when he became infirm. He lent the
Institute dignity and prestige. I doubt whether he
knew much of Mendelism, or had followed the work
of the past five years. He knew little of what we
were doing, and initialed our vouchers without ever
demurring. Of course he tried to keep in touch with
us, and I will confess that our routine work was
mainly a cover for the daring plan that Lazaroff
had, bit by bit, outlined to me.

"You see, Pennell," he explained in self-justification, "the work must be done. And where are there such opportunities as here? Science cannot be bound by the provisions of a dead man's deed. It is not likely that Sir Spofforth would object, either, but the Trustees might have intelligence enough to pick up the idea from the quarterly reports if we were entirely frank, and a biologist with imagination is called a charlatan. And we must work quickly, while we have this chance. When Sir Spofforth dies the Trustees will probably pick some fussy little busybody who will want to poke his nose into everything and take personal charge. Then — what of our experiment?"

The idea aroused me to as much enthusiasm as Lazaroff. And yet there was disappointment in the knowledge that we should never know the results of it.

In brief, Lazaroff's scheme was this: If animal tissues, removed from the entire organism, can exist in a condition of suspended vitality for an indefinite time, at a temperature suited to them in conditions which forbid germ life to flourish, why not the living animal? Lazaroff had selected three monkeys from among our stock for the experiment. They were to be sealed each in a vacuum cylinder of special design, and left for a century.

"The more I think about the plan, the more enthusiastic I become, Pennell," Lazaroff cried. "If the unconscious cell life survives indefinitely, why not the entire organism plus consciousness?"

"Much may happen in a hundred years, Lazaroff," I answered.

"True, Pennell. But they will never find the vault. Even now, before it is sealed, it would not be looked for, built as it is into the cellar wall beneath the freezing-plant. It was to this end, you know, that I brought down workmen from London, instead of employing local talent. Well — we shall leave papers. Earthquakes and revolutions may happen overhead, but a hundred years hence, when the papers are opened, a search will be made. Our traveling simians will be found by a very different world, I assure you, Pennell!"

He had the light of an enthusiast in his eyes, and his mood aroused my own imagination.

"What use is that, Lazaroff?" I cried. "We shall not know the results of our experiment. And what message can monkeys carry to that world concerning ours? If monkeys, why not men?"

He looked at me fixedly, smiling ever so little, and I perceived that he had drawn the expression of that thought out of the depths of my own mind by his strong will. Now he nodded in approbation.

"Pennell —" he began, with hesitation, "do you want to know why I myself do not — ?" He stopped. "I am almost ashamed to tell you what it is that makes me wish to live out my life among my contemporaries," he continued. "How strong the primal instincts are in all of us, Arnold! Nature, with her blind, but perfectly directed will, warring on mind, and mind rising slowly to dominate her, armed, as she is, with her dreadful arsenal of a thousand superstitions, instincts, terrors. It is a fearful battle, Arnold, and many of us fall by the way."

He turned aside abruptly, as if he regretted the half-confidence. I thought I knew what he meant, and I was stirred too.

We dined that night with Sir Spofforth and Esther in their new house within a stone's throw of the Institute. Esther was the only child; her mother had died during her infancy. We four had been intimates during the whole five years of the Institute's existence; strangely alone, we four, in the busy Surrey town. The memory of that last night is the most poignant that remains to me. How far away it seems, and how long ago! If I could have known then that our companionship was ended!

The argument to which I have referred began after dinner, over our coffee. It was our usual hour for disputations, but they had never been so keen, nor Lazaroff so outspoken. Sir Spofforth was a man of the old school of thought, religious, tolerant, and withal more disquieted than he himself was aware, by the dominant materialism of the younger men; and Lazaroff had all the tactlessness of his Jena training. There were rumors of war with Germany, but Sir Spofforth was too old to adjust his mind immediately to this conception. He grew heated, as always, on the cynical scheme of the democratic government, dictated by its greed for power, to force Ulster beneath an alien yoke, upon the loud and stunning silence of our English pacifists and lovers of oppressed nations where their sincerity would be best proved. He deplored the new and dangerous doctrines that were permeating society, the decay of morals, the loss of reverence and pride in service. Civilization, he said, seemed dying, and democracy its murderer.

"Dying! It is still struggling in its birth throes!" cried Lazaroff impetuously. "I grant that the democracy of today has proved its futility. But there is a new democracy to come. We are enslaved by the traditions of the past, by a worn-out religious system based upon the primitive animistic notion of a soul. There is the fatal weakness of our democracy. Science has never found the smallest trace of a soul; on the contrary, we know beyond doubt that we live in a mechanistic universe of absolute determinism."

I see Sir Spofforth's tolerant, yet eager look as he answered him.

"I grant you that the soul is not to be found in the dissecting-room, Herman," he answered. "I, as you know, have devoted my life to the empirical investigation of truth, and I do not decry the method. But you cannot ignore the interior way of analysis, through the one thing we know most intimately — consciousness."

"A by-product of matter," answered Lazaroff contemptuously. "Or, if we want to be precisely true, the sum and substance of cell consciousness."

"Well, throw the blame on the cell, then, in the modern fashion," said Sir Spofforth, smiling. "I doubt, though, whether you have solved the one big problem by creating some million smaller ones. On the contrary, you are postulating a hierarchy of intelligences, quite in the Catholic fashion. If brain consciousness is not a specialized form of omniscient consciousness, how does the brainless amoeba find its food and engulf it, or the vine its supports? If you have robbed us of the abortive hope of saving the little empire of the brain beyond the change of death — and I deny even that entirely — some of us have identified consciousness with a non-material personality functioning through all life and fashioning it."

"Vitalism!" scoffed Lazaroff.

I watched Esther's eager face as she looked from one speaker to the other. Sir Spofforth seemed more agitated than the situation warranted, and I saw him glance at his daughter a little nervously before he answered.

"Herman, I repeat that I have given my life to scientific investigation," he replied. "But I have always recognized the validity of the metaphysical inquiry. I believe Faith and Science have found their paths convergent. Lodge thinks so, too. Kelvin took that stand. James, your great psychologist, shifted before he died. Science must confine her activities within their natural bounds and not seek to play a pontifical part, or the excesses of the Scholastics will be repeated in a new and darker age."

"I cannot agree with you," cried Lazaroff vehemently. "An age is dawning when, relieved from their chains, men will look open-eyed into Nature to learn her secrets. Today civilization is being choked to death by the effete, the defective, whom a too benign humanitarianism suffers to live beneath the shelter of a worn-out faith. The fearful menace of a race of defectives has laid hold of the popular imagination. Soon we shall follow the lead of progressive America, and forbid them to propagate their kind. Here any statesman who dared suggest sterilization would be hounded from office. But England is awakening.

"It will go, that relic of degrading, savage superstition called the soul, the barbarous legacy of the ages enshrined in a hundred fairy stories. Science will rule. Man will be free. The logical State, finely conceived by Wells, without its rudimentary appendixes and fish-gills, will be the nation of the future. For we are outgrowing childish things. Man is coming of age. If only I could live to see it! But I was born a century too soon!''

The expression on Lazaroff's face at that moment was so singular that I could not take my eyes away from it.

"It will be a world of physical and mental perfection, too," he cried. "Of free men and women, freely mating, separating when the mating impulse is dead —"

"Yes, he is right, Father," Esther interposed eagerly. "Whatever else may come, the hour of woman's liberation is striking."

"That hour struck many times in the ancient world, my dear," her father answered. "And it brought, not liberation, but slavery." He turned to Lazaroff. "You want a world of men and women reared like prize cattle and governed by laws as mechanistic as your universe," he said. "Well, Herman, you have had that world. That was the pre-Christian world. Your free love, your eugenics has been tried in Rome, in Sparta, in many an ancient kingdom. And we know what those civilizations were.

"If you eugenists only knew the dreadful crop of dragon's teeth that you are scattering today upon the fertile soil of the unthinking mind! Because we, fortunately, live in the millennial lull of a transitional age, you think that human nature has changed; that the fury of the Crusades will never be renewed in fantastic social wars, and the madness of religious fratricide in the madness of Science become Faith. All the old evils are lying low, lurking in the minds of men, ready to spring forth in all their ancient fury when the wise and illogical compromises, evolved through centuries of experience, have been discarded. I sometimes think that Holy Russia has man's future in her charge. For without Christianity the moral nature of man will be where it has been in ages past. Social and economic readjustments leave it unchanged."

"A religion of slaves, of the weak and incompetent," said Lazaroff loudly.

"You think, then, that human passions have become emulsified by education? What a delusion!"

"Unquestionably. Permit me to refer to myself as an example of the crass materialist. For I do not believe in anything but matter. Matter is soul, as Hæckel proves. Yet, I am not on that account a man of base impulses. I do not want to wound, to kill, to steal, to torture —"

"Are you quite sure you know yourself, Herman?"

"But I utterly reject the efficacy of your Christianity, except in this low order of civilization. It is a dead faith, with its foolish miracles, its preposterous and unscientific dualism."

"And I say," cried Sir Spofforth, rising out of his chair, "that it is precisely the Christian norm, the unattainable ideal of Christ, working in the human heart, that has freed civilization from cruelty and shame. Why, look backward before Christ lived, and forward: don't you see that we are actually indwelling in Him, according to His promise? Think of the Christians burned as living torches in Nero's time, and read the writings of contemporary Romans, men of disciplined lives and a mentality as great as ours. Read Pliny, Tacitus, Seneca; read of the hopelessness of life when Rome was at her highest, and see if this stirred them. Picture Marcus Aurelius, the noble Stoic, presiding over the amphitheater. Study the manners and morals of Athens when her light burned most brightly. Contrast a thousand years of man's abasement, and try to set the Inquisition against that.

"Future ages will say this: that nobody, not one of our statesmen saw the course that had been set when the civil State was first established. Never before in history had tribe or nation existed but grew up round the focus of some god. The churchless State is a body without a soul. Warnings multiply — in France and in America — but who can read them? When religion goes, the spirit of the race is dying.

It is just the ideal of Christ, enshrined in the minds
of a few leaders of character and trained conviction,
that has kept the world on its slow course of progress.   And nothing else saves us from the unstable
tyrannies of ancient days."

I was so stirred by Sir Spofforth's eloquence that
I clapped my hands vigorously, although I did not
wholly agree with him.   Esther was staring at
Lazaroff; she was partly convinced and wanted him
to answer her father.   But Lazaroff, ignoring her
gaze, scowled at me across the table.

"So you are of the same mind, are you, Pennell?"
he asked, not trying to disguise his sneer.   "And
you don't imagine that it is your missing five centimeters?   Well, I hope that you may have your
chance to find out for yourself.   I hope you may,
indeed."   He nodded and smiled in a rather evil
fashion.

"Well, I must really offer you all an apology,"
said Sir Spofforth, penitently.   "Enough of these
debatable subjects for a week at least.   We two shall
never agree on politics or religion, Herman.   Let
us go upstairs."

CHAPTER II

SINCE Sir Spofforth was a little infirm, and leaned on my arm to make his slow ascent of the stairs, we entered the drawing-room a full minute after the others. The room was empty; Esther and Lazaroff had gone into the big conservatory that opened out of the south side. I heard the rustle of the girl's dress as she moved among the palms, and Lazaroff speaking earnestly in a low voice.

"Sit down, Arnold," said Sir Spofforth, subsiding stiffly into his arm chair. "Thank you, my boy. I feel old age coming swiftly upon me nowadays. No, I am not self-deceived. It is strange, this sense of the daily diminution of the physical powers, and not at all unpleasant, either. It seems familiar, too, as if one had passed through it plenty of times before. It is something like bedtime, Arnold, but I hope and believe there will be a tomorrow, for I assure you I have an almost boyish zest for life, though rather contemplative than energetic for a while, till I have rested. There is a little forgetfulness of names and places, but memory seems to become more luminous as it falls back upon itself. Well, some day you will experience this. You two

16

must carry on the work of the Institute. Herman is an able fellow, in spite of his mechanistic notions. But I wonder whether any woman could be happy with him?"

He watched me rather keenly as he said that.

"There's only one thing makes me want to live a little longer, Arnold," he continued, "and that is Esther's future. It would be a great satisfaction to me to see her settled happily before I go. Forgive an old man's frankness if I say that sometimes I have almost thought you two cared for each other."

"You are quite right in part, sir," I replied. "I do care for Esther a good deal."

"And she, I am sure, has a very warm feeling for you, Arnold. There is nobody whom I would rather have for Esther's husband than yourself."

"Well, sir, the fact is, we are not sure that our views are altogether harmonious," I confessed. "I am, as you know, rather sceptical about the newest views for revolutionizing woman's status, while Esther — "

"Is a full-fledged suffragist and has exalted notions about the race of the future. Tush, my boy! Never hold back proposing marriage because of intellectual differences. The race spirit, sitting up aloft and pulling the strings, is laughing at you."

"But, Sir Spofforth, to be candid, it was not I who held back," I answered.

"Hum! I see!" he answered, nodding his head. Then, very seriously, "My boy, I want you to win her. It would embitter my last days to see my daughter the wife of Herman Lazaroff. I have watched and tried to study him: it isn't his materialism, Arnold, it's his infernal will. He'll break everything and everybody that conflicts with it when he wakes up and knows his powers. Now he doesn't understand himself at all. He can see nothing interiorly, as good old Swedenborg would say. I tell you, Herman Lazaroff, able fellow as he is, and splendid brain, is a machine of devilish energy, and, unfortunately, fashioned for purely destructive purposes."

Like most old men, he had the habit of falling into soliloquy, and toward the end of his speech his voice dropped, and he spoke rather to himself than to me. Though I remembered his words afterward, at the time I regarded his indictment as the prejudice of an octogenarian. He was in his eightieth year, and there was no doubt his keen mind was failing. I was searching for a reply when Esther and Lazaroff came back from the conservatory.

Esther's face was flushed and she looked utterly miserable. But I was amazed to see the expression upon Lazaroff's. He was deathly white, and his black eyes seemed to gleam with infernal resolution. At that moment it did occur to me that Sir Spofforth might be wiser in his judgment than I. Lazaroff came forward quietly and sat down, and I tried to make the occasion for conversation. But he, seated motionless and abstracted, seemed hardly to hear me, and rose from his chair after a few moments, looking toward Esther, who was standing near the conservatory entrance. Her brown-colored gown gleamed golden in the lamplight.

"Sir Spofforth, Miss Esther is interested in our new freezing-plant," he said. "I thought, with your permission, that I would take her to see it lit up by electricity. You'll come too, Pennell?"

"Wouldn't daytime be better, Lazaroff?" I suggested, and I did not know what was the cause of the vaguely felt distrust that prompted my words. Certainly I had no fears of any sort, or reason for any. Yet, looking at Lazaroff's face, now flushed and somehow sinister, I remembered Sir Spofforth's words again.

"Let us go tonight," said Esther, and it seemed to me that there was a note of penitence in her voice, as if she wished to make Lazaroff amends.

She came slowly across the room toward us. She looked at Lazaroff—I thought remorsefully, and at me with an expression of understanding that I never had seen in her eyes before. My heart leaped up to meet that message. But that was the instant signal-flash of souls, and the next moment I detected in her glance the same sense of foreboding that mine must have shown her.

It is strange how instantaneously such complexities present themselves with convincing power. Though the knowledge lay latent in my mind, I am sure now I was aware that I should never set eyes upon Sir Spofforth, in life or death, again.

He rose up slowly. "Don't be long, my dear," he said to Esther. "I shall not wait up for you. Good night, Herman. Good night, Arnold." He passed the door and began to ascend the stairs. He turned. "Arnold!" he began. "No, never mind. I will tell you tomorrow."

He never told me. He was gone, and we three went downstairs, out of the house, and crossed the garden toward the Institute, whose squat form blocked the view of the road. Croydon, in the distance, hummed like a huge dynamo. The Bear dipped slantingly above; the wind was shaking down the fading petals of the rambler roses. I remember the picture more vividly than I perceived it then; the intense darkness, the white lights of the distant town, the yellow lamp glow on the short grass, cut off squarely by the window-sash and trisected by the window-bars. Lazaroff led the way, walking a little distance in front of us, toward the annex, a building just completed, in which was the new freezing-plant, with our few guinea-pigs, and the monkeys that had been bought recently, out of our own money, for the great experiment. He drew a key from his pocket and began fumbling with the lock. Esther stopped in the shadows at my side.

"He asked me to marry him," she said. "I told him never — never! That was the word I used. I used to think that I could care for him, Arnold, but in that instant I knew — yes, I knew my heart."

I knew mine too, and I took her in my arms in the shadow of the Institute. She lifted her mouth to mine. All the while Lazaroff was fumbling with the lock. Yet I am sure he was aware, by virtue of that intuition which tells us all vital things.

When he had opened the door he turned a switch, and the interior leaped into view round twenty points of light that pierced the shadows.

"Come in, Arnold," he said, turning to me — and I thought there was blood on his lip. "I will lead, and you and Miss Esther can follow me. Don't be alarmed, Miss Esther, if you hear the monkeys screaming. They grow lonely at night."

"Poor little things! How dreadful!" Esther said.

"We shall not keep them here very long," Lazaroff answered in extenuation. He stooped over a cane chair and picked up a warm shawl. "You will need to put this about you," he continued, standing back and leaving me to adjust it about Esther's shoulders.

So he had planned to bring her here; his subtle mind had foreseen even this detail. He left nothing to the unexpected. He lived up to his principles.

We passed between two silent dynamos. The freezing-plant was already in operation, but George, the machinist, went off duty at six, after stopping the dynamos, and the temperature did not rise much during the night. It was very cold. The moisture on the brick walls had congealed to a thin film of ice, and a frosted network covered the ammonia pipes. Lazaroff stopped in front of a large wooden chest, with a glass door.

"In this very ordinary-looking icebox we keep our choicest specimens," he said to Esther.

"Don't open that!" I exclaimed.

He laughed disagreeably. "I had no intention of doing so," he answered. "You applauded Sir Spofforth's mediaeval vitalistic views tonight, Pennell, and the transition from the dream to the reality might prove too disturbing for your peace of mind. Dream on, by permission of those five missing centimeters. It is such an extinguisher of the soul theory to see parts of the organism flourishing in perfect health, all ready to work and grow, devoid of consciousness and brain attachments. We have two-fifths of a guinea-pig's heart, Miss Esther, that is yearning to begin its pulsations as soon as it is placed in a suitable medium."

He passed on. Esther's fingers gripped my wrist tightly. "What an abominable man!" she whispered. "Arnold — my dear — to think I didn't know my mind until an hour ago! When he asked me, something seemed to strip the mask from his face and the scales from my eyes. I hate him — but I'm afraid of him, Arnold."

I drew her arm through mine and held her hand. Lazaroff preceded us down a flight of new concrete steps which had just dried. The cellar into which we descended had been used for storing packing-cases, and we had always gone down by a short ladder. It was here that the experiment was to be made. I had been shown nothing of Lazaroff's preparations.

The cellar had been paved with concrete since my last visit, and I thought it looked smaller than formerly. As we went down we heard the monkeys begin to chatter. Lazaroff switched on a light. I saw a cage of guinea-pigs close at hand. They squealed and scurried among their straw. Two monkeys, awakened by the light, put their arms about each other and grimaced at me. A tiny marmoset stretched out its black, human-like arms between the bars appealingly. It looked very lonely and child-like as it blinked at us. What a terrific journey into the future Lazaroff, like some god, planned for that atom of flesh.

He stopped at the end of the cellar. I perceived now that the brick wall was new; it seemed to be an inner wall, bounding a partition; that was why the cellar looked smaller. The half-dried mortar clung flabbily to the interstices.

"Can you find the entrance, Arnold?" asked Lazaroff.

"The entrance?" The light was not strong, to be sure, but still it seemed impossible that there could be an ingress into that solid wall.

Lazaroff touched a brick, and a large mass swung inward, like a door. In fact, it was a door, with bricks facing it, the outer edge contiguous with the outer edge of the fixed rows, so that the deception was perfect.

"You didn't tell me that the chamber was completed, Lazaroff!" I exclaimed in surprise.

"No, Arnold? Well, but I don't tell you everything," he answered.

We stepped through the doorway, and Lazaroff switched on a tiny light within. Now I perceived that we were standing in a long and very narrow space, with cement-faced walls and roof, making the chamber impervious to sound and light. It was below the level of the ground, and thus, as Lazaroff had said, earthquakes might happen above, and it would never be discovered, not even though the annex were pulled down, unless one blasted out the foundations.

The sole contents were three large cylinders of metal, looking like giant thermos bottles. Each was about six feet long — too long for a monkey, it seemed to me — and had a glass plate in front. Lazaroff drove his heel against the glass of the nearest cylinder with all his might.

"It is quite unbreakable, you see," he said. "It will turn a rifle bullet. 'Suffragette glass,' the maker calls it."

"But what are these for?" asked Esther.

"These, Miss Esther, are to convey three monkeys into the twenty-first century," answered Lazaroff. "By instantaneously suspending animation at a temperature of twenty-five degrees, we hope to maintain the bodily organism without change until the time for their awakening comes. The problem is, whether that mysterious by-product of matter called consciousness will return."

"How dreadful!" exclaimed Esther, shuddering.

"But the temperature will rise, Lazaroff," I interposed, "and however carefully your cylinders are made it is impossible to hope to maintain the internal heat at only twenty-five degrees during a century."

"You forget that our monkeys will be sealed in a vacuum," he answered. "There is an inner and an outer case of vanadium steel mixed with a secret composition which will resist even thermite. And even if the temperature does rise — well, if a homely instance may be allowed — you are aware that canned beef, as the Americans term it, will remain fresh in an air-tight tin even in the tropics. That is dead matter, while our monkeys will be millions of living cells. The vacuum is created by simply screwing on this cap."

"But not a perfect vacuum,". I interposed. "That is impossible."

"Sufficiently near to eliminate the aerobic bacilli which flourish on oxygen, and the infinitesimal amount of that remaining in the cylinder is probably absorbed and transmuted by the surface capillaries and lungs, leaving simply carbon dioxide, neon, crypton, et cetera."

I examined the cylinder nearest me with interest. A small dial was set into its cap. Lazaroff anticipated my question.

"That is the most ingenious part of the mechanism," he explained. "It is a hundred-year clock, made specially for me by Jurgensen, of Copenhagen, and, to salve your conscience, paid for, like the cylinders, out of my private purse. It runs true to within three-tenths of a second. The alarm can be set to any year, if necessary. A good alarm clock for lazy people, Miss Esther. This one, you see, I have already set to a hundred years ahead. This is at sixty-five; I shall set that to a hundred presently, for we don't want one of our monkeys to awaken several generations ahead of his friends. This one is not set. Now, observe, I turn the hands on the dials. The large figures are years. The smaller ones are days. Now as soon as the cap is screwed on, the internal vacuum causes this lever to fall, catching this cam and starting the mechanism. We have then a bottled monkey in an indestructible shell, for really I do not know what could make much impression on steel of this thickness, which is both resistant and malleable, and fireproof too. It is impossible, in short, to release the inmate before the appointed time, and, even then, immediate death would ensue."

"Why?" I asked.

"Because resuscitation must be gradual. I base my hopes upon the chance that the lungs and heart will automatically resume their functions, being in their most perfect medium. But if air were admitted before the bodily machine had become, so to say, synchronized, the swarm of micro-organisms would make short work of our subject. Besides, the hasty respiration produced by this rush of air would produce immediate death by its transformation into carbon dioxide. The air must enter under slight pressure, in minute quantities, during a period of

about ten days. Very well! As the timepiece gradually runs down, the cap slowly unscrews, and a tiny
quantity of filtered air leaks in. It is so arranged
that, at the exact end of the period, the cap flies off,
and the subject awakes."

"Herman," said Esther, hurriedly, "I don't like
this. It isn't right. And I am sure my father does
not know about it."

"My dear Miss Esther, I assure you that it is a
very ordinary scientific experiment," Lazaroff answered, laughing. "Come, Arnold," he added, "why
not get in yourself and try how it feels? You are
not afraid?"

"In my clothes?"

"Certainly."

"Arnold, I don't want you to get into that thing,"
Esther protested.

"Of course, if our friend is afraid that I am going
to screw him up for a century —" began Lazaroff.

"I am not at all afraid," I returned, a little nettled.
"How do I get in?"

"I'll have to help you," Lazaroff answered. "It
was not made for a big man in clothes. Button your
coat. Now — put your arms down by your sides."
He rolled a cylinder upon the floor, and I put my feet
inside rather reluctantly and squeezed down to the
bottom. Lazaroff looked at me and burst into loud
laughter.

"Not much room to turn round, is there?" he said, raising the cylinder with an effort and standing it on its base again.

"Come out, Arnold," pleaded Esther; and I saw that her face was white with fear.

But I was quite helpless, and above me I saw Lazaroff, smiling at my predicament.

"Now if I were going to be so unkind as to send you into the next century," he said, "to be the only animist, with a defective skull, in a world of vile materialism—"

"Please, Herman, for my sake!" Esther implored.

"I should put on the cap," he said, and fitted it.

He must have touched some mechanism that I had not seen, for instantly the cap began to whir on the screw. Through the glass face I caught a last glimpse of Esther's terrified eyes. The image blurred and vanished as my breath dimmed the glass and frosted it. I heard the swift jar of the cap mechanism end in a jarring click. I gasped for air; there was none. My head swam, my throat was closed; the blackness was pricked into flecks of fire. I groped for memory through unconsciousness— and ceased.

CHAPTER III

I HAVE heard patients, emerging from the chloroform swoon, describe how, before awakening, they had seemed to view themselves lying unconscious upon their beds, detailing the posture of their motionless bodies and inert limbs. In this way, now, I seemed to see myself.

I am sure that was no dream of the vague borderland between death and life. I saw the pallid face, so shrunken that the skin clung to the edged bones, and the dry hair, the pinched lips and waxen hands. I saw myself as if from some non-spatial point, and with singular indifference, except that one fragment of knowledge, detached from my serene omniscience, troubled me. I had to return within that physical envelope; and behind me lay dim memories, quite untranslatable, but ineffably rapturous, which made that projected incarnation an event of dread.

Vague images of earthly things began to float upward out of the dark, as it were, symbols of physical life whose meaning remained obscure. I pictured a spring-board, on which a swimmer stood poised, waiting to dive into the sea and set the plank behind him quivering, and a large roll of some material, like a carpet, blocking a cellar door.

Gradually, through an alternation of dreams and blankness, I began to be aware of the parched and withered body that cloaked me. The point of consciousness had shrunk within its earthly envelope. Soon it diffused itself throughout my members. Now I could translate my symbols into ideas. That coiled-up substance that blocked the door was my tongue, fallen back into the throat. And the spring-board on which the swimmer stood—that was my heart, waiting to beat. And unless and until the swimmer —I—made that plunge into life's ocean, it could not. Slowly the need of physical resurrection urged me onward.

A thousand darts were stabbing in my flesh, like purgatorial fire. No motor nerve had yet awakened, but the capillaries, opening, pricked me like red-hot needles. Faint memories of the past flashed through my mind, and, though I recalled no intervening period, I was sensible that those events had happened infinitely long before.

Suddenly I plunged. I felt as if a sword had pierced my body. I felt the waters of that living ocean close over my face, and gasped. I breathed. Simultaneously, with a loud click, the cap of the cylinder flew off, air rushed in, a stabbing light broke through my closed eyelids; I fainted.

It was, of course, the gradual unscrewing of the cylinder cap as the mechanism ran down, and the consequent admission of minute quantities of oxygen, that had begun to restore me. I must have passed several days in semi-consciousness before the cylinder opened. When the last thread of the screw was traversed, the inrush of air caused the respiration to begin.

I was breathing when I became conscious once more, and my heart was straining in my breast. I got my eyes open. There followed hours of light-tortured delirium, during which I struggled to regain the motor powers. With infinite endeavor I placed one hand upon the other and passed it up the wrist and forearm. The muscles were all gone. The ulna and radius were perfectly distinguishable, and I could encircle either with my fingers, after I had managed to flex them. I noticed that my joints creaked like rusty hinges.

I tried to bend my elbows, and this next grim battle lasted an incalculable time. Gradually I became aware of some obstacle on each side of me. Then, for the first time since my awakening, I knew that I was inside the cylinder. But I did not know that it had fallen upon its side until it slid forward, and my puny struggles dislodged me and flung me free into a pool of water. I drew in a deep breath, feeling my lungs crackle like old parchment, and plunged my face and shoulders beneath the surface. My skin sucked up the moisture like a sponge, and I contrived to get a few drops past my swollen tongue. I had just sense enough and time to turn my face upward before I became unconscious again.

I must have slept long, for, on my next awakening, the light was brighter and still more torturing. Memory began to stir. I recalled my conversation with Sir Spofforth, our journey into the annex, Lazaroff's invitation to me to enter the cylinder. He must have shut me in for a moment by way of a practical joke, and gone away with Esther, persuading himself and her that I could free myself and would follow. I tried to call him. But only a croaking gasp came from my lips. I tried again and again, gradually regaining the power of vocal utterance. But there came no answer, and each time that I called, the echoing, hoarse susurrus brought me nearer to the realization of some terror at hand which I did not dare to face.

I looked about me. Beside me lay the cylinder, almost buried in mud. I was still within the secret vault, but a part of the brick partition had fallen inward in such a way as to screen the few visible inches of the steel case that had housed me, so that nobody would have suspected its presence in the mud of the little chamber. I remembered that there had been two more; I looked about me, but there was no sign of them.

Now I began to realize that there had been a considerable change in my surroundings since I became unconscious. The light which had distressed me came through a hole in the roof of the adjoining cellar, filtering thence through the aperture in the broken wall, and was of the dimmest. In place of the concrete floor there was a swamp of mud, with pools of water here and there, and the dirt was heaped up in the corners and against the walls. Moss and splotched fungi grew among the tumbled bricks, and everywhere were spore stains and microscopic plant growth.

I was bewildered by these signs of dilapidation everywhere. The guinea-pigs and monkeys were gone; the cellar was empty, save for some low, rough planks of wood fitted on trestles and set about the floor. On the wall at the far end hung something that gradually took form as I strained my aching eyes to a focus.

It was a crucifix. The cellar had become a subterranean chapel. The cross was hewn coarsely of pine, and the figure that hung upon it grotesquely carven; yet there was the pathos of wistful, ignorant effort in the workmanship that bespoke the sincerity of the artist.

I made my difficult way upon hands and knees

I made my difficult way toward the stairs

through the gap in the wall, across the mud floor of the cellar, toward the stairs, resting several times from weariness before I reached my destination. But when I arrived at the far end, where the stairs should have been, I received a shock that totally unnerved me. The stairs were gone. In place of them was a debris of rubble and broken stones, as firmly set as if workmen had built it into the wall. The mass must have been there for years, because, out of the thin soil that had drifted in, a little oak tree sprang, twisting its spindling stem to rear its crown toward the patch of daylight.

At last I understood. I had come to realize the fact that my sleep had been a prolonged one; it might have lasted weeks — even months, I had thought, as with cataleptics; but an entire century! that idea had been too incredibly grotesque for consideration. That Sir Spofforth, with whom, it seemed, I had dined almost yesterday, had gone, ages ago, to his long home; Lazaroff; Esther, whom I loved; that generations had come into birth and died . . . . it seemed too cruel a jest. I wept. I raved and called for Esther. Surely a hundred years had never passed, turning her brown hair to gray, lining her gentle face, bringing at last the gift of death to her, while I lay underground, encased in steel and air!

I cried aloud in terror. I hammered helplessly

upon the walls.   Again I called Esther, Lazaroff, George.   There was no answer of any kind.

Presently a ray of light quivered through the hole, falling upon the heap of debris that blocked the stair-way.   The yellow beam moved onward, and now it bathed the thin branches of the little twisted tree that, by the aid of those few minutes of sunlight daily, had ventured into life.   It had grown cunningly sidewise, so as to expose the maximum of wood to the light.   I watched the ray till it went out; I wanted to show the plant to Lazaroff, to ask him whether the mechanics of heliotropism could suffice to answer the problem of the tree's brainless consciousness; and my chagrin that this whim could not be fulfilled assumed an absurd significance.   It was, in fact, the realization of this loss of responsiveness to the reality of the situation that constantly urged me to find some way of escape when I might have relapsed otherwise into an acquiescence which would have brought insanity and death.

The stairs being gone, I turned my consideration to the cellar roof.   To reach this it would be necessary to drag one of the planks beneath the hole and scramble up, clinging to the sides with my fingers and bracing my feet against the wall.   This feat was not a difficult one for a normal man, but for me clearly impossible.   I must wait until I became stronger.

It is a strange thing, but I had not associated the need of waiting with the idea of food until I found the box of biscuit. I stumbled upon the box by the accident of scratching my wrist against the edge as I crawled along the wall. I saw the corner projecting from a mound of earth, and, scraping some of the dirt away, I lifted the pine-wood lid.

Inside the box I found a quantity of biscuit which seemed to have been baked recently. It was crisp, and too hard for me to break. I dipped a piece in the stagnant water, and, as I swallowed the first morsels, became aware of my ravenous hunger.

I can hardly estimate the duration of the imprisonment that followed. It was of days and nights which succeeded each the other in monotonous succession, during which, like a hibernating beast, I crouched and groped within the cellar, dozing and shivering, and gnawing incessantly at my food. Only those few minutes of sunshine daily saved my reason, I am convinced now. My evening clothes, which at first had appeared to have suffered no injury during my century of sleep, had begun to disintegrate, and hung upon me in tattered fragments. It was a period of despair, with very little alternating hope. Sometimes I prayed wildly beneath the crucifix, sometimes, in an access of madness, I cried for Esther and Lazaroff again. And for whole hours I convinced myself that this was a dream.

But my strength returned with amazing swiftness. As in the case of a typhoid convalescent, every particle of food seemed to build up my body. I must have put on pounds each day. The barrel framework of my ribs filled out, the muscles showed their old outlines beneath the skin, the fluid rushed into the joints and restored their suppleness. And daily I practiced exercises. I managed to drag one of the benches beneath the hole at last, and, standing on this, tried often to draw myself up; but on each occasion my struggles only brought down a shower of earth and stones, and I resigned myself to a period of further waiting, watching for dawn like a troglodyte, and for the sun like a fire-worshiper.

In the end my escape developed in a manner the least imaginable. It began with my discovery of a second box in another of the mounds. I opened it hastily, in the greedy anticipation of finding something more palatable than biscuit.

Instead of this I found a number of strange batons of wood. They resembled policemen's truncheons, but each had a tiny rounded plate of glass near the head, and there evidently was some sort of mechanism near the handle, for there was a push-button, fitted with a heavy guard of brass, so strong that I could not raise it with my fingers. It was indeed providential that I was unable to do so.

I carried the strange implement beneath the hole

in the roof and laid it on the bench, intending to examine it more carefully as soon as the sun appeared. Meanwhile, this being the time for my daily exercise, I mounted the bench and tried to pull myself up. I failed; yet I detected a considerable improvement in my muscular power, and, becoming exhausted, I prepared to descend. Inadvertently, but without anticipating any serious result, I placed my foot against the truncheon in such a way as to elevate the guard.

I heard it click as it rose into position, and, in setting down my foot again, depressed the pushbutton.

The truncheon tipped to the ground, pointing upward. I saw a ray of blinding light, of intense whiteness tipped with mauve, shoot from the head, and, with a crash, a shower of stones fell on me, bearing me to the ground and enveloping me in a cloud of dust.

I must have lain half stunned for some minutes. I was aroused by feeling the sunlight on my eyelids. I started to my feet. The hole in the roof was nearly twice the former size, and a heap of fallen stones and pieces of brick afforded me a perfect stepway. I was scratched by the falling debris, but happily the explosion, as I deemed it, seemed to have been in an upward direction.

In a moment I was scrambling up the stones. I

slipped and clutched and struggled; I got my head and shoulders in the air and pulled my body after me; I trod upon leaves; I looked about me.

I was standing in the midst of what appeared to be an ancient forest of oak and beech trees, whose bare boughs, covered with snow, shook under a gray sky above a carpet of withered, snow-spread leaves, and under these were endless heaps of disintegrating bricks. In vain I looked about me for the Institute. There was no sign of it, nor of Sir Spofforth's house. Nowhere was anything to be seen but the same forest growth, the dead leaves scurrying before the chill wind, and the vast brick piles. I had emerged from the cellar into a trackless wilderness.

And now at last my final doubt, which had bred hope, was gone. I ran through the forest, on and on, shouting like a madman and beating my breast, stumbling over the brick heaps that lay everywhere, plunging through thorny undergrowth, heedless of any course. I must have been running for ten minutes when my strength failed me, and I collapsed beside an ancient road, overgrown with shrubs and saplings, yet discernible in its course between the tall trees that bordered it. Before me, far away through the vista line, I saw a white bank against the gray horizon.

I flung myself upon my face and prayed, with all my will, to die.

CHAPTER IV

A SHADOW swept over me, and, looking up, I saw an airplane gliding noiselessly above; it stopped, hung poised and motionless, and then dropped slowly and almost vertically into the road, coming to ground within a dozen yards of where I lay.

There stepped out a man in a uniform of pale blue, having insewn upon the breast a piece of white linen, cut to the shape of a swan. He came toward me with hesitancy, and stood over me, staring at me and at my clothes with an expression indicative of the greatest bewilderment.

"Where's your brass, friend?" he inquired after a few moments, speaking in a high-pitched, monotonous, and rather nasal tone. He rubbed his smooth-shaven face in thought. "Where's your brass?" he repeated.

I perceived that he wore about his neck a twisted cord whose ends were tied through the loop of a brass plate, stamped with letters and figures.

"For God's sake tell me what year this is!" I cried.

At the profane expletive, which had been drawn from me by my anguish, he recoiled in dismay; he

41

seemed less shocked than frightened; he glanced about him quickly, and then cast a very searching look at me. But next he began to smile in a half-humorous, kindly way.

"You're one of the escaped defectives, aren't you?" he inquired. "You have nothing to fear from me, friend. We airplane scouts have no love for the Guard. You can go on your way. But where are you lying up? Are your friends near?"

"Will you tell me what year this is?" I demanded frantically.

"Yap, certainly," he answered. "This is Thirty-seven, Cold Solstice less five." He shook his head and began staring at me again.

I laughed hysterically. "I don't know what that jargon means," I answered, "but I went to sleep in the vault of the Biological Institute in the year 1915."

Perplexity had succeeded alarm. The airscout shook his head again. He was one of those deliberate, slow-moving men whose resolutions, tardily made, harden to inflexibility; I recognized the type and found the individual pleasing. He was a good-looking young fellow of about eight and twenty, with straight, dark hair and a very frank countenance. He looked like a sailor, and the rolling, open collar, which fell back, sailor fashion, revealed a muscular throat, tanned, like his face, to the color of the bricks around us.

"I don't know what to make of you," he said thoughtfully. "I don't want to trap you, but you were better off in the art factories. I don't know what to do with you."

I sprang to my feet, and for an instant I ceased to realize my predicament. "Will you take me to my friends in London?" I asked. In my mind was the memory of a university acquaintance who lived in St. John's Wood. But then the swift remembrance came back to me, and I hung my head and groaned.

"Back to London!" exclaimed the airscout. "But you'll be put to the leather vats. Doctor Sanson is furious, and the police are searching for you everywhere. You're crazed! What's the sense of running away from painting pictures and going back to sweat ten years over the hides?"

"Take me to London!" I implored. "I have nowhere to go. Perhaps — I don't know —"

I was hoping wildly that somebody whom I had known might still survive. But by this time I was beginning to pull myself together. I resolved to wait for his decision.

"Now, friend," he said, as if he had made up his mind, "your top got stuffed making those factory pictures, as was very natural. Now, I think you had better go back to London, and I'll take you there, since your friends have shaken you. But of course it must be the police station. I can't risk my own liberty. Once more, are you sure you want to go? If not, I haven't seen you."

"I'll go," I answered indifferently.

"Yap? Step in, then!"

I took my seat beside him. It will seem incredible, but I had never ridden in an airplane before. In my other days only a few had seen these craft. It was hardly more than six years since the Wrights had flown when my long sleep began. In spite of my oppression of mind, or perhaps because the days of horror that I had spent in the cellar produced the unavoidable reaction, I began to feel the exhilaration of the flight as we ascended to a height of perhaps a thousand feet and drove northward. The sensation was that of sitting still and seeing the trees flit by beneath me, and would have been pleasing but for the intense cold, which pierced through my rags and numbed me. I perceived that the airplane was under perfect control, and could be stayed without falling. After a while I realized that there was no motor.

My companion saw me looking at the machine. "Improved solar type," he said, patting her caressingly. "Better than a bird, isn't she?" He turned toward me. "You've been sleeping in the wood these three days?" he asked. "And find the factories best? I don't score you for that. Where's the rest of you? Five, weren't there? Why didn't you keep together? Where's that bishop of yours?"

But, seeing that he could elicit no comprehensible answer to his repeated questions — in truth, I did not know how to reply — he relapsed into an equal silence. And now the white bank that I had seen on the horizon began to assume crenellations, which in turn became buildings of immense height and symmetrical aspect. And I forgot my situation in admiration and amazement at the panorama that began to unfold beneath us.

The county of Surrey appeared to be an extensive forest, ending about a waste of dismantled brick, the suburbs of old London, which extended on each side as far as I could see. Then the modern town began: an outer ring of what I took to be enormous factories and storage warehouses; an inner ring, no doubt, of residences; and then the nucleus, the most splendid city that the imagination could have devised.

London seemed to be smaller than the metropolis of a century ago. I could see from the height of Hampstead, in the north, to the region of Dulwich, and from Woolwich to Acton, all clearly defined, like a great map unrolled beneath me, though I could recognize none of the old landmarks, save the unchanging Thames. The interior city was laid out in squares, huge buildings, sometimes enclosing interior courts, occupying the blocks formed by the parallel and intersecting streets. As we drove inward from the outskirts, the buildings became higher, but always uniformly so, the city thus presenting the aspect of a succession of gigantic steps, until the summit, the square mile comprising the heart, was reached.

This consisted of an array of enormous edifices, with fronts perfectly plain, and evidently constructed of brick-faced steel-work, but all glistening a dazzling white, which, even at that height, made my eyes water, and rising uniformly some forty-five or fifty stories. The flat roofs were occupied by gardens or what I took to be gymnasia, sheltered beneath tarpaulins. I saw innumerable airplanes at rest, suspended high above the streets, while others flitted here and there above the roofs, and a whole fleet lay, as if moored, some distance away, apparently over the center of the city, above a singular building, which awakened associations in my mind, though I was unable to name it.

It had a round dome, being, in fact, the only domed building that I could see. This covered only the central portion of the enormous architectural mass, and appeared to float in the air above an aerial garden, laid out with walks that radiated from a flat building, which filled the space between the floating dome and the roof beneath it. I surmised that this must be the new House of Parliament. The entire mass was surrounded by a double wall, with a roofed space of perhaps ninety feet from rear to front, castellated. Mounted on this were what appeared to be a number of large, conical-shaped implements, of great size. Long, graceful bridges on arches connected this wall with the domed building; and wall and building glistened from top to base so brilliantly that the glow seared my eyes like sunlight.

As we were now flying at a low altitude, I turned my attention to the streets, which appeared like canyons far beneath. Along these swarmed a multitude of travelers, dressed in two colors only, white and blue, the latter vastly predominating. I could see no vehicles, and I imagined, what proved to be correct, that the streets themselves were moving. Most of those journeying seemed content to lean back against the railings, the lowest bars of which projected, forming a continuous seat, and rest. Nearly all the streets were traveling in the same direction, those that reversed this movement being small and comparatively empty. From the presence of what seemed to be iron stanchions, set along the edges of these moving ways, I surmised that they were roofed with crystal.

Along the front of the buildings ran single tracks, connecting at regular intervals with the streets beneath by means of elevators, which shot up and down continuously, bearing their freight. These tracks were placed above each other at ten-story intervals, so that there were three or four rows of these aerial streets, ranging from the ground to the upper portions of the buildings, all filled with travelers. The buildings, each comprising an entire block, the elevated streets, with their graceful bridges flung forth across the chasms, the absence of any of the old poverty and dirt, and that huge gathering of human beings, going about their business in so systematic a fashion, fascinated me, and even aroused my enthusiasm.

Signs evidently indicated to persons approaching in airships the purpose of each building and landing-stage, but these were in characters entirely unintelligible to me.

My companion stayed the vessel in the air and tapped me on the arm. I started, to see him regarding me with the same expression of humorous perplexity.

"I must put you off here, friend," he said. "I think I have done the best I could for you. You would have died in the forest, while here — well, there's a chance for you. And it's better to go to the leather vats for a few years than to die and go nowhere. I'll know you if we meet again. What's your name?"

"Arnold Pennell," I answered, clasping the hand that he held out to me.

He almost jumped. "Don't tell that to the Council, unless you want the Rest Cure," he said.

"Don't tell them my name?"

"Not both names, friend. You know what I mean. If you don't know—" He shrugged his shoulders. "Mine's Jones," he said. "My father's was Williams. My grandfather's was Jones again. They say it's one of our oldest names — common in the days before civilization. Now down we go."

The airplane swooped down and came to rest upon the roof immediately beneath us. On this I saw a number of men, apparently practicing gymnastic exercises; and hardly were we at a standstill when two of them came running up to us. They were clad in blue uniforms resembling that of the airscout, but instead of a swan each wore a shield-shaped piece of linen upon his back and breast.

"What's this?" they demanded in a breath, pointing at me and bursting into bellowing laughter.

"One of your defectives," answered Jones. "I found him in the forest while patrolling."

They rushed at me and dragged me from the airplane, swiftly patting me about the body, as if in search of weapons. Satisfied that I was unarmed, they turned to the airscout.

"You'll share the reward!" they cried, again simultaneously.

"Keep it!" replied the airscout tartly, and rose into the air, waving me a cordial good-bye.

They rushed me across the roof through a crowd of other men, similarly clad, down an elevator, and into the street. They dragged me upon one of the moving platforms and conveyed me a short distance, descending at the entrance to one of the innumerable shining buildings, over which was inscribed something in the same undecipherable letters.

But, quickly as we had gone, the report of my arrest seemed to have preceded us, for our way was blocked by a vast and constantly increasing crowd, that came running up with lively and shameless curiosity, and, attracted by my rags, I suppose, pressed closely about us and uttered hoots of laughter. I heard the word "defective" bandied from mouth to mouth.

I looked at these people attentively. There were both men and women present, all wearing clothing of the same pale blue color, which seemed to be prescribed, although the cut of each garment was to some extent individual. In effect, the men wore sack suits of a coarsely woven woolen material, with short, loose trousers fastened with laces about the ankles, and square-cut coats having wide lapels extending to a broad, turned-back collar that fell over the shoulders like a sailor's, revealing a neckpiece of blue linen. The women's short skirts reached to the tops

I glanced from one to another, and
sr

mirthless eyes, and mouths twisted in
ry

of their high boots, and the fashion seemed to run to large buttons and loose sleeves. They wore no hats. Upon the breast, near the shoulder, each person wore a small linen badge, indicative of his occupation.

What disconcerted me was the shrewd, mocking smile upon each face. I glanced from one to another, seeking to find something of the same friendly interest that animated me, and met hard, mirthless eyes, and mouths twisted in sneering mockery.

Another thing that startled and almost terrified me was the absence of a certain conventionality of restraint that had ruled everybody in that other world of mine. For instance, among those gibing at me was a gray-bearded man who danced before me like a small urchin. Another made an expressive pantomime of death. A girl stuck out her tongue at me. I remembered the plaint, that never since the glorious age of Greece had the code of public morality coincided with that privately held. This we all knew; the statesman in parliament was not on bowing terms with the same statesman in the smoking-room. Some said it was Christianity, others respectability that bound us in this organic hypocrisy; but now the two codes seemed to have coalesced. A grandfather grimaced at me; a gray-haired woman put out her foot to trip me; if there had been stones I think they would have flung them at me. But suddenly a youngish lad in white appeared, and the crowd, hastening to make a path for him, shrank back with servile demeanor. Taking advantage of this, my captors, linking their arms in mine, made a rush forward, scattering the mob right and left, and bore me through a swinging door into a small rotunda, in which a number of other policemen were seated with their blue-clad prisoners.

CHAPTER V

INSIDE the rotunda a burly man in blue, with the white shield on his breast, was standing on guard in front of a second swinging door, above which was painted something in the same strange characters. A few words to him from my captors apparently secured us precedence, for he stared at me curiously, opened the door, and bawled to some person inside. I was pushed into a large courtroom. It contained no seats, however, for spectators or witnesses. The only occupants were the magistrate and his clerk, and a group of policemen who lounged at one end of the room, joking among themselves. The clerk, a little, obsequious man in blue, was seated at a desk immediately opposite that of his chief, a pompous, surly fellow in white, wearing about his shoulders a lusterless black cape, which seemed to be a truncation of the old legal gown. Placing me on a platform near the clerk's desk, the two policemen who were in charge of me stepped forward and began an explanation in low tones which was not meant to meet my ears, and did not.

The magistrate started nervously, and, putting his hand beneath his desk, pulled up a truncheon similar to those that I had seen in the cellar. He handled this nervously during our interview.

"Well, what have you to say, you filthy defective?" he shouted at me, when the police had ended.

I heard a suppressed chuckle behind me, and then became aware that all the police had gathered about me, convulsed with amusement at my rags.

"Stand back, you swine!" bellowed the magistrate. "Give me the Escaped Defectives Book," he added, to his clerk.

The clerk handed up to him a small publication which I could see contained numerous miniature photographs in color. He began studying it, looking up at me from time to time. Occasionally, at his nod, one of the policemen would seize my face and push it into profile. At last the magistrate thrust the book away petulantly.

"This isn't one of them," he announced to the policemen. "Who are you?" he continued, glaring at me. "You're not on the defectives' list. Where do you come from? Tell the truth or I'll commit you to the leathers. Why are you in masquerade? Where's your brass? Your print? Your number? Your district?"

The clerk wagged his middle finger at me and, drawing a printed form from a pile, pushed it toward me. I took it, but I could make nothing of it, for it was in the same unknown characters.

"I can only read the old-fashioned alphabet," I said.

The room echoed with the universal laughter. The magistrate almost jumped out of his chair.

"What!" he yelled. "You're lying! You know you are. You have an accent. You're from another province. What's your game?"

The clerk, ignoring his superior's outburst, pulled back the form, and, taking in his hand a sort of fountain pen, began to fill it in with a black fluid that dried the instant it touched the paper.

"Number, district, province, city, print, and brass?" he inquired. He paused and looked up at me. "Brach or dolicoph? Whorl, loop, or median? Facial, cephalic, and color indexes? Your Sanson test? Your Binet rating?"

But, since I made no attempt to answer these utterly baffling questions, the clerk ceased to ply me with them and looked up at the magistrate for instructions. The magistrate, who had been leaning forward, watching me attentively, now smiled as if he had suddenly grasped the situation.

"I'll tell you what you are," he said, shaking his finger at me. "You're a Spanish spy, masquerading as a defective in order to get into the workshops and corrupt the defectives there."

"Now I should call him a Slav," said the clerk complacently. "He's a brach, you see, Boss. And that makes his offense a capital one," he added complacently.

"Put him up for the Council, then," growled the magistrate. "Standardize him," he added to the policemen, "and commit him to the Strangers' House pending the Council's ascription."

My captors hurried me away. In the street a large crowd, which had assembled to see me emerge, greeted me with noisy hooting. And, looking again into these hard faces, I began to realize that some portentous change had come over mankind since my long sleep, whose nature I did not understand; but, whatever it was, it had not made men better.

However, the moving platform quickly carried us away, and the mob dwindled, so that when we reached our destination only a nucleus remained. This, however, followed me persistently, gathering to itself other idlers, who ran beside me, peering up into my face, and fingering my tattered clothes, and pulling at the tails of my coat in half-infantile and half-simian curiosity.

The building which we entered contained a single large room on the ground floor, with desks ranged around the walls. Behind each desk a clerk in blue was seated, either contemplating the scene before him or listening disdainfully to applications. I was taken to a desk near the door. One of the policemen now left me, and the other, who had contrived, without my knowledge, to possess himself of the gold watch that had been in my pocket for the last century, placed it upon the desk before the clerk, who came back slowly and resentfully from a fit of abstraction.

"Committed stranger?" he inquired.

"Yap," said the policeman. "He had this."

The clerk stared at the watch, raised it, and let it fall on its face. The glass splintered, and he jumped in his seat as if a pistol had been discharged.

"What is it?" he screamed.

"It looks like an antique chronometer," said the policeman, examining it curiously. "See the twelve hours on the dial."

"Well, they aren't listed," the clerk grumbled.

"You lie, you thief," retorted the policeman.

With some reluctance, but without resentment, the clerk opened a large book in a paper cover, closely printed in fine hieroglyphics interspersed with figures. He turned from place to place until he found what he was trying not to find.

"Museum chronometers, first century B.C. Listed at two hektones," he mumbled, and began unlocking a drawer.

"B. C.!" I exclaimed. "What do you mean?"

He paused in the act of pulling the drawer out and glared at me.

"I said 'museum chronometer of the first century

before civilization,' you fool!" he snarled. "That's what it is, and that's what it's listed at. Here!"

Extracting some metal counters from the drawer, which he closed with a bang, he thrust them toward me.

"What am I to do with these?" I asked.

The policeman winked at him, and I caught the word "Spain." The clerk's amazement changed to malignant mirth.

"The value of your chronometer," he screamed in my ear, as if I were deaf.

"But I don't intend to sell it," I retorted.

A shriek of laughter at my side apprised me that the crowd had gathered about me. The space about the desk was packed with the same sneering, mirthless faces, and fifty hands were raised in mimicry or gesticulation.

"What a barbarian!" murmured a young woman with a typewriter badge on her shoulder.

The clerk looked at her and winked maliciously. Then he addressed me again.

"If you don't understand now, you vill before the Council ends ascribing you," he said. "However, I'll explain. Your museum chronometer, not being an object of necessity, is the property of this Province. This is a civilized country, and you can't have hoard-property here, whatever you can do in Spain. Strangers' effects are bought by the Province at their listed value, and your chronometer is listed at two hundred labor units, or ones — in other words, if you have ever heard of the metric system, two hektones."

"Ah, give him the Rest Cure!" said the girl with the typewriter badge, swinging about and stalking away contemptuously.

I picked up the metal counters and began examining them. They were crudely made, and without milled edges. Two of them appeared to be of aluminum; on one side was an ant in relief, and under it the inscription,

LABOR COMMON
37

on the other side, in bold letters, were the words,

HALF HEKTONE
FIFTY ONES

There were two smaller pieces, of a yellowish-gray, each stamped,

TWENTY-FIVE ONES

It did not take me more than a moment's calculation to see that if the hektone was a hundred units of currency, or labor hours, I had only a hektone and a half instead of two. I told the clerk of the deficiency.

"Don't lie! Sign that!" he shouted, pushing an inkpad and printed form toward me.

"I shall not sign, and I shall bring this theft to the attention of — Doctor Sanson," I said, suddenly recollecting the name.

It was a chance shot, but its effect was extraordinary. The mob, which had begun to jostle me, suddenly scurried away in the greatest confusion. The clerk turned white; he picked up the money with trembling fingers.

"Why, that is so!" he exclaimed. "It was a mistake, Boss. I didn't mean it. I'm sorry. I — I thought you were a blue," he muttered, looking up at me beseechingly. And he returned me a whole half-hektone too much.

I tossed this back to him and returned no answer. I was looking about for a pen with which to sign the receipt when the policeman took hold of my thumb in a comically obsequious manner and pressed the inkpad against it. So I made my mark upon the paper.

In the corridor outside he turned toward me humbly.

"Are you a trapper, Boss?" he asked.

"A what?"

"A switch. A wipe. I mean a council watcher."

"A spy, you mean?" I asked. "Certainly not."

He shook his head in perplexity, and seemed uncertain whether to believe me or not. "He thought you were," he said. "That was an old list he used. You should have had more. Of course I couldn't get in bad with him by telling you, but you'd have had nothing if I hadn't stood up for you. Isn't that worth something, Boss?"

I offered him one of the smaller pieces, rather in fear of giving offense, but he pocketed it at once, and then, with a new aggressiveness toward the gathering crowd, took me upstairs to the Strangers' Bureau. Here I was stripped and examined by two physicians, and photographed in three positions; my finger prints were taken, and the three indexes. Then a dapper little clerk in blue passed a tape measure in several ways about my head and beckoned to me mysteriously to come to his desk.

"It's too bad," he exclaimed.

"What is too bad?" I inquired.

"The difference is five centimeters, and — well, I'm afraid you're a brach. I'd like to help you out, but — well, if I can —"

The meaning of the word suddenly revealed itself to me. "You mean my head is brachycephalic?" I asked.

"There is, unfortunately, no doubt," he answered, and, coming closer under the pretense of measuring me again, began to whisper. "You know, the measure is flexible," he said, glancing furtively about him.

"The revising clerk passes all my measurements without refèrring back to the doctors. There's an understanding between us. Now I could get you into the dolicoph class—"

"The longheads?"

"Yes," he murmured, looking at me with an expression of mutual understanding.

"But what advantage would that be to me?" I inquired.

"They say," he whispered, "that the Council is going to penalize the brachs several points. It is Doctor Sanson's new theory, you know, that the brachs are more defective than the dolicophs. Now I'd risk making you a dolicoph for—would it be worth a hektone to you?"

I flushed with indignation. "Do you suppose I am going to bribe you—?" I began loudly.

The clerk leaped back. "This subject is a brach!" he yelled, and gave the figures to a clerk at the next desk, who made a note on a form and looked at me with intense disgust.

So I was set down as broad-headed. Then I was made to sit before a Binet board, containing wooden blocks of various shapes, which had to be set in corresponding holes within a period timed on a stopwatch. Word associations followed, a childish game at which I had played during the course of my medical training; we had regarded this as one of those transitory fads born in Germany and conveyed to us through the American medium, which came and went and left no by-products except a little wasted enthusiasm on the part of our younger men. I accomplished both tasks easily, and I thought the physicians seemed disappointed.

Finally I received a suit of bluish-gray color, the strangers' uniform, I was informed, and a pair of high, soft shoes. A metal badge, stamped with letters and figures, was hung about my neck by a cord, and I was turned over to the charge of a blue-clad, grizzled man of shortish stature, with a kindly look in the eyes that strongly affected me. For I realized by now that all these persons about me, all whom I had seen, with whom I had conversed, had lacked something more than good-will; they gave me the impression of being animated machines, res-ervoirs of intense energy, and yet not . . . . what? I could not determine them.

There was a patient humility about his bearing, and yet, I fancied, a sort of stubborn power, a con-sciousness of some secret strength that radiated from him.

He came up to me after conversing with the doc-tors, blue-clad men with white capes about their shoulders, all of whom had eyed me curiously dur-ing their speech with him.

"I am the District Strangers' Guard," he said

to me. "You are a foreigner, I understand, and waiting to be ascribed by the Council. It is not necessary to make any explanation to me. I am the guard, and nothing more, and it is my task to provide you with food and lodging in the Strangers' House until you are sent for, S6 1845."

"I beg your pardon?" I asked, before I realized that he was addressing me by the number on the brass badge that hung from my neck.

"My pardon?" he answered, looking at me with a puzzled expression. "That is an antique word, is it not?"

"I mean, I did not know the significance of these numbers," I replied.

"Your brass," he said, still more bewildered. "That is, of course, your temporary number until the Council assigns you to your proper place in the community. It means, as you must be aware, Stranger of the Sixth District. My unofficial name is David. What is yours, friend?"

He almost jumped when I told him, and glanced nervously about him. We had just passed through the doorway, and he drew me to one side, looking at me in a most peculiar manner.

"You must know only one name is legal in this Province," he whispered. "Surely you will not hazard everything by such bravado. I mean — "

He checked himself and searched my eyes, as if

he could not understand whether my ignorance was assumed or real.

"Arnold," he said suddenly, as if he had reached a swift and hazardous decision, "you are to be my private guest. If you are assuming ignorance for safety, you shall learn that there is nothing to fear from me. And when you trust me, you shall give me the news of Paul and all our friends. If you are actually a Spaniard — no, tell me nothing — it is essential that you should learn what all our inmates know, before you go to the Council. Doctor Sanson is not tolerant of strangers unless they learn to conform . . . . I shall help you in every way that is possible. The Bureau Head has asked me to watch you carefully. It is a special order from headquarters. There is some rumor about you . . . . but it will be all right in my own apartment."

I felt too heartbroken more than to thank him briefly. The sense of my isolation in this new world swept over me with poignant power. David must have guessed something of my feeling, for he said nothing more. We halted for a moment at the entrance to the building, and he pulled a watch from his pocket. I saw that the dial, which was not faced with glass, and had the hands inset, was divided into ten main sections, each comprising ten smaller ones.

"Ten hours and seventy-four," he said. "We dine at one-fifty. Seventy-six minutes to get home."

CHAPTER VI

DURING my brief journeys through the streets earlier in the day I had been too conscious of my surprise and perplexity to examine my surroundings with any concentration of mind. Now, standing on the middle platform of what seemed to be one of the principal streets and traveled at a speed of about eight miles an hour, I looked about me with increasing astonishment. I do not know which attracted my attention more, the crowds or the buildings. I asked David for information as we proceeded, stating that I was unable to read the signs, as I was acquainted only with the old alphabet. Seeing his incredulity, I added:

"When you are willing, I shall be glad to tell you my history, though I shall hardly hope to be believed. For the present, let me say that I know nothing at all of your modern civilization."

"But surely in Russia——" David began, and checked himself. Thereafter he seemed to admit the possibility that I was not dissembling, and to consider me as a bona fide traveler from some interior Russian province.

"Our writing is syllabic," he said. "We have

66

gone the round of the circle and now make the syllable the unit instead of the letter, as the Assyrians did, and the Chinese."

"And what is the purpose of this blue paint on the buildings?" I asked, shielding my eyes from the dazzling, blue-white luster.

"Blue?" repeated David in surprise.

"There—and there."

"Why, that is glow, of course," he answered. "Surely you are not color-blind, Arnold? Or can it be that in—where you came from they have only the old seven colors in the spectrum?"

"From red to violet."

He shook his head and looked at me whimsically. "We have had nine for at least twenty years," he said. "Mull, below red, and glow, above violet; what our ancestors called ultra-violet and believed to be invisible, though it was staring them in the face everywhere all the time. There used to be a theory that the color sense has developed with civilization. Don't make any reference to that color-blindness of yours, Arnold," he continued, after a brief pause.

It occurred to me that he had not explained the choice of this color, though he had named it.

"Here is the Bureau of Statistics," he went on, as we traveled past another of the interminable buildings. "This is the Bureau of Prints and Indexes; there are more than a thousand million records within. This is the Bureau of Economics; this of Pedigrees and Relationships; this of Defective Germ-Plasm; and this is our Sixth District School."

The streets were scrupulously clean; they occupied only the central part of the space between the fronts of the buildings, that which would have been called the pavement formerly, being used as resting and lounging places.

"Here is our district store," he added. "Would you like to look inside?"

I assented, and we stepped off the moving portion of the street into an open space surrounded by telephone funnels, at which small groups of men and women were listening. As he halted, a loud voice began calling:

"Latest news! Rain is expected. Don't forget Freedom Day! Muster for your amusement in Picnic Park, or the Council will make it hot for you! The escaped defectives all caught and sent to the leathers. A foreign spy captured this morning after a desperate resistance and now under guard. The miserable defective has confessed, involving numerous others. He is a low-class brach and a filthy degenerate. Boss Lembken is on the job. Praise him!"

"Hurrah!" shouted the mob.

"Come," said David, plucking me by the sleeve. It was only then I realized that the reference was to me. I must have uttered an indignant exclamation, for he drew me away hurriedly.

"Hush! You must keep your tongue guarded in public," he whispered. "One can hear at both ends of the telephone."

"But it is a lie!" I said indignantly. "Who can spread such news as that, and why?"

I noticed that one or two people were watching me curiously. Then, glancing up, I was amazed to see my face outlined upon a screen beneath a hood that formed a dark circle around it. It was an execrable caricature, designed to arouse hate and contempt; and yet the likeness was plainly discernible.

Somehow David got me away. "It will be all right," he kept repeating. "It doesn't mean anything. See, here is our store."

Bewildered, I allowed him to lead me toward the entrance of a large building, before which a woman sat within a cage of crystal.

"Change pieces!" she cried at intervals, in a high-pitched voice. "Change pieces or show brasses!"

"We change our money here," David explained. "Purchases of more than half a hektone are made on the credit system. Our brasses are identification checks. The district clearing-house keeps the complete record of each citizen's financial status."

I had expected to see all the products of the world

spread out within. I found, instead, only a single sample of each kind of merchandise, the goods themselves being stored in warehouses. Seeing an excellent blue overcoat of fine cheviot, I paid thirty ones for it, and David ordered a similar coat to be sent to me at the Strangers' House.

"Watch the street!" he said, as we emerged.

I perceived the passengers scrambling off the moving portion of the roadway. A moment later the track began to travel in the opposite direction.

"We reverse our streets according to the stream of travel," said David. "The mechanism is controlled by solar power, transmitted from the Vosges."

We journeyed for some five and twenty minutes by the new reckoning — what would have been a quarter of an hour. We changed streets frequently, and it seemed to me, although I could not be sure of it, that David purposely selected a roundabout route. At length, we stopped in front of a large building of the uniform height and style. Upon the front was sculptured a man in a laborer's blouse with a protecting hand laid upon the head of one who cowered before him — presumably the stranger.

"I shall take you in by the basement and internal elevator," said David, "so as to give you a glimpse of our traffic system."

We had passed numbers of subway entrances, with

gentle ramps descending into clean, white-walled passages, along which I had seen an endless series of trucks proceeding on single rails. Beneath the Strangers' House I saw the termination of a branch line; and, as we stood watching, a porter in blue seized a small truck which had detached itself from the rail, and, with a slight push, sent it spinning into a goods elevator.

"Gyroscopic action," explained David. "Above this is the House kitchen, connecting with the district sub-kitchen by means of a two-foot tube."

And every now and then he would stop in the midst of his explanations and cast that searching look at me, as if to inquire whether I could be ignorant of all this.

We stepped into an elevator, David pressed a button, and the cage shot up to the top story. Opposite us was a door with a bell at the side, as in the old-fashioned apartment. David rang, and the door opened, revealing a girl about eighteen years of age, who looked at me with parted lips and an expression that was unmistakably fear.

"Arnold, this is my daughter Elizabeth," said David, kissing her. "Arnold is under our special care," he continued. "He comes from a very distant city outside the Federation, and is waiting to be ascribed. He knows no more about civilization than if he had just awakened after a sleep of a century."

The girl shot a quick, dubious, searching glance at me. I met it steadily, and she turned her eyes away. Again she looked at me, and my gaze apparently reassured her, for she gave me her hand in a very unaffected manner, and we went through a living-room into a simply furnished dining-room. It much resembled one of my own century, except that the furniture was in good taste; the curves and spirals and volutes of our machine-carved chairs and tables were gone; the wall was of a plain gray, without paper or pictures; the carpet was plain, and the absence of curls and twists even on the handles of the cutlery was extraordinarily restful. Between the two rooms was a small enclosed space containing a telephone funnel with knobs and levers disposed about it, and a dumb-waiter. The table linen was of a peculiar lusterless black. Looking out of the window, I saw that the uppermost street ran past it, and occasionally the hatless head of a pedestrian appeared.

"Anything new to you, Arnold?" inquired my host, as we took our places at the table.

"Principally the color of the table linen," I answered. "Black seems strange to me."

"Black! Do you call that black?" asked David in surprise. "Why, that is mull, and not at all like black to me. For my part I prefer the old-fashioned white, but two years ago, when the plans to dress us in mull instead of blue were rescinded, the Wool and Linen bosses had accumulated a large quantity of mull goods in the warehouses on speculation, the loss of which would have hurt them badly — so we were asked to use mull-colored table linen."

"Do you like chicken?" inquired Elizabeth. "It is of last year's freezing, and I got it as a special favor, for the supply for 34-5 is not yet exhausted, and they are supposed not to draw on the new cellars. If father had told me that he was going to bring home a guest —"

"But I didn't know it myself," said David. "Of course, I could have telephoned, but —"

"Never do that!" exclaimed Elizabeth impetuously; and I saw the look of fear upon her face again.

A bell sounded, the shaft door clicked open, and a tray lay in the orifice. Elizabeth carried it to the table, and a well-cooked meal was smoking before us.

"You may be surprised to know that this tea was made two miles away," said David, "in the district sub-kitchen. It came to us at seventy miles an hour. Before we had the gyroscopic attachments, fluids were occasionally spilled."

"And how do you clean the apartment?" I asked Elizabeth.

"In the old-fashioned way," she answered, smiling. "I am an expert with the solar vacuum and duster."

"I believe our friend is accustomed to the existence of a servant class," said David, laughing at me.

But there was a subdued melancholy about him, as well as about Elizabeth. The sense of it, and the constraint it bred, grew on me momentarily. After dinner the dishes were sent down the shaft, and David handed me a typical twentieth-century cigar.

"In a sense, this is one of our compromises," he said, as we sat down in the adjoining room. "Doctor Sanson wants to forbid the use of nicotine as impairing the productive efficiency of the race. But the Council thinks the narcotic has a restraining influence —"

He broke off as Elizabeth looked at him rather significantly.

"I understand, then, that the old tendencies toward the illogical and the unnecessary have not been entirely conquered?" I asked.

"No, no!" said David emphatically. "Private apartments, for instance, instead of the phalanstery. And then the tabloid floods! The human stomach still demands bulk as well as nutriment. Still, it is claimed that with education —"

"Do you remember the legend of the man who educated his ass to live on a single straw a day?" asked Elizabeth.

We laughed; but I was still conscious of the restraint.

"Then, of course, people are too lazy, when hungry, to weigh their food and calculate it in calories," David continued. "Doctor Sanson is fighting the abuse of protein. He claims that its decrease will set free more workers to apply themselves to more productive labor instead of food-raising, and will also lengthen the productive life of the individual. But we are still protein gluttons."

"The chicken—" interposed Elizabeth.

It seemed to me that the girl had some serious purpose in her interruptions. I was beginning to realize that she still feared me; I wondered why.

"And you may have observed that the eternal feminine has baffled Doctor Sanson's desire to abolish the skirt," continued David. "In fact, human nature seems to flow on in much the same old way beneath the surface of civilization. I am inclined to think that our economic changes have not seriously amended it."

"Father, if you are going to talk like a heretic, I shall leave you!" exclaimed Elizabeth, rising.

She left the room, and David followed her. Presently he came back alone.

"Arnold," he began, seating himself and knocking the ashes from his cigar, "my daughter is troubled about my frankness with you. You know there is a period of necessary restraint just now, owing to the final adjustment being incomplete.

Some of the oldest men remember the former régime. The Council is strict, and — in short, Arnold, I am putting my own safety in your hands because I trust you, and also because —" He broke off in confusion. "You need to know so much before you face the Council," he resumed. "Arnold, some time I will receive your confidence, and then — well, this misunderstanding will be cleared away."

I shook his hand warmly. "I suppose I am not permitted to leave the apartment?" I asked.

"By all means. Go where you will. Your gray uniform shows you to be an unascribed stranger, and every policeman has your photograph in his thumb-book by now. Only, remember that you must decline to enter into conversation with anyone who may accost you. Please remember this point scrupulously, for your own sake. But, Arnold, do you know, I think you can spend the rest of your day very profitably in learning to read."

"Learn in a day?"

"To some extent. There are only thirty-five principal characters, and all the sub-characters are readily discernible as coming under these heads. I believe Elizabeth has an old spelling-book, and she will be delighted to instruct you."

The idea aroused his enthusiasm, and a few minutes later Elizabeth had begun to give me my lesson. By supper time I had already mastered the elements, and we continued to study in the evening under the soft solar light, which, issuing from small, shaded, glass-covered apertures in the walls, made the room as bright as day.

Soon after dinner the dumb-waiter shaft clicked open and a package lay there. Inside was my overcoat.

At least, it was meant for me. But instead of the fine cheviot, I discovered a wretched mixture of cotton and shoddy. I was indignant.

David advised me to do nothing. "A stranger sometimes gets poor service," he explained.

"It is a deliberate fraud, then?" I demanded.

He placed his hand restrainingly on my arm. "Is it worth while quarreling with the Wool Boss before you go to the Council?" he asked.

He went on to explain that each industry was autonomous, and had its own boss, elected annually by the workers, in theory, but for life in practice. The Wool Boss, like the other bosses, received one per cent upon the value of every article made by his department.

"At present our social organization is a little upset," he explained again. When the Russian troubles are ended we shall resume our normal life. There will be more spaciousness, more freedom . . . . liberty will be enlarged . . . ."

We went to bed early. I was grateful to discover

that the old-fashioned bed had not been sent into limbo. But then the bed, of course, antedates history.

David apologized for mentioning bedtime.

"Nine is the curfew hour," he explained. "At nine-half the solar light goes out. It is only a temporary restriction until—" Again he checked himself.

I mused so long that the solar light, which flooded the bedroom within and made London a vivid picture in a black frame without, was suddenly turned off, leaving me to grope my way into bed in the darkness. I lay thinking of Esther, who had died so long ago, and I knew that when the first bewilderment of the new life had passed away my loss would seem as unbearable as before. I was as helpless as a savage in this fantastic city. It seemed incredible that I had been groping in the cellar that same morning.

I thought of Elizabeth and the terrified look in her eyes; I heard a city clock strike ten, and, an hour later, one, and it was long before I remembered that ten was midnight; my last resolve was to try to forget my former life and fling myself with all my power into the new. At last I fell asleep, to be awakened by the sun shining into my eyes along a canyon that stretched between the high buildings as far as I could see.

CHAPTER VII

IT WAS not until a week had passed that the first stimulus of the amazing life into which I had been plunged abated, leaving me a prey to melancholy reflections. The memory of Esther, which I had tried so hard to put away, began to recur incessantly. I felt shut off from humanity, a survival from a generation whose memory, even, had become legendary.

They seemed to understand my feelings, although they could not know their cause, and tried to keep me from brooding. By tacit understanding no references were made to my past. They accepted me as a stranger, and yet there was the same latent suspicion on Elizabeth's part. And I could not help seeing that some heavy grief or apprehension hung over them. And I felt that I was an intruder upon it. At night I would hear David pacing his room for hours, and sometimes a groan would break from his lips.

He gave me to understand that the summons to appear before the Council might be delayed for days or weeks. It was always presented unexpectedly, and always peremptory, he said. During the week following my arrival at the Strangers' House I never went out alone. Whenever I made the suggestion, David either volunteered to accompany me or found some excuse to detain me. In particular, he requested me to stay within doors during the four hours when he was at the Bureau, in the morning.

Finally I became almost exasperated. "You have told me that I am free," I protested.

"And you are free, Arnold," he answered. "It is for your own sake that I make this request of you. There are hidden things, shadows against the sunlight of our civilization, and transitory, I hope, which you would hardly understand. You must learn them by degrees, Arnold. To me they have seemed necessary in this transitional epoch; but they are hard, Arnold; hard to endure."

And he sighed in so melancholy a fashion that I suspected one of those shadows rested on his own home.

Yes, there were hidden things, and I got no nearer the heart of them, although I had hints as to their nature. For instance, there was the Animal Vivisection Bureau. I wondered why David spoke of the Animal Vivisection Bureau, and not of the Vivisection Bureau.

I never had realized before how large a share animals played in our lives. The horse, I was told, had not existed in the British Province for a generation.

Cats disappeared when the rodent virus was invented, and were now only to be found in a wild state in the woods. There seemed to be no dogs, and I did not ask David about them.

There was no social life at all. The other inmates of the Strangers' House were lodged on the different floors and ate in common, living under the watchful care of the deputies, who occasionally came to David for advice or instructions. Our only neighbor on the top floor was a little woman with two children who had come from a northern city and intended to return as soon as passes for leaving London, which had been stopped, were again issued. Inspectors from the Children's Bureau visited her nearly every day, always leaving her in a condition of terror, as I inferred from a remark dropped by Elizabeth. Her husband had dropped dead in the street two months before. David told me that these sudden deaths were common, and were considered a triumph for medical science.

And yet I knew that David had visitors after the solar lights went out. My room was at the end of the apartment near the street; but I heard strangers tiptoe along the passage, and whispered colloquies in David's room. My host would appear abstracted the next morning, and watch me very thoughtfully. At such times I felt more than ever an intruder in the household.

Yes, it was a world Lazaroff would have appreciated, could he have had his wish fulfilled, to be born into it. Would his viewpoint have changed, I wondered? It was a world from which all the amenities and charities of life seemed to have been banished. I tried to lead up to that subject in my talks with David, but he appeared unable to understand me.

Was it an atheistic world? I had not ventured to question David about this. But I knew that there was no Sunday upon the calendar, and that the tenth day was the civil holiday. That day had fallen already, and endless crowds had marched through the streets, to the music of bands, to play-places in waste spots outside London. The Council supervised the games, which were compulsory. Of all the paternal regulations of the Council, this seemed to me the most arbitrary and oppressive.

"We have to keep the people under discipline," David explained. "Once they were allowed to wander at will; but they tore up the trees and flowers and strewed paper and broken bottles everywhere."

That was true. I remembered the public fields of my own age. I recalled how one writer had seen in them a complete indictment of democracy itself.

I was amazed and alarmed increasingly by what I saw in my journeys about the town with David: the large brass tags that gave each person his label, the occupation badges, the insolence of the whites, pass-

ing with bodyguards of blues who elbowed all out of
their way. And once there came a frantic scramble
to make a passage for a tall, black-bearded man in a
dark-blue uniform, who passed in the midst of his
retinue with clanking sword.

I had noticed these men in uniform about the
streets. They strode like conquerors amid a servile
populace. I learned that the tall man was Mehemet,
a Turk in command of an international force, the
bodyguard of Sanson, and devoted to him.

Perhaps it was as well that, before my enlightenment came, I completed a cursory survey of the new
civilization. At my request David took me to one of
the public schools. I was astonished to discover that
no history prior to 1945 was taught, and no geog-
raphy. The greater part of the curriculum was
devoted to scientific and economic subjects. So great
had been the progress in knowledge that, on opening some of the text-books, I discovered that I was
quite unable to understand them.

I learned that Oxford and Cambridge had disappeared, with the old public schools, in 1945, after
a revolution, the anger of the people having been
kindled against them on account of their moral influence and the distinctive stamp of character that they
produced. To prevent tutors of personality from
imparting to their pupils the elements of humane
tradition, David told me, the text-books were so

written as to eliminate entirely the personal element in instruction, a reform that the prophet Wells had urged rather furiously, and perhaps invidiously, in his own century.

"The Council shapes each citizen's education from the cradle to the workshop," said David. "It is very anxious to secure precision of knowledge. For instance, it is a criminal offense for mothers to teach their children fairy stories. It is the duty of the inspectors to question children rigorously, in order to ascertain whether they are acquainted with any of this unscientific, heretical folk-lore."

"Which has doubtless all perished," I said.

"On the contrary," he answered, "an immense quantity of it has come down to us, practically unchanged, through all the revolutions of the past century, and not only that but new tales have arisen. The authorities are at their wits' end to discover who is responsible for the existence of this masonic secret among the younger generation."

From the school we went to the workshop. On the way home we stopped at one of the open-air moving picture shows, and saw two or three dramatized versions of public affairs. Ingenious mechanism synchronized the movements of the figures upon the screen, which were in stereoscopic relief, with speeches made through the telephone funnels. These, David said, took the place of newspapers when the socialized State destroyed the printed news-sheet by the simple process of killing the advertising.

We also looked inside the district art gallery. None of the pictures antedated the year 1978, and each illustrated some phase of the new civilization in an educational way. I must not forget to say that later I found a novel in David's home, which Elizabeth must have read in her schoolgirl days. The scene was laid in the early twentieth century, and the story dealt with the adventures of a young man of property, depicting the romance of his care-free life. A moral at the end, and copious footnotes, inserted by the Council's order, drew attention to the improvement in the human lot since that barbarous period.

So, day by day, I waited, and my eyes were opened more and more to my environment. Daily I expected the Council summons that did not come, and daily the constraint grew. I was thinking of suggesting to David that I should be located among the other strangers in place of continuing to accept his hospitality; but before I could decide to approach him an incident occurred which revealed to me the existence of conditions which, unintelligible though they were, made me decide to approach David again with a view to a mutual understanding.

David was at the Strangers' Bureau and would not return for at least two hours. Under Elizabeth's

instruction I had made swift progress in understanding the combinations of syllables that make up the
written language. I had just begun, in fact, to master the ingenious Brebœuf system, whereby the sim-
pler of the syllables have been combined to form the
written speech of four of the five Provinces. David
had told me that the Council's inability to enforce
the invented language Spekezi as the universal
tongue, had been one of the severest shocks that the
new civilization had received. Then came Brebœuf
with his universal syllabic symbols.

Now, if the written language were merely picto-
rial, it could have been used to represent all the languages on earth. But since it is syllabic, and therefore depicts words instead of ideas, it was a supreme
achievement to have invented a written language
adapted to four tongues. The Brebœuf system is
based, of course, upon the common Latin and San-
skrit elements. Brebœuf, who was one of the last of
the classical scholars, was rewarded, as is well
known, by being freed from the defectives' art
factories in his old age, and pensioned.

However, it was not my purpose to touch upon
this matter. My interest was beginning to flag, and
I was paying more attention to Elizabeth than to the
lesson. I was trying to trace in her features some
elusive resemblance to Esther. I was wondering
whether I could ever become a normal citizen of

this strange world. Suddenly the telephone funnel shouted Elizabeth's name.

She sprang from her chair and rushed into her bedroom, which was next to the external elevator shaft. Her expression and gestures alarmed me so greatly that I ran after her. When I reached her door I saw her standing in the middle of the room, deathly white, and clenched in her hand was a knife, which she was aiming at her heart.

I ran into the room and wrested the weapon from her grasp. She fell upon the floor unconscious. All the while this was happening the funnel was shouting stridently, "Elizabeth!" "Elizabeth!" together with the string of letters and figures that completed her nomenclature.

I went to the funnel and lied to the voice. "She is not here," I said.

"Then tell her, when she returns, that the price of the dress will be five units more, on account of the new wool schedule," the voice responded.

Such was the half-comic ending of what had nearly been a tragedy. I revived the girl and explained the matter to her, but for some time she remained in a condition approaching collapse. When she began to regain consciousness she wept hysterically.

It was only the fear of causing David anxiety that enabled her to resume her accustomed demeanor by the time he returned. She begged me to make no mention of the matter to him, and I agreed on condition that she would never use the knife except in the last extremity. But I was working in the dark, for, though she consented to the bargain, when I begged her to tell me what it was she feared, she remained mute, shaking her head and closing her mouth obstinately.

"Will you not trust me, Elizabeth?" I pleaded.

Then, to my surprise, she looked accusingly at me. "Will you trust me?" she asked. "Will you not trust my father and me? Haven't you news of Paul?" Her expression was indescribably beseeching.

"We don't know who you are," she went on rapidly. "My father trusts everybody. But I know your assumed ignorance is impossible. You don't trust us, Arnold, and you are playing with us. You have been here three weeks and the Council has not sent for you. If you were what you claim to be you would know your danger. Trust us, and, if you are what we hoped you were, tell me about Paul. Is he safe? Is he well?"

"I never heard of him," I stammered. "I—"

She looked at me with reproach and glided quietly away. I heard her sigh mournfully. And still I groped in a fog of mystery and could learn nothing.

CHAPTER VIII

HOW THE WORLD WAS MADE OVER

DAVID possessed a small library of books, nearly all of a scientific nature. Among them, however, I found two histories, and, in spite of their obvious bias and violent character, I was enabled to understand what had happened in the world since my long sleep began.

I learned of the great war that had begun a few days after I entered the cylinder, when Russia and the democracies of Europe stamped out German autocracy and laid the foundations of democratic government. I learned how this democratic spirit burst out in 1945, when all the experiences of the social order, accumulated by mankind since the dawn of history were jettisoned, with all their lessons and all their warnings.

It was extraordinary to me that none of us had realized the changes which had been impending. Warnings there had been, as there always are. They were the decay of parliamentary government in all lands, the breaking down of tradition and authority in every phase; only there was nobody to heed them. Then, previously, whether by acknowledgment or in spite of denial, society had always been founded on servile labor. The harnessing of the tides, and, later, the control of solar power, threw millions out of employment, millions of hungry men with time to think and nothing to reverence.

The book said that the movement could have been stayed by wise measures. But it was doubtful, for a frenzy for change was spreading like wildfire over the civilized world. Now only Spain, restored Russia, and monarchical and prosperous South America resisted it, among Occidental nations.

I read that in 1945 democracy initiated the millennium by bursting all the dykes. Millions were slain. London, Paris, Berlin, New York, Chicago, Winnipeg were burned to ashes, with scores of other cities. Peace was restored fifteen years later by a few military chiefs who came into power owing to the universal exhaustion. At that time whole populations were turning cannibal. All organized industries had been destroyed. The path for reconstruction was clear.

Men called that the period of reaction, but it might have been the period of reconciliation. Both sides failed in the ensuing years; the mob, because it lacked idealism; the leaders, because they failed to recognize the unassailable truth in the old Socialist propaganda, that the era of machinery and of an inexhaustible supply of industrial power had made the systematization of production inevitable. With half the people workless, it was ridiculous that they should suffer and starve because they could not buy the goods rotting in the stuffed warehouses. The system did not fall because it was ridiculous, however, but because it had become unworkable. Production had to be for use, not profit. When profit went, rent had to go, and interest, that leech of society, so long forbidden by the Catholic Church, and no doubt the direst result of the Reformation. Failure to realize this need dragged down the old order in 1978. It fell forever, and with it died all hope of a civilization built on that of the past.

It was then that the writings of the great Wells, since called the Prophet, were discovered and proved the inspiration of the new order. In place of the illogical instinct of nations there was to be a New Republic, based on pure reason, and shining with facets of unanswerable facts. The world was to forget its past as thoroughly as it had forgotten the Stone Age. The new revolution was led by Sanson, I gathered, and swiftly conquered. There ensued two years of worse anarchy than before. India was lost to Britain, and became a democracy, convulsed with civil strife. Our savage wards reverted to barbarism. Australia fell to China. All the world's archives were destroyed. Picture galleries went up in flames; statues were smashed to pieces; monuments were blasted. The Parthenon perished, the

British Museum, the Louvre; east of the Bosphorus there remained hardly a memorial of the past, except St. Peter's and Cologne Cathedral. But, at the end of the two years, the five Provinces of Britain, France, Skandogermania, Italy, and Hungary found themselves the nucleus of the future Federation of Man, under a pure democracy.

Here, amid fulsome plaudits, the tale ended; but I went to David to ask him for some more particulars. He had seen me reading, and I think he had been prepared for my question.

"I shall be glad to explain anything, Arnold," he said.

"I have been reading about the new Federation," I said. "England is, then, no longer independent? And the United States? And Russia and Spain?"

He smiled. "Of course, if you do not know these things, Arnold —" he began. "But surely you are at least aware of the history of your own country?"

"I know nothing," I answered.

"Well, then, the United States is an independent nation. We have made proposals for a union, but the bosses have not yet come to terms. Spain stamped out her revolution. We were on the point of compelling her to come in when she discovered the secret of the Glow Ray, which would have made the effort unremunerative."

"What is this Ray?"

"It is a combustion by old light, stored solar energy being transmitted for that and all other power purposes from the great solar works on the Vosges Mountains. Its invention made the old warfare obsolete. Our small-arms are miniature Ray mirrors, charged with a single unit; our big ordnance is supplied from the Vosges by cable connection. The Ray destroys everything that it encounters, not protected by the glow paint which you may have observed on the fronts of our buildings. This is the last and greatest of the coal tar discoveries, and its manufacture is based upon the exact relationship between the disintegrating glow rays and an exact color having a fixed number of vibrations.

"Russia," he continued, "crushed her revolution, too, as she had crushed earlier anarchistic outbreaks. But though she has discovered the glow paint, she has not the Ray. The Federation is consequently at war with her, for her antiquated ideals make her a menace to civilization. Besides, we need her wheat-fields. We have an army of ten thousand men, two from each of the five Provinces, and have cooped up the young Tsar, Alexander, with his army of a million men, in Tula. His surrender is expected daily."

"Ten thousand against a million?"

"Yes, with the Ray. However, even ten thousand were difficult to secure, though the pay of each soldier is five units hourly. Twelve men have been killed already. That is the weak point in our civilization, Arnold. In spite of daily lectures by the most gifted orators that the Council can obtain, showing that the desire for immortality is an inherited perversion, and that we are immortal anyway, in the germ-plasm, man is unwilling to die. In time the Council hopes, by reason and education, to rid men of this ancient terror."

"What is the ethical basis of our government?" I asked.

"Science, which alone survived the destruction of knowledge. The scientific books were saved from the twelve million tons of printed paper, chiefly from the British Museum shelves, that burned for twelve days upon Blackheath; and from the contents of the Bibliotheque Nationale that heated Paris during an entire month.

"A commission quickly synthesized the discoveries of earlier investigators. World councils of scientists laid down the dogmas of universal knowledge in the Vienna Creed, which was adopted without dissentients after those who objected had been put to death. The famous quarrel whether Force is of the same substance as Matter, or a like substance, was decided here. The Sames conquered the Similars, by virtue of a proclamation from Boss Rose.

"We know now that Science has given Nature's

complete and final revelation to mankind. We tolerate no heresies, no independent judgment. In vital matters toleration means only a dead faith. The Modernist idea of criticizing the basic principles of our Science becomes a capital offense, if preached, because the Boss is himself the repository of all knowledge, and the pronouncements of Boss Lembken supreme. It is not that we are bigoted, you understand. It is, indeed, suggested that Science unfolds like a flower, revealing herself in larger scope to each generation. But new discoveries can only be adaptations of what is already known."

I almost thought that there was irony in his tone; but he met my gaze steadily, challengingly, as if to say, "If these are not your views, declare them."

"One thing I want to know is this," I said. "The history books make no mention of the blues and the whites. On what do you base the division of the State into these two groups of citizens?"

"That is Doctor Sanson's doing," he answered. "The blues are the defectives, the whites the perfect specimens of the race. The whites alone are admitted to posts of responsibility. But most of them prefer not to labor, and live in seclusion upon State pensions for the sake of the race.

"This is considered Doctor Sanson's crowning achievement for humanity," David continued. "Before his advent to power, defectives had been living among the normal population since the dawn of history unrecognized. We have now an intricate system of points of deficiency whereby they can be detected infallibly, based partly upon heredity, partly on measurements, partly craniometry and the Binet-Sanson tests.

"Doctor Sanson has long been anxious to pass his sterilization measure, but he has been unable to persuade the Council to face the fierce, ignorant, popular resentment that it would incur, although this practice is of respectable antiquity in China and the Mohammedan world, and was reintroduced to the Occident by progressive America a whole century ago. Of course, the morons and all below a certain grading are not allowed to reproduce their kind; but Sanson wishes to include the high-grade defectives also. However, that would reduce the total productivity, and thus the question bristles with difficulties."

As I listened to all this jargon I felt more and more bewildered.

"You appear to have created a new aristocracy, then, based on·physical perfection," I said.

"No, there you are wrong, Arnold," said David. "Our democracy will never endure hereditary privileges. What it has introduced is hereditary disabilities. We simply disqualify from the white, or normal class, the ninety-five per cent who are below the standard. It was progressive America that first conceived the plan of raising man to the level of the hound and the blooded horse.

"Yet," he continued, "defectives do crop up, even among the offspring of the whites. They are hard to discover; but by the Sanson tests we can discover defectives who are, to all appearance, flawless. This class exists especially among those of unusual mental power, which is in itself a stigma of deficiency. Then there are the men who write our books and paint our pictures in the art factories. They present an anarchical longing for personal license. But they are isolated and never allowed to mingle with the world. Yes, there are odd kinks in the human brain. For instance, there still exists a preposterous sense of nationality, which is being remedied by a system of forced emigration. The Prophet Wells did not entirely estimate in its exactness the tenacity of this illogical notion.

"Then there was that extraordinary outbreak, the Name War. Who could have anticipated that human beings would object to being classified under letters and numbers, for the sake of statistical simplicity? Yet a misguided fifty thousand chose to meet death rather than give up their names. However, Britain is said to be the province of compromises, and it was agreed that the whites should retain two names, and the blues one."

"But surely," I said, "the people did not vote for these restrictions?"

"You do not understand our system of government, Arnold. Naturally there can be no voting in matters of science, sanitation, or statistics. Yet, even here there is an indirect control, for our rulers, who are whites, are elected by ballot annually, by the high-grade defectives of both sexes. The Federal Council, which is not now in session, meets once a year in London, the capital, and consists of five lay bosses, of whom Lembken is chief, and five Science bosses under Sanson. You will appreciate the stability of our government when I tell you that for twenty years every nominated boss has been re-elected."

I was almost certain of an undertone of irony in his words now.

"You see," he continued, "non-votes are counted as ayes. Then those opposing the Council must give their reason, which is filed in the Bureau of Complaints. And again all such objections have been found to be invalid, since they have invariably been made by undetected morons, who have been sent to the workshops for life in consequence. Every applicant at the Bureau of Complaints is examined by physicians. That was Sanson's idea."

A most ingenious one. Suddenly I became sure that David was testing me; the whole tenor of his conversation had been ironical, hesitating, perhaps, and carefully weighed, lest he was running into danger, but corresponding in no wise to his convictions. But why was he afraid of me?

"Who is this Doctor Sanson?" I asked him.

To my surprise his voice dropped, and, before answering, he cast a cautious glance toward the telephone funnel. Then, rising, he stuffed a sofa cover into it.

"An illegal act," he said, reseating himself. "If that were known I should be liable to forced labor in the leather factories for several years. Now, Arnold, you see my faith in you. Well, then, I cannot answer you. He is a man of superhuman powers, more feared than any man has ever been feared. There is a popular belief that he was born a thousand years ago, and has wandered from land to land, waiting for the new age to dawn. The Christians called him Antichrist. Nothing has ever been learned as to his origin. He appeared like a conqueror, about the year 1980, to lead the hosts of the revolution to victory."

"He is the ruler?"

David shook his head. "Boss Lembken is the titular head. But all know that Sanson is supreme, although he chooses to let Boss Lembken hold the reins of power. He could do anything, make any laws he wished, become supreme ruler of earth. He is believed to be immortal, and to have the power of renewing his youth whenever he wishes. Arnold, the people believe that he can bestow immortality upon them and overcome their last enemy, death. That is the secret of their terror of him. And—"

His voice sank to a whisper:

"You have come at a critical time. For this expectancy has set a date. None knows how the rumor started, but during the next few months, 'soon after the Cold Solstice,' the prophecy runs, a Messiah is to come to earth, ignorant of his destiny. When he learns it he will offer mankind its ancient liberty. Sanson will offer immortality in place of it. Then will come the most titanic of all struggles, and the result is not known."

His voice quavered and ceased. And, staring at him, incredulous at first, I realized that David was repeating no foolish, popular tale, but what he himself believed.

Even Science had not succeeded in banishing faith from the hearts of men. She had made it superstition instead. My brain reeled as the dreadful picture David had drawn came home to me.

"David," I exclaimed impulsively, "you are an educated man and an intelligent one. Why do you not wear the white uniform? Surely you are not a defective?"

"Yes," he replied. "Under the Sanson law. My

father had epileptic seizures in his youth. He had to hide — but some day I will tell you about that. It penalizes me twelve points, and Elizabeth six, thank God!"

And, just as the airscout's face had expressed fear at my own expletive, so David recoiled in horror at the word that had burst from his lips.

"Arnold," he said, taking me by the arm, "there is a book — an illegal book, to possess which would mean death. I am going to lend it to you — and after you have read it you can tell me your story."

CHAPTER IX

I FOUND the book beneath my pillow. David had been afraid to hand it to me, and I was not surprised. For assuredly the anonymous author would have received the utmost penalty from the Council.

He was a Christian, and he took the ground that democracy, in itself bad, had become impossible when the atheistic deism of the eighteenth century pervaded the minds of the voting masses and took the form of Haeckel's materialism and that of his school of thinkers.

He claimed that, so far from indicating the spread of enlightenment, it was due to national decay, and had always preceded periods of national reconstruction, instancing Rome and Athens, and the America of a century ago, where democracy had become incompatible with free speech and assembly, an independent judiciary, and a broad and secure freedom.

Written for circulation among those opposed to the Sanson régime, it was a fervent prayer for the deliverance of the world. In it I gathered more of the meaning of the new civilization than I had learned from David.

102

I read that the War of the Nations was caused by one thing alone: the breaking down of Christianity in Germany, and the revival of the old pagan doctrines, with the ensuing challenge against all that humanity had built up during two thousand years.

But in that period of ferments only a few had seen this meaning. The challenge had been interpreted as one of aristocracy against democracy, largely because democracy, then in the saddle, was the creed of the loudest publicists. For this the writer Wells, known posthumously as "The Prophet," a man whose penetrating judgment and synthetic mind were fogged by class consciousness, was largely responsible.

The hope of democracy was fair in those after-years, when nations, purged by their ordeal of blood, revived the noble hopes of liberty. Men would have sacrificed everything for their brethren during that first decade of peace. There was a splendid spiritual awakening among the nations. Democracy was the young, smiling god, the guardian of universal peace.

If only, the writer said, that spiritual enlargement had been joined to Christian faith. But the backwash of nineteenth century atheism swamped it. The doctrines of materialism were rooted in the masses. The German virus could not be rooted out without trained leadership and ideals. I recalled

Sir Spofforth's words when I read that. "It must not happen again!" all men had said, when at last peace triumphed. No, not if the spirit of Christ, governing all men, had drawn them into brotherhood. But what if insults had been heaped upon the German people? What hope of peace was there when hate such as this ruled in the mind of the leader of the new faith?

Instead of Christ, these blind philosophers set up their democratic god. They labelled war "dynastic," and believed democracy would destroy it. Had they not used their eyes? Did they not know that war was the embodiment of hate? Had they never looked on a mob, shouting for war, or was human nature to be changed by education, and through prosperity, so that no nation would ever again gather to itself false doctrines, with hate, and scorn, and pride, and go forth to destroy?

As every century produced its dominant illusion, so now in the twentieth this singular delusion of a democracy progressing through graded virtue unto a perfect day possessed the race. And here the writer paused to draw another instance from America, not, as he was painstaking to explain, because her inhabitants were different from other men, but because they were the same.

He showed how decadence had spread exactly as democracy had spread. He told of the two counties

of Ohio where investigation showed the inhabitants
to have sold their votes universally — merchants and
clergymen, professional men and laborers. Corruption radiated from the English-speaking centers.
Law, principle, and integrity had gone first in New
England and the South, in the withered branches of
Anglo-Saxondom that had broken from the bough.
One by one all the traditions of civic honesty had
died; and if life was still tolerable in the early twentieth century, when justice was a byword and faith
in public men had almost ceased, it was because the
State was still largely an abstraction and people
could still keep aloof from politics.

All the while there existed the same pitiable belief
that this democracy would some day become honest,
all-good, all-wise; but this was democracy and the
fruits of it, and nowhere had it had a fairer chance
to inaugurate the millennium. And the same mob
that ran blindly after its blind leaders, responsive to
every prejudice, to the old Moloch of race-hatred and
the old Mammon of dishonesty, would, had it been
allowed, have followed an ideal with its fund of
inexhaustible loyalty and self-sacrifice.

Men had not changed. The Amazon and Congo
valleys were drenched with the blood of murdered
natives, and democracy yawned, just as the blood
of Polish women and children, massacred by State
troops, cried from the Colorado mining camps. In

former days Christian orders arose to uphold justice and to keep down the devil in man. When Christendom was one, labor guilds had arisen under Catholic auspices whereby all men could live in freedom; now the Pope, impotent, could only issue an encyclical against that oppression of labor which, in its turn, begot hatred and war. The sword of Justice had been snapped in the scabbard.

Was this the hope of the world, he asked, this barren, Christless democracy? How many hearts had it broken? How many idealists had sacrificed themselves before this idol, dying with blind faith in a deity that devoured its votaries? Was there no higher hope? Were millions of colored men and women in America to be born forever, black cattle without hope, and die without a part in life? Had not the race at last turned on itself, when the eugenics madness thrust the sword into the heart of every family and made life a more loathsome slavery than any the world had known? What a sinister end to human hopes!

The persecutions of the mob always struck to degrade humanity. And when England developed, in proportion to her democracy, the same corruption as the United States, the same lack of loyalty and public sense, the same violence and the same vindictiveness, that was suspected which happened afterward — that the same types of men would rise to leadership, and her faithful, loyal heroes vanish like smoke in a gale.

And all the time the remedy was at hand; no Moloch of hate, no stock-farm theory of human bodies, but the principles of Christ, imposed to save the world by leaders who had abdicated their responsibility. The mob could never understand the need of abstract justice nor subordinate greed to duty. But for some ideal, however dimly seen, it could obey and sacrifice itself with matchless zeal, even to death.

Truly the Prophet Wells had prophesied of the years to come: "Not only will moral standards be shifting and uncertain, admitting of physiologically sound menages of very variable status, but also vice and depravity, in every form that is not absolutely penal, will be practiced in every grade of magnificence, and condoned."

A shadow fell across the book. I looked up and saw David. He had been glancing over my shoulder as I read, unconscious of him; and he had reached these words with me.

His eyes flashed, he shook his fist in vehemence of passion. "No, Arnold!" he cried. "We'll fight as long as we live to remain something better than the beasts; if life is a lie, or a dream, we'll fight for that!"

CHAPTER X

THE DOMED BUILDING

"ARNOLD! Arnold!"

The funnel in the room was calling me, not in its customary strident tones, but with a muffled, intimate appeal.

David was at the Bureau, and Elizabeth had gone out on one of her infrequent journeys. It was as if the voice knew I was alone, for it had never spoken to me before, and had never called in that particular tone of intimacy and understanding.

"Arnold, I am your friend," the voice continued. "You will come to no good in the Strangers' House. Go out quietly by the external elevator at once and proceed toward the Temple, where everything will be explained to you."

My bewilderment changed to intense expectancy. The Temple was, I knew, the domed building that seemed to dominate London; I had seen it from afar each time David and I had gone out together, and each time David had seemed sedulously to avoid approaching it, proceeding and returning in a circuitous manner.

"See for yourself the heritage of the new civilization," the voice continued. "Do not allow yourself

108

to be made a prisoner by those who wish you no good. Go out at once by the external elevator. Turn to the right. Walk slowly. Look about you. Your friends are watching you."

I went out and descended the building by the external elevator. A minute later I was upon the traveling street, feeling like a runaway schoolboy, and animated by an intense desire to solve the secret that lay before me.

Presently, remembering that I was to proceed slowly, I had the curiosity to step off the traveling platform into a large, open space on which a crowd was seated. I took my post beside one of the funnels that surrounded it, and saw that I was at one of the moving picture performances. Spelling out the title upon the curtain, I understood that news from Russia was to be given.

There was none of that blur of vision which was a common defect of the old-fashioned pictures, and the words spoken from the funnels synchronized so perfectly with the actions on the screen that the illusion was complete. Upon the parapet of the fortress reared by our besieging troops I saw machines with conical tops, faced with large, glow-painted shields. As I watched, there rushed across the field of vision a number of men of the most degraded, savage aspect, armed with long swords, which they brandished furiously, while the funnels yelled like demons.

"These are the Russian savages, filthy defectives who are attacking the army of the Federation," announced the funnel at my side, in such a personal way that I started, imagining for a moment that someone had spoken to me.

As the horde neared the fortress a short command was uttered, and from each of the conical machines a glare of light shot forth. The Russians wilted and crumpled up. They did not fall; they were rather consumed like lead dropped into fire, and the next line wilted too as the Ray caught them, tumbling in charred masses upon the bodies of their companions. Higher and higher rose the dreadful pyramid of mortality, until the field was empty.

"The victory of Science over Superstition," announced each funnel simultaneously. "The Russians do not possess the Ray. They are degraded outcasts, refuse from the pre-civilization period, starving in Tula, and will all die unless they surrender soon. What a pity to have to destroy so much potential productivity! It is the Tsar's fault. He is a dirty moron, full of germ life, and has never produced a hektone in his life. We shall next see him before the Council. Boss Lembken is on the job. Praise him!"

"Hurrah" yelled the spectators, rising in their seats to cheer.

The curtain darkened, and the next scene of the

drama was displayed. It was laid in the Council Hall; but inasmuch as the Council was not in session, and the Tsar was not yet captured, it possessed a certain unreality for me which the audience did not seem to share. With considerable interest I watched the ten about the Council table. At the head sat a figure of enormous girth, dressed in white, with a black, or probably mull robe about the shoulders. The face, appalling in its grossness, must be that of Lembken, titular ruler of the Federation, a fat old man with huge paunch and shrunken throat, on which the sagging cheeks hung like a dewlap. A fit head for such a people!

Beside him sat a man of about the same age, per-haps sixty years, but lithe and lean and muscular, and with the keenest, cruelest face that I ever had seen. His whitening hair was brushed back from his forehead, and his expression was so full of sinis-ter and malignant power that I knew this could be none other than Sanson, the devil of this devil's world, who ruled the superstitious multitude by the terror of "Science become Faith," as old Sir Spof-forth had so aptly phrased it.

And, as I looked at him, I seemed to see the fea-tures of Herman Lazaroff, as he might have been in his old age. There was the same self-confidence, become arrogance, and self-assertion grown with power, the same demoniac energy and will, trained by its use upon a servile multitude. Thus Lazaroff might have been, if he could have had his wish to live again.

What struck me, as I gazed upon the strong, clean-shaven faces about the Council board, was that they seemed to reproduce the aspect and gestures of the degenerate emperors of Rome. Was history repeating itself; a state-fed mob, state-governed industries, the fist of autocracy beneath the glove of impotent democracy, and those terrific incarnations of cruelty and insane pride in power?

I saw the Tsar, a dwarfish, wretched figure in a tinsel crown, dragged, groveling, to Lembken's feet, while Lembken assumed an attitude of inflexibility; and then once more the curtain darkened.

"Praise your Boss!" hooted the funnels. "He is the people's friend. That's how he deals with kings! He shows no mercy to the people's enemies. The Tsar is a low-grade moron. His heredity is horrible. He cannot pass Test I upon the Binet board. He is a wretched brach, and will now work in the leathers till he dies, producing for you."

"Hurrah!" screamed the spectators. "Out with him! To the Rest Cure!"

And the absurdity of the display came home to none except myself. These citizens were in deadly earnest. How shrewd the mind that had contrived a pabulum so well calculated to appeal to the mob palate! The contrived crudeness, the planned abuse betrayed an intimate and assured acquaintance with the people's psychology.

"Praise louder!" whispered the intimate voice beside me. "Why do you not praise when the others do?"

And then I realized that the funnel was speaking to me! Nobody else had heard, nobody else was meant to hear. I knew that the funnels had a tele-photophonic attachment whereby one could see as well as hear. Somewhere, then, the person who had spoken to me that morning was watching and playing with me. For an instant I felt caught in a trap.

"You do not seem to be an admirer of Boss Lembken," said a voice upon my other side; and I swung around to see a little, sallow man in blue, with a plank badge on his shoulder, indicating that he was a carpenter. "I see you are a stranger," he continued, with a glance at my gray uniform. "What do you think of London?"

"I have not seen much of it as yet," I answered, remembering David's warning.

"Ah, you are diplomatic," he returned suavely. "One has to be diplomatic in these days, do you not think? You are of the same opinion as many of us, only you lack the courage to say it, that certain features of our civilization are over-developed. Now let us take Doctor Sanson, for instance — do you not consider that he is pushing his prosecution of morons to undue lengths? Has he not, in other words, a mania about them?"

"I think," I answered, hotly, "that a man whose chief amusement consists in torturing his fellow-men needs to have his own mentality investigated."

"A worthy sentiment," answered the little man, nodding his head briskly. In short, you are with us on that subject. And as for Lembken?"

"I know nothing of him," I answered shortly.

"No, of course not. You are wise not to commit yourself," said the little man eagerly. "One must not pass judgment without investigation. But still, our democracy has, in some respects, retained the features of the old despotisms, do you not think? And then, do you consider that the people are really omnipotent?"

He cocked his head as he spoke, and he had the objectionable habit of thrusting his face forward, so that he had been forcing me, step by step, around the circumference of a circle.

"The truth is, you say, we are actually in a condition of slavery," he persisted. "We are no better off than our ancestors, for all our boast of civilization. Is that not so, to your way of thinking?"

"You are very quick," I answered, "to put words into my mouth before I speak them."

"But you think them. Don't you think them?"

he urged, cocking his head again and watching me with intense eagerness.

The little man had ceased crowding me, and suddenly I saw that he had contrived to have me speak almost into the mouth of the funnel. It was only then that the meaning of his pertinacity and of his repulsive trade grew clear to me.

"Take yourself away!" I cried in anger.

"Oh, certainly! By all means! Yap, yap, if you wish it," he answered, drawing back and watching me with a sarcastic smile.

I went upon my way, filled with indignation. I wondered whether the Council was watching me before summoning me, and why they attributed so much importance to my views. I stared about me at the streets and the crowds, the dazzling fronts of the high buildings, and even then I half believed that this was a dream. Life could not have grown so accursed as this.

Before I became aware of it I had drawn near to the domed building, toward which the street was running. The houses suddenly fell away, and the splendid structure, which had seemed to float above the house-tops elusively, revealed itself to me. I was near the summit of a rather steep hill, whose superior portion consisted of a smooth glacis composed of neatly-jointed stones, across which the converging streets moved toward the castellated fortification, each terminating before a gate in this wall. The gate in front of me was composed of huge blocks of stone, probably with a steel foundation, and swung upon thin hinges of some metal that must have had enormous tensile strength. It was open and, like the fortificatión, was covered with glow paint or plaster, a dazzling mirror, now white, now blue, and bright as sunlight. Above the wall were the great conical, glow-painted Ray guns.

I passed through the gateway under a massive arch. Now I saw that the double wall enclosed a barracks or circular fortress, surrounding the inner courtyard, and connected with the dome by long bridges, stretched upon arches. The court within was laid out in grass plots, and was most spacious.

I stood still and gazed in admiration at the stupendous architectural scheme of the great building that occupied the center of the circular space. The dome covered only a small portion of the entire mass, and on each side was a succession of halls and porticos, approached between Corinthian columns, and, I thought, intercommunicating. The part immediately beneath the dome appeared to be of older date than the rest, and formed the nucleus of the complete conception.

As I stood staring in astonishment, suddenly I knew what the domed building was. It was St. Paul's Cathedral; but the cross was gone.

My wonder grew as I watched it. The dome designed by Sir Christopher Wren remained intact; yet it no longer rested on the summit, but seemed to soar, supported on numerous low pillars, and, twenty feet beneath it, on a flat under-roof, was a garden of luxuriating palm trees, and therefore presumably enclosed by invisible crystal walls. I saw the gorgeous coloring of tropical flowers, and scarlet creepers that twined around the trunks of old trees. What a magnificent pleasure-ground for the Council of the Federated Provinces, high up above the London streets in the December weather!

An elderly, bent man in blue, with the sign of a hammer on his shoulder, came slowly toward me.

"Can one obtain a permit to go to the Council garden?" I inquired of him.

He stopped and looked dully at me. "Eh?" he inquired.

"I want to go up and see the aerial garden," I responded, pointing.

"You want to go up there?" he exclaimed, and then began to chuckle. He slapped first one knee and then the other.

"Ho! Ho!" he roared. "That's good. But listen! You don't know who you're talking to. My daughter lives up there. I'll never see her again, but I like to walk here and look up and think about my luck. It gives me standing. I've got to earn a hektone and a quarter monthly, haven't I? But I tell you I don't earn fifty ones a month, and I lay off when I want to, and there's not a Labor Boss dares say a word to me. And down I go on the register for my hektone and a quarter every month, as sure as the sun rises."

His hard, shrewd laughter convulsed him again, and he slapped his legs and leered at me. Then he drew closer to me and laid his hand on my arm confidentially.

"You've heard of this new freedom the people are whispering about?" he asked, glancing apprehensively about him. "They're never satisfied, the people aren't. They want to get back to the old, bad ways of a hundred years ago, when there wasn't food to go around, and the rich sucked the poor men dry. I've read about those days. But the people are forgetting. Sanson will crush them when they're ready to break out. Do you know what they want? Do you? Do you?

"They want God back again, after we've put him down. They want their heaven after their rotten hides are turned into fertilizer. I know. I know those Christians. London's full of them today. The defective shops are full of them. They're talking and planning for an uprising that will turn back the hands of the clock. But Sanson will oust them when he gets ready. He'll give them the Rest Cure.

"They say there's a Messiah coming to mate the

Temple goddess and bring back the old, bad days. Do you know what Sanson means to do? He's going to mate her himself. And then he's going to make us all immortal. We'll have our heaven on earth then, and keep our bodies too. What's the use of a heaven when you haven't a body to enjoy it with? Sanson will make us all young again. We don't want freedom, we want immortality."

I was so astonished by his gabbling that I remained silent after he had ended, not knowing how to answer him. He began scanning me slowly from my feet upward.

"You're a stranger," he said, with slow suspicion.

"Yes," I replied. "Now tell me how I can go up to the Council garden."

"Garden," he replied, in apparent stupefaction. "Don't you know that's Boss Lembken's palace? That's the People's House, where Boss Lembken lives. People can't go up there. Don't you know that's the People's House? Who are you?"

Suddenly he started back and a malignant look came over his face.

"You're a wipe!" he shrieked. "You want to trap me and send me to the Comfortable Bedroom because I'm too old to work. Never a month passes but I put up my hektone and a quarter. Look on the register. You want to switch an old man who minds his own business and puts up his hektone and a quarter, you rotten moron!"

His old face worked with fear and excitement, and he raised his fist in a threatening manner; then, suddenly changing his intention, he swung on his heel and hurried away toward the gate. I saw him glance back furtively at me and then increase his speed.

As I turned to look at him I perceived that a small wooden gate on the interior side of the circular fortification stood partly open, and inside I saw a troop of the international guards at drill.

I crossed the court and came to a halt before the Corinthian columns that I had seen; and now I perceived that the pedestal of each contained a bas-relief, a conventionalized figure beneath which was engraved a tribute to some great leader of mankind. The engravings were in the old Roman characters, which seemed to have been retained on statues, coins, and brasses, just as we in our day still inscribed coins and statue pedestals in Latin. I walked around the columns, reading these inscriptions.

The first that caught my eye was in honor of Darwin, and read simply, "The Father of Civilization."

The next was to Karl Marx. "He interpreted

history in the light of materialism, and gave us the social State, with food for all," I read.

There was one in honor of Wells, "the Prophet of the Race."

There was one to Weismann, "who gave us immortality, not in a ghostly heaven, but in the germ-plasm.".

The next was to Mendel, who had "interpreted man's destiny in terms of the pea." Poor, patient, toiling Abbot, what were you doing in this galaxy?

And there was one to Nietzsche, "the scourge of Jesus of Nazareth, a peasant god."

CHAPTER XI

THE man in blue with the machine badge on his shoulder, who was waiting for me at the entrance, surveyed me with a smile of tolerant amusement.

"You are now at the heart of civilization," he began. "Let me act as your guide, for I see that you are a stranger. Is it not wonderful to contemplate that here, upon a space of a few hektares, man has erected a monument that shall endure forever! This wing," he added, "is Doctor Sanson's domain, while Boss Lembken exercises his priestly function from the People's House, under the dome."

He led me within the portico and through a swing door on the north side of the building. I found myself within a circular chamber like a hospital theater, with marble seats rising almost to the roof around a small central platform, on which were a crystal table, a large silver tank, and a cabinet with glass doors, through which I could see surgical appliances.

"This is the Animal Vivisection Bureau," said my guide. "It is not open to the public while demonstrations are being given. The Council does not permit the laity to acquire medical knowledge. We have several hundred dogs constantly kenneled beneath, in the sound-proof rooms; they are born there and, in general, die here."

"You use only dogs?" I asked.

"At present, yes. Their trustfulness and docility make them the best subjects, for we are demonstrating to our classes the nature and symptoms of pain. Now here—"

I followed him through another swing door into a similar room, but at least twice the size.

"This is the Vivisection Bureau," he continued, taking his stand beside a table of reddish marble mottled with blue veins, with a cup-like depression at the head. The people call it, jocularly, of course, the Rest Cure Home. You can guess why. Criminals and other suitable subjects are never lacking for experimentation. Doctor Sanson is said to be making investigations which will prove of a revolutionary nature. Then, the supply of moron children appears to be inexhaustible. Again, of course, there is the annual Surgeons' Day, when we round up the populace. The date being movable, the ignorant are kept in a state of wholesome apprehension. But let us follow that throng."

Through the glass of the swing door I perceived a large crowd pouring into another part of the building, following in the wake of an old man, perhaps eighty years of age, who was being conducted by two of the blue-coated guards. Behind him trailed a little rat-faced man in blue, who glanced furtively about him with a smile of bravado. We went with the mob into a third chamber.

It was about the size of the second, and in the center was a large structure of steel, with a swing door. The brass rail which surrounded it kept back the spectators, who lined it, heaving and staring, and uttering loud exclamations of interest and delight. The room was filled with the nauseating stench of an anaesthetic.

One of the guards raised a drop-bar in the rail, and the old man passed through and walked with firm steps toward the steel structure. His white beard drifted over his breast, his blue eyes were fixed hard, and he had the poise of complete resignation. At the door he turned and addressed the spectators.

"It's a bad world, and I am glad to go out of it," he said. "I remember when the world was Christian. It was a better world then."

He passed through, and the anaesthetic fumes suddenly became intensified. I heard the creak as of a chair inside the structure, a sigh, and the soft dabbing of a wet sponge. That was all, and the mob, struck silent, began to shuffle, and then to murmur. I saw the rat-faced man slinking away.

"This," said my guide, "is popularly called the Comfortable Bedroom. The old man can no longer produce his hektone and a quarter monthly, and his grandson, who has the right to take over the burden, has just been mated. Most of our old qualify for life in senility, but no doubt he dissipated his credit margin in youth. Again, many prefer to go this way. Now if he had been a woman he would have been accredited thirty hektones for each child supplied to the State. That is Doctor Sanson's method of assuring productivity."

But I broke from the man in horror, forcing my passage through the crowd, which was dispersing already. I ran on through hall after hall, approaching the central part of the building, until I was again blocked by a crowd, this time of young men and women in blue, who were reading a lengthy list of letters and figures, suspended high in the center of this chamber. Most of these young people were in pairs, and, as they read, they nudged each other and exchanged facetious phrases.

But one pair I saw who, with clasped hands, turned wretchedly away and passed back slowly toward the entrance.

"This is more cheerful than the Comfortable Bedroom," murmured a voice at my side.

The new speaker was a dapper young fellow with a small, pert mustache and an air of insinuating familiarity. He placed his hand upon my arm to detain me as I started to move away.

"The kindly Council, which relieves old age of the burden of life, also provides that the life to come shall be as efficient for productivity as possible," he said. "I see you are a stranger and may not know that these young people are here to learn the names of their mates."

"Do you mean that the Council decides whom each man or woman is to marry?" I asked.

"To mate? Yap, in ordinary cases. There is no mating for one-fourth of the population — that is to say, those of the morons whose germ-plasm contains impure dominants, and who are yet capable of sufficient productivity to be permitted to reach maturity. Grade 2, the ordinary defectives, who number another fourth of the people, are at present mated, though Doctor Sanson will soon abolish this practice. The sexes of this class are united in accordance with their Sanson rating, with a view to eliminating the dominants."

"And these are defectives of what you call Grade 2?" I asked.

"No, these are all Grade 1 defectives," he answered, regarding me with amusement. "Defectives such as us. We number forty-five per cent of the population and form the average type. They are free to choose within limits. The Council prepares periodically lists of young men and young women in whom the deficiencies are recessive, and those on one side of the list may mate with any of those upon the other side. Monogamy is, however, frowned upon. I suppose you, in your country, never heard of this plan?"

"Yes, it used to be called the totem, or group marriage, and was confined to the most degraded savages on earth, the Aborigines of Australia," I answered. But the little man, who had evidently not heard of Australia, only looked at me blankly. A rush of people toward the next hall carried us apart, and, not loath to lose my companion, I followed the crowd, to find myself in the immense central auditorium, within which orators were addressing the people from various platforms.

Upon that nearest me a lecturer was holding forth with the enthusiasm of some Dominican of old.

"Produce! Produce!" he yelled, with wild gesticulations. "Out with the unproductive who cannot create a hektone and a quarter monthly! Out with the moron! Out with the defective! Out with the unadaptable! Out with the weak! Out with him who denies the consubstantiality of Force and Matter! No compromise! Sterilize, sterilize, as Doctor Sanson demands of you! There are defectives in the shops today, spreading the moron doctrines of Christianity. There are asymmetries and variations from the Sanson norm, cunningly concealed, legacies of malformations from degenerate ancestors, impure germ-plasm that menaces the future of the human race. Let us support Sanson, citizens! Go through the city with sickle and pruning-hook for the perfect race of the future, in the name of democracy! Praise the great Boss!"

"Hurrah!" shrieked the mob enthusiastically.

"Will you not go up and see the Temple goddess?" whispered a voice in my ear.

I started, but I could not discern the speaker. I looked up. On either side of the auditorium a high staircase of gleaming marble led to a gallery which surrounded it. Doors were set in the wall of this in many places, and above were more stairs and more galleries, tier above tier. At the head of each stairway one of the guards was posted. He stood there like a statue, picturesque in his blue uniform, which made a splotch of color against the white marble wall.

"Go up and ask no questions," whispered somebody on my other side; and again I turned quickly, but none of those near me seemed to have spoken.

I went up the stairway, passing the guard, who did not stop or question me. As I stopped in the gallery, high above the auditorium, a door opened, and there came out a man of extreme age, dressed in white, with a gold ant badge on either shoulder. He propped himself upon a staff, and stood blinking and leering at me, and wagging his head like a grotesque idol.

"A stranger!" he exclaimed. "So you have come to see the goddess of the Ant Temple! Would you like to stand upon the altar platform and see her face to face? It only costs one hektone, but it is customary to offer a gratuity to the assistant priest."

I thrust the money into the shaking hand that he stretched out to me. At that moment I did not know whether I was still free, or whether this was that peremptory summons to the Council of which David had warned me. I realized that the spies who had dogged my path were all links in some subtle scheme.

The old man preceded me into a large room on the south side of the auditorium, beyond which I saw another door. This seemed to be a robing-room for the priests, for white garments with the gold ant badge hung from the walls, which were covered with mirrors, from each of which the horrible old face grimaced at me.

"You are to go through that door," said the old man, pointing to the far end of the room. "It is a great privilege to look upon the face of the goddess. Not everyone may do so, but you are not an ordinary man, are you?"

He shot a penetrating glance at me.

"Thus the Messiah will look upon her when he comes," he continued. "At least, so runs the prophecy, and remember, you may be he, for it is foretold that he will come unknowing his mission. But wait!" — for I was hastening toward the door — "you must put on a priest's robes. It is not proper for a layman to look upon the goddess."

He indicated a white robe with the ant badge that hung on a table beside me.

"Don't be in a hurry," he mumbled. "It is a great pleasure to me to talk with strangers from remote countries. Where do you come from? You look like a man of the last century, come back to life. How the barbarians of that period would stare if they could see our civilization!"

"What is this Temple?" I inquired. "Do men worship an ant, and are you its priest?"

He chuckled and leered at me. "Oh, no, I am a very humble old man," he answered. "I am only an assistant priest. Boss Lembken is the Chief Priest. And you ask about the Ant? The people worship it, but it is not known whether they see it as the symbol of labor, or whether they think it is a god. The religious ideas of the people were always a confused and chaotic jumble, even in the old days of Christianity. But the Ant is only the transition stage from God to Matter. We know there is no God, nothing but Matter, and man is born of Matter and destined to be resolved into it. But the people are still ignorant, and it keeps them calm, to have an ant to pray to. Besides, if there were not the Ant they would turn to Christianity again and set back the clock of progress.

"I remember Christianity well. In my young days it used to be a power. I used to go to church," he cackled. "Not that I believed in God, any more than the rest. Only the aristocrats and the intellectuals did that. I didn't believe in the Devil either, but I do now. Do you know the Devil's name? It is human nature."

I remained speechless beneath the spell that the wretch cast over me.

"Yes, the Devil is human nature," he resumed. "For it would thwart progress forever, groveling before its idol of a soul. But already. when I was a young man, only the intellectuals believed in Christianity. Once it had been the masses. But Science proved that there was nothing but Matter, and the momentum of the materialistic impulse was too strong for the reviving faith. The aristocrats should have guarded their faith instead of letting the people rise to control. But they were fools. They set up in little rival bodies when Christ prayed for them to be one. They permitted divorce when He said no. They tried to compromise with Him, all except Rome and barbarous Russia, and that is why St. Peter's still stands as a Cathedral while St. Paul's is the Ant Temple. I remember it all.

"Christ knew. He knew they would go under if they tried to sail with the wind. When Science said there were no miracles they cut out the miracles. And when the visionary Myers made his generation think there might be miracles after all, they put some of them back again, but very cautiously. They didn't know that the people weren't going to follow them into rationalism and then out again. Nobody was going to believe when the leaders themselves didn't believe.

"When He taught them how to heal the sick they preferred to mix His prescription with drugs. They couldn't believe in one thing and they couldn't believe in the other. He told them to leave Caesar's things to Caesar, and they went into politics. They tried to bargain with Socialism when it became strong, but it wouldn't have anything to do with them. Then they preached housing reform and a good living, when He praised poverty and told them to preach resignation. They couldn't obey in anything; they thought they knew better; they tried to follow the times after they split into pieces; of course they went under."

"Is there no Christianity anywhere?" I asked.

"In your native Russia," he jeered. "In St. Peter's, because the Italian Province segregates the evil to keep it under observation. In Cologne, because the bishop learned the secret of the Ray. And in the defectives' shops. They say they have the Scriptures hidden in there, but the Council has put dozens to the torture and has never found them. It is hard to clear the human mind of its inherited rubbish. After the Revolution, Christianity continued to be taught among other myths. But it aroused anti-social instincts. Christians were the enemies of human progress. They used to go into the Rest Cure Home and ask to be vivisected in place of the wretched morons there. You can't build up a progressive civilization out of people like that. So the teaching was made a capital offense. That was after we burned the bishops."

"What!" I cried.

"Death by burning came to us from the great trans-Atlantic democracy, you know," he said, leering at me. "Europe had forgotten it. But we set up the stakes again. I saw Archbishop Tremont, of York, and the Roman Catholic Archbishop of Westminster burned side by side in the ruins of Westminster Hall. Then there was Bonham, of London, and Bethany, of Manchester, and Dean Cross, of Chichester; we put them in plaster of paris and unslaked lime first. The morons could have fled to Skandogermania, which was not free then. But they went, all three, into the Council Hall, and preached to the Council. That was in Boss Rose's time. So they had to go. And they blessed us while their bones were crackling. You can't make a progressive nation out of people like that."

I hurried toward the door. I pushed it open, and it swung back noiselessly behind me.

Within the vastness of the Temple I heard a murmur rise, a wail of misery that made the ensuing silence more dreadful still. For here I encountered only thick gloom and emptiness, and soundless space, as though some veil of awful silence had been drawn before the tabernacle of an evil god. My knees shook as I advanced, clutching the rail beside my hand.

I found myself upon a slender bridge that seemed to span the vault. It widened in the center to a small, square, stone-paved enclosure, like a flat altar-top, surrounded by a close-wrought grille that gleamed like gold. I halted here, and, looking down, saw, far beneath, a throng whose white faces stared upward like masks. Again that chant arose, and now I heard its burden:

"We are immortal in the germ-plasm; make us immortal in the body before we die."

Then something beneath me began to assume shape as my eyes grew used to the obscurity. It was a great ant of gold, five hundred tons of it, perhaps, erected on a great pedestal of stone; where should have been the altar of the Savior of the world, there the abominable insect crawled, with its articulated, smooth body, and one antenna upraised.

The symbol was graven clear. This was the aspiration of mankind, and to this we had come, through Science that would not look within, through a feminism that had sought new, and the progressive aims of ethical doctrinaires that had discarded the old safeguards; Christ's light yoke of well-tried moral laws, sufficient to centuries; through all the fanatic votaries of a mechanistic creed; polygamy and mutilation, and all the shameful things from which the race had struggled through suffering upward. All the old evils which we had thought exorcised forever had crept in on us again, out of the shadows where they had lain concealed.

I stood there, sick with horror, clinging to the rail.

How far from gentle St. Francis and St. Catherine, and all the gracious spirits of the dead and derided ages, progress had moved! Were those things false and forgotten, those saintly ideals which had shone like lamps of faith through the night of the world? Was this the truth and were those nothing?

I heard a sobbing in the shadows beneath. I looked down and perceived, immediately before the Ant, an aged man prostrate. He muttered; and, though I heard no words that I could understand, I realized that, in his blind, helpless way, he was groping toward the godhead.

Then I looked up and saw something that sent the blood throbbing through my head and drew my voice from me in gasping breaths.

At the edge of the platform on which I stood, out of the gloom, loomed the round body of the second cylinder. And inside, through the face of unbroken glass, I saw the sleeping face of Esther, my love of a century ago.

The cap of the cylinder was half unscrewed.

CHAPTER XII

THE LORDS OF MISRULE

I SAW her eyelids quiver and half unclose an instant, and, though there was no other sign of awakening upon the mask-like face of sleep, I knew she lived. The indicators upon the dials showed that five days remained before the opening of the cylinder. And, as I stared through the glass plate, so horror-struck and shaken, some power seemed to take possession of me and make me very calm. An immense elation succeeded fear and rendered it impotent. Esther was restored to me. We had not slept through that whole century not to meet at last.

How many years we two had lain side by side within our cylinders, down in the vault, I could not know. Yet there had been a sweetness behind those misty memories of my awakening as if our spirits had been in contact during those hundred years of helpless swoon.

The eyelids quivered again. But for the emaciation and the dreadful pallor I might have thought she was only lightly sleeping, and would awaken at my call. The love in my heart surged up triumphantly. For her sake I meant to play the man before the Council.

I meant to go there now. I think my instinct must have been the courage born of hopelessness, such as that which had carried the bishops to their death. For only a desperate stroke could win me Esther; and such a stroke must be made, should be made. With steady steps I returned to the priests' room.

The dotard was waiting for me, and he came forward, smiling and blinking into my face, searing my soul with eyes as hard as agates.

"I am going to the Council," I said quietly.

He looked at me in terror. He seized me by the arm.

"No, no, no!" he exclaimed. "You are to go to your friends. The Council is not in session."

"It is in session. I have been held for it."

"You don't understand. That is the Provincial Council. This is a matter for the Federal Council, and Sanson is not your friend. Don't you understand now? Sanson is working on the problem of immortality and doesn't suspect. Boss Lembken is your friend. Don't you know he is your friend?"

"No," I answered contemptuously.

The old man clutched me in extreme agitation.

"If you are headstrong you will go to ruin," he cried. "Boss Lembken is your friend. He sent for you. Not Sanson. Boss Lembken discovered who you were while Sanson was dreaming over his victims. If Sanson knew he would get you into his power and overthrow the priesthood. He means to destroy the Ant and have no god. He is going to mate the goddess when 'she awakens—"

He saw me start and clench my fists, and a deep-drawn "Ah!" of relief came from his lips. For I had betrayed my identity beyond all doubt; and it was to make sure of this that I had been sent into the Temple. I could see it all now.

"Now listen to me," he said, coming near and thrusting his repulsive old face into mine. "Boss Lembken wants you. He wants to help you and give you power. But he was not sure of you; and so he had to use craft and caution. When the Messiah comes Lembken will overthrow Sanson and make the world free again. It was Lembken who sent for you."

He was becoming incoherent with fright at my obduracy.

"The People's House is above the Temple," he continued. "Boss Lembken lives there. He has a beautiful palace. You will be happy there. And Sanson has no palace and no delights. He wants nothing except to vivisect the morons. So you will not want to go to Sanson. He can offer you nothing. We must be cautious, and if he is in the Council Hall we must wait till he has gone, for he controls the Guard, and if he saw you he would have you

seized. That is why I gave you a priest's robes—
because Sanson dares not stop the priests, who are
under Lembken. Come with me, then."

I accompanied him out into the gallery above the
auditorium, in which the orators were still declaim-
ing to a lessening crowd. Sanson or Lembken, it
mattered little to me. I felt enmeshed in some plot
whose meaning was incomprehensible. But I meant
to win Esther. I walked like a somnambulist, feeling
that the dream might dissolve at any moment. A
shaft from the western sun struck blood-red on a
window. A pigeon that had perched among the columns fluttered to the ground. Above me I saw tier
upon tier of galleries.

We ascended the marble stairway, the guards making no attempt to stop us, nor were we challenged.
I noticed that they were armed with Ray rods, similar to those that I had seen in the cellar; and they
raised them in salutation as we passed.

We ascended flight after flight, and always the
guards posted at the top of each saluted us and
stepped aside. We passed across a little covered
bridge and presently entered a small rotunda, in
which a dozen guards were seated, sipping coffee
and chatting in low tones. Behind them was an
immensely high door marked in large letters

COUNCIL HALL

To the right and left of it were smaller doors.

We entered the door on the right, and the priest, stopping, whispered to me:

"You must make no sound. If Sanson is in Council he must not discover us."

I found myself in a small room, with the inevitable door at the farther end. Upon one side were two apertures in the wall, disclosed by sliding panels that moved noiselessly — spy-holes, each as large as the bottom of a teacup. The priest stooped before one and I looked through the other.

The immense Council Hall was dim, and it took a few moments for my eyes to grow accustomed to the obscurity. Then I saw at the distant end a raised platform, on which stood two high chairs, like thrones.

There were three men upon this platform, one occupying each chair, and the third standing.

One was unmistakably Lembken, the obese old boss of the Federation. He wore a trailing gown of white, with a short mull cape about his shoulders, and there were golden ants — as I discovered afterward — stamped all over the fabric. He was lying rather than standing, and his feet rested upon a stool. He was smiling in evil fashion, and he was stout to the verge of disease. I could not see his face distinctly.

Upon the second throne sat a man with a fanatic's face and a square beard of black that swept his breast. He had a large ant badge on either shoulder of his white gown, and on one finger was an immensely heavy ring of gold that projected beyond the knuckles. This was the Deputy Chief Priest.

Standing between the two in the shadows, lolling back half-insolently against Boss Lembken's chair, to whisper in his ear, and again turning to the priest, was Sanson. I could not mistake the whitening hair brushed back, the gestures of intense pride and power, though I could hardly see the face. He wore a tight tunic of white, without a badge, and he bore himself with a complete absence of self-consciousness. There was not a trace of pose in the completeness of that manifested personality, with its alert poise, cat-like and tense, as if each nerve and sinew had been disciplined to serve the master-soul within.

As I watched I heard a strident, metallic voice call in loud tones:

"Wait till the Goddess awakens and the Messiah comes! He'll make an end of Sanson and his cruelties, and give us freedom again!"

Now I perceived that behind Sanson and between the two thrones stood a telephone funnel, attached to some mechanism. It was from this that the voice had issued. It was followed by the clacking sound of a riband of paper being run off a reel. Sanson stepped back, picked up the riband, and ran it through his fingers, glancing at it indifferently.

"The speaker lives in District 9, Block 47, but we do not yet know his name. A trapper is watching," said the voice in the funnel.

A bell rang, the door on the left of the Council Hall was opened by a guard, and a girl of about eighteen entered. She was robed in white and on her shoulder was the sign of a palm tree. She stood before Boss Lembken's throne with downcast face and clasped hands, trembling violently.

"They sent for me," she said in a low voice.

I saw the smile deepen on Lembken's face. He sat leering at her; then he shifted each foot down from the stool and gathered himself, puffing, upon his feet. He put his hand under her chin and raised it, looking into her face. The girl twisted herself away, screamed and began running toward the door.

"Let me go home! Please—please!" she cried.

The guard at the door placed one hand over her mouth and dragged her, struggling, through a small door behind the funnel, which I had not seen.

I clenched my fists; only the thought of Esther held me where I was.

"Ascribe the heretics," said Lembken to the deputy priest, and puffed out behind the guard.

Sanson stepped backward and touched the funnel mechanism, which instantly began to scream.

"Heresy in the paper shops!" it howled. "Exam-

ine District 5. They say there is a God. Weed out
the morons there!"

The writing mechanism began to clack again. I
saw the paper riband coil like a snake along the floor
between the thrones. Sanson stopped the machine,
which was beginning to screech once more. He
moved to the vacant throne and sat down.

Again the bell tinkled, and there came in a man
of about thirty years, in blue, leading a little boy by
the hand. He looked about him in bewilderment,
and then, seeing the priest, flung himself on his
knees and pressed his lips to the hem of his robe.

"It is not true that I am a heretic, as they say," he
babbled. "I believe in Science Supreme, and Force
and Matter, coexistent and consubstantial, according to the Vienna Creed, and in the Boss, the Keeper
of Knowledge. That man dies as the beast dies.
And that we are immortal in the germ-plasm,
through our descendants. I believe in Darwin,
Hæckel, and Wells, who brought us to enlightenment—"

"That boy is a moron!" screamed Sanson, inter-
rupting the man's parrot-rote by leaping from his
chair.

He dragged the child from the father, switched
on the solar light, and set him down, peering into
his face. He took the child's head between his hands
and scanned it. His expression was transformed; he

looked like a madman. And then I realized that the man was really mad; a madman ruled the world, as in the time of Caligula.

The father crept humbly toward Sanson; he was shaking pitiably.

"He is a Grade 2 defective," he whispered. "You don't take Grade 2 from the parents. He is Grade 2 — the doctors said so —" He repeated this over and over, standing with hands clasped and staring eyes.

"I say he is a moron!" Sanson shouted. "The doctors are fools. He is a brach. Look at that index and that angle! Look at the cranium, asymmetrical here — and here! The fingers flex too far apart, a proof of deficiency. The ears project at different angles, my eighth stigma of degeneracy. He is a moron of the third grade, and must go to the Vivi —"

With an unhuman scream the father leaped at Sanson and flung him to the ground, snatched up the boy in his arms and began running toward the door. From his throne the priest looked on impassively; it was no business of his. The guard appeared.

But before the man reached the guard at the door Sanson had leaped to his feet and pulled a Ray rod from his tunic. He pointed it. I heard the catch click. A stream of blinding, purple-white light flashed forth. I heard the carpet rip as if a sword had slashed it. A chip of wood flew high into the air. On the floor lay two charred, unrecognizable bodies.

I confess my only impulse then was of fear. How could I confront that devil, or Lembken, in his hell, when for Esther's sake I must be cautious and wise? I plunged toward the farther door. The priest caught at me, but I shook him off and flung him, stunned, to the floor. I opened the door and rushed through.

I was amazed to find myself upon a long, slender bridge that spanned the central court of the vast structure. I stopped, bewildered, not knowing where to turn, and the whole scene burned itself upon my brain in an instant.

The immense mass was divided into four separate buildings. The Council Hall, from which I had emerged, was on the southern side, and, looking beyond it, I saw the Thames, winding like a silver riband into the distance. Facing me was the north wing, by which I had entered, containing the Vivisection Bureau and other halls of nameless horrors, with Sanson's quarters. On my left hand the Temple towered high over me. Above my head I saw the outlines of the noble dome, and the palm trees behind their crystal walls. A blood-red creeper trailed down through a chink in the wall.

Upon my right was a massive fortress that I had not hitherto perceived, floating above which was a whole fleet of airships, evidently the same that I had seen when I flew into London. There must have been more than a hundred of them, ranging from tiny scoutplanes to huge monsters with glow shields about them, projecting conical machines like those that studded the top of the enclosing wall, but smaller. On their prows were great jaws of steel, in some cases closed, in others distended, fifteen feet of projecting jaw and mandible, capable, as it looked, of crushing steel plate like eggshells.

The bridge on which I stood ran from the Council Hall to the wing where Sanson dwelled. A bridge from the Temple building ran straight to the fortress of the airships at right angles to this, the two thus crossing, forming a little enclosed space in the center. At various spots, bridges from the enclosing fortress crossed the court and entered the pile of buildings. And the whole concept was so beautiful that even then I stopped to gaze.

But I did not know whither to turn. In front of me, where the bridge entered Sanson's wing, a guard stood watching me. As I approached the central place where the two bridges met he raised his Ray rod with a threatening gesture.

I turned to the right. Here, where the bridge from the Temple entered the fort of the airships, I saw an airscout in blue, with the white swan on his breast, watching me. Again I stopped. My mind was awhirl with the horrors that I had seen; I could not think! I did not know what to do. All exit seemed barred to me except that whereby I had come.

Beneath me lay the court, a broad expanse of white, inlaid with geometrical figures of green grass. On it crawled tiny figures in blue. I was halfway between the court below and the Temple dome above; yet everything was so still that the voices below came up to me.

A group had gathered, chattering excitedly, about something that lay hard by the Temple entrance. As they moved this way and that I saw that it had been a woman. She had been young; her garments had been white; there was a gold palm on a torn-off fragment that a gust of wind drove up toward me. I caught at it, but it went sailing past and fluttered down in the central court between the buildings.

I saw the spectators look up toward the aerial gardens. The blood-red creeping vine now swung from an open crystal door. That paradise of tropic beauty, those flame-colored flowers were such as blossom in hell.

The crystal door above me clashed to and reopened as the wind caught it. It seemed to clang rhythmically, like a clear tocsin, high up beneath the dome, a bell of doom to warn the blood-stained city. Again it sounded like a workman's hammer; and the silence that covered everything made the sounds more ominous and dread, as if Fate were hammering out the minutes remaining before she slashed her thread.

An old man pushed his way through the gathering crowd. He peered into the white face, and wrung his hands, and wept, and his voice rose in a high, penetrating wail.

"It'll all be ended," I heard him cry. "I can't work now. I can't make up my time. I've spent my credit margin. I'm old and outed and done with. I'll have to go to the Comfortable Bedroom."

It was the old man whom I had seen earlier that day. The crowd jeered and pressed forward, those who were behind craning their necks and rising on their toes to see the joint spectacle of death and grief. The old man shook his gnarled fist at his dead daughter.

"You've killed me," he sobbed in rage. "Why couldn't you have stayed up there till Sanson has made us all immortal? I'm going to the Comfortable Bedroom now, and my body will die like a beast's, and I'll be ended."

And he broke into atrocious curses, while the crowd screamed with delight and mocked his passion.

The little gate on the inner side of the fort opened, and a troop of the Guard emerged, carrying a stretcher. At the sight of them the mob scuttled away. The guards picked up the body and carried it within the gate. One began scattering sand.

Out of the crowd leaped an old man with flowing hair and beard. He stood out in the court and shook his fist toward the Temple dome.

"Woe to you, accursed city!" he screamed. "Woe to you in the day of judgment! Woe to your whites and harlots when the judgment comes!"

The crystal door banged and clashed open. A woman in white put out her hand and closed it. A latch-click pricked the air. The sun gilded the dome and turned it to a ball of fire. Down in the court the madman cried unceasingly.

"Woe to you, accursed city!" he screa
to your whites and h

to you in the day of judgment! Woe
the judgment comes!"

CHAPTER XIII

THE PALACE OF PALMS

THE sun dipped behind the western buildings, and the glare of the glow on fort and Temple and encircling wall was like phosphorescent fire. I saw the guards stirring in their enclosure. The Airscouts' Fortress shone, hard and brilliant, against the sky.

I gathered my wits together. I had seen the hidden things, and, because I knew of none other to whom to turn, I resolved to appeal to David. Esther, the prey of these insane degenerates when she awakened . . . . David's own secret troubles . . . . could we not aid each other? Might not two men accomplish something in these evil days?

I turned to the right across the bridge that led to the Airscouts' Fortress. The sentinel stood still, watching me. He raised his Ray rod, not to threaten me, but to salute, and I remembered that the airscouts had no love for the Guard, and hence must be under Lembken's control. He took me for a priest. But the weapon shook in his hand, and the astonishment upon his face matched that on mine. I recognized the man Jones, who had brought me to London.

"I want to leave this hell!" I cried. "Which way? Which way?"

"You want—you want—?" he stammered.

"The Strangers' House. I am lost here—"

He looked at me in utter perplexity.

"Help me!" I pleaded. "Show me the way!"

The door behind him opened, and there stepped out a man of about fifty years, dressed in white, with a golden swan on each shoulder. Jones stepped aside and saluted him. The newcomer approached me. His hard, clean-shaven face was impenetrable, and his eyes burned with a dull fire. Behind him crept a second figure; it was the old priest.

"There he is! Seize him!" he shrieked.

The first man laid his hand on my shoulder. "I am Air-Admiral Hancock," he said. "You are to accompany me to Boss Lembken."

I went with him across the bridge into a doorway set in the west side of the Temple building. I expected again to see the vast interior beneath me, but we entered a narrow corridor and stepped into a small automatic elevator. In a moment we had shot up and halted inside the Palace entrance. Hancock opened the door of the cage.

We were standing in a spacious hall, bare, save for the hanging tapestries and heavy Persian rugs on the mosaic floor. It was half dark, and there was a perfume that made my head swim. Before the curtained aperture opposite us stood a negro boy, with a Ray rod in his hand. As we approached he threw the curtain aside and saluted us.

There were soft solar lights in the next room, which was rose-red, and decorated and furnished in the style of Louis Quatorze. Another negro stood in the doorway opposite; he, too, saluted and threw the curtain back.

The third room was enameled in blue. The blue lights gave it an unearthly aspect, which was increased by the baroque style of its ornamentation. The perfume was stronger.

The negro at the door of the fourth room was a giant. He wore the uniform of an eighteenth century grenadier. His scarlet coat and white pigtail formed vivid spots against the dull-gold curtain. The room within was dark. We waited on the threshold.

At first I could see nothing. Then, gradually, the outlines of the room came into sight. There were low divans and rugs, and mirrors on every wall multiplied them. I heard a rasping sound, and a blotch of crimson and green became a brilliant macaw that scraped its way with its sharp claws from end to end of a horizontal perch. Behind it I now saw the white gleam of Lembken's robe; then the couch on which he lay; then the girl who crouched, fanning him, at his feet; then the rotund form of the old man, the sharp eyes and the heavy jowl with the pendulous cheeks.

"I have executed your orders, Boss," said the Air-Admiral.

The old man rose upon his feet heavily and came puffing up to us. His heavy soft hands wandered about my robes, patting me here and there, while he puffed and snorted like some sea monster.

"You haven't a knife or a Ray rod?" he inquired suspiciously. "You haven't anything to harm me? I am an old, weak man. I am the people's friend, and yet many want to kill me."

He seemed to satisfy himself with the result of his inspection, and withdrew to his couch, picking up a Ray rod and resting it across his knee.

He dismissed Hancock and the girl. She rose to her feet briskly, with a mechanical smile. She was about twenty years old, it seemed to me, but there was a hardness and cruelty about her mouth that shocked me, and the soul behind the mask of youth seemed centuries old.

"Amaranth wanted to stay, to hear what I was going to say to you," said Lembken, "but I make everybody mind his own business in the People's House. Besides, she might have fallen in love with you. I like to have good-looking people about me." He looked at me and at the Ray rod, and then at me again; then, with a petulant gesture, he sent the weapon flying across the room.

"There! You see I trust you!" he said, smiling. "Sit down beside me. We understand each other, so we will be frank. Men such as we are above deceptions. You ought to be about a hundred and twenty-eight years old!"

He spoke jocularly, and yet I could see that he wished to be sure I was the man he sought. Evidently he knew my history. He heaved a sigh of immense satisfaction when I acquiesced.

"I was not sure it was you," he said. "One has to be cautious when so much depends on it. And Sanson was beginning to suspect, but he does not know that I discovered Lazaroff's papers. Sanson does not know everything, you see, Arnold. What do you think of his Rest Cure, as the people term it? It is his, not mine, you know."

"I think he is Satan himself," I answered quickly. Yet I was not sure that I preferred this perfumed degenerate to Sanson, with his maniac cruelty.

A smile crept over the flabby face. Lembken looked pleased. He placed his hand upon my shoulder.

"A classical scholar," he said. "You refer to the mythical ruler of the infernal realms. Assuredly we shall soon understand each other. Sanson is a strong man. When I meet strong men I let them be as strong as they want to be. They break themselves to pieces. In a democracy like ours there is no room for strong men. Sanson doesn't understand that. He thinks the Mayor of the Palace is going to step into the shoes of the Roi Fainéant. But the Roi Fainéant always wins — if he sits still. I am the Roi Fainéant."

I was so amazed at the strange psychology he was disclosing that I found no answer ready. I knew he was dissembling some deep-laid purpose, but why he had need of me I could not imagine. And the man's affectation of good-will almost began to delude me.

"Do you like David's daughter?" he began, so suddenly that I started. "Ah!" he continued, shaking his finger waggishly, "one seldom sees a woman approximating so closely to the Sanson norm. There is an attachment, if I know young men. How would you like her for your own? I hit the mark, then?"

Before I could reply he was on another tack.

"Now, there is Hancock," he resumed. "He is a Christian, and ought to go to the defectives' shops, according to the law Sanson made. But I don't care. I would just as soon have Christianity as the Ant, or Mormonism, as they have in America. I don't like tyranny. If I had my way everyone would be perfectly free. Sanson doesn't see that he has embittered the people.   He is harrying them with his laws, and they blame me.   I am the people's friend."

With a sudden, hoarse scream the macaw flew from the bar and perched on Lembken's shoulder, where she sat, preening her plumage and croaking at me.   "The people's friend," she screamed, and broke into choking laughter.

"So you see it is entirely to your interest to help me and not Sanson," Lembken continued.   "Reasonable men cement their friendships with self-interest. Come, let me look at you."

He touched some switch near him, and the room was illuminated with a blaze of solar light.   The golden ants upon his robes leaped into view.   He turned on the divan heavily and stared into my face.

"Yes, I can trust you," he said in approbation. "Well, Sanson will learn his error in four days' time. You shall live here with me and have a life of pleasure.   You need never think about the world below. We do exactly what we please; that is my rule in the People's House."

"The People's House!" screamed the macaw, leaving his shoulder and fluttering back to her perch, from which she surveyed us coldly, head on one side. "The People's House!   The people's friend!" she alternated, in a muttering diminuendo.

"My head aches today," said Lembken petulantly.

"That is why I am sitting here. There has been an accident: one of our ladies fell down through an open door. It made my head ache."

I knew he lied when he spoke of an accident. I knew that she had thrown herself down. The lie brought back my mind to its focus; and in that instant my lips were sealed, and my half-formed intent to throw myself on Lembken's mercy, pleading for Esther and our love, died.

"So we shall talk tomorrow," Lembken continued. "For the present you are one of us. You see your interest lies in joining us, and the part you have to play in return will be short and not difficult for a man of your discernment. That small part will be paid, four days hence—"

I was sure that it concerned Esther now. "And will be all, and afterward your life will be free from all laws and bonds. You never need leave the People's House unless you want to. Here everyone does as he pleases. Come, Arnold, I will show you the gardens."

He stood up, puffing, and gave me his arm like an old friend. The man's manners were fascinating. I could well understand how he had worked his way to power. There was the good-fellowship of the twentieth-century demagogue, but there was more; there was discernment and culture; and there was more still; there was a corrupting influence about his candor that seemed to strike its deadly roots down into my moral nature and shrivel it.

We passed out through the empty rooms. The Palace was level with the Temple roof; there were no steps. There was no stairway at all, for the whole structure, which seemed to extend from side to side of the vast roof, consisted of a single story. We passed out between two giant negroes, who stood like ebony statues. And now I saw that the four rooms in which I had been, comprised only the smallest portion of the building, which was set out irregularly, receding here to leave space for a little lawn, projecting there, evidently to enclose a garden. And I discovered why the interior was so dark; there were no windows — at least, on this side of the Palace.

It was a fairyland. I thought of the old palaces at Capri. Here, high above the swarming streets, a man might take his pleasure in ease indeed. The crystal walls must have been sound-proof, for not a murmur from below reached us. I heard the music of bubbling brooks, the cries of birds among the trees, the faint tinkle of a guitar or mandolin struck somewhere in the recesses of the ramified buildings.

We were traversing a graveled path that ran between the Palace and the crystal wall. Looking down, I could see the glow circle of the fortress. It had grown dark; the lights which lit our way, that I had thought daylight, were from the solar vents,

concealed so skilfully that they shed a soft, diffused
radiance everywhere, as of afternoon. We turned
the angle of the building, and I stopped short
and looked in involuntary admiration at the scene
before me.

We might have stepped into the heart of some
Amazonian forest, for we were in a tangled wilderness of palms and other tropical trees. The air was
filled with the scent of orange flowers, and in a grove
near me clusters of the bright fruit hung from the
weighted boughs. From the dank earth sprang clusters of exotic, flaming flowers, and ferns. Huge
vines knotted themselves about the trunks of trees,
through whose recesses flew flocks of brilliantly
plumaged birds. The path became a trail, meander-
ing between the trees and crossing rushing brooklets.
The vast concavity of the dome above was like an
arched heaven of blue, studded with golden stars.

"What do you think of the People's House,
Arnold?" Lembken inquired, turning heavily upon
me.

"It is a paradise," I answered.

I was amazed to see two tears roll down his cheeks.
It was the same strange yielding to emotional impulse
that I had discerned before. So might Nero have
wept over his fiddle.

"It is the reward of those who are the chosen of
the people," he answered. "It will be your reward,

Arnold. You must dream over this tonight, and tomorrow we will make our compact. I have reserved quarters for you. You will meet nobody you do not wish to meet. That is the chief charm of the People's House; we meet only for our festivities; otherwise we are quite free. Come, Arnold!"

The scene, the atmosphere, the fearful personality of Lembken seemed to appeal to some being in me whose hideous presence I had never suspected. A deadly inertia of the spirit was conquering me. Esther, my love of a hundred years, became in memory elusive as a dream to me. The sensuous appeal of this wonderland swept over me.

We had threaded the recesses of the groves, passing secluded arbors of twisted vines, pergolas and rustic cottages about which clung the scarlet trumpets of pomegranate flowers; now the crystal walls came into sight again, and, as we approached, a gust of wind blew the door open. Instantly, to divert my senses from that soul-destroying dominance, there rushed in, the murmurs of the city, the voices of the multitude below, and, above all, clear and distinct, the wild accents of the whitebeard, who had denounced the pleasure-palace that afternoon.

"Woe to you, London, when your whitecoats sit with their harlots in the high places! Woe! Woe!"

I could not see him; through the door I saw only the circle of the enclosing walls, a luminous orb

beneath, and the glare of the huge Ray guns; beyond
were the mighty buildings.　Lembken put out his
hand and closed the door.　The voices were cut off
into silence.　I glanced at him, but his brow was
untroubled and serene.

He led me across a little, shelving lawn, through
a small gateway.　There was nobody in the tiny close,
surrounded by a high marble wall.　There were no
windows in the little house before me.　It might have
held two rooms.

"Three rooms," said Lembken, as if he had read
my thoughts.　"Good night, Arnold.　Remember,
we do what we like to do in the People's House.
There are no laws, no bonds.　Dream of this paradise that shall be yours, and open the third door
softly."

He left me.　I pushed the first door open and
entered.

It was a bedroom, furnished in the conventional
style which had not changed appreciably during the
century, but all in ebony or teak, and luxurious
almost beyond conception.　The floor was covered
with a thick-piled Bokhara rug, of red and ivory,
and exquisite texture.

I passed through the inevitable swing door.　The
second room was fitted as a combination library and
dining-room.　There was an ebony bookcase, filled
with magnificently bound books, a sideboard on

which stood wines and distilled liquors, a heavy dining-table, arm-chairs.

This room had a window, and, looking out, I was surprised to see beneath me the bridge that led to the Airscouts' Fortress, and, at the end of it, a figure in blue, the white swan on his breast brilliant in the glare of the solar light over his head.

I passed on. But instead of the swing door the further wall contained a door of heavy, iron-bound wood, with bolts of steel. Then I remembered Lembken's words: "Open the third door softly."

The bolts moved in their sockets with hardly a sound. I drew them; I opened the door and passed into a tiny chamber.

A girl in white, with the palm badge upon her shoulder, was standing there. The room had been dark; the sudden influx of the solar light from the library showed me the pallid face and blazing eyes of her whom I had least thought to see before me — Elizabeth!

CHAPTER XIV

THE HOUSE ON THE WALL

SHE stared at me with eyes that seemed to see nothing; and then a look of recognition came into them, and a twitching smile upon her lips. She put her arms out and came unsteadily toward me. She threw her right arm back. I caught her hand as it swung downward, and the dagger's razor edge grazed my shoulder.

The next moment she was fighting like a trapped panther. I could not have imagined that such strength and fierceness existed in any woman. She twisted her wrists out of my grasp time and again, and we wrestled for the dagger till the blood from my slashed fingers fouled my priest's robe. Each of the stabbing blows she dealt so wildly would have driven the dagger in to the hilt.

I grappled with her, caught her right arm at last, and forced it upward, but we swayed to and fro for nearly a minute before I mastered her. Even then she had one last surprise in store, for, when she saw that she was beaten, she drew her dagger hand quickly backward, and I seized the point of the blade within an inch of her breast. I forced her fingers open brutally, and the steel fell to the floor.

164

Then she wrested herself away, and crouched in the corner, watching me, motionless, but still ready to leap. Her gasping breaths were the only sound in the room.

"Elizabeth!" I cried. "I am not here to harm you. Look at me; listen to me!"

Her eyes were fixed on my face in terror that precluded speech. How she watched me! Only once did her glance waver, and that was toward the dagger on the floor. I kicked it backward with my heel.

"Elizabeth, listen to me!" I implored her. "I did not know that you were here, and I do not know how you came here. I want to help you. I want to take you home to David!"

"Ah!" she said, shuddering. "This is what you whites call a romance in the style of the first century B.C., a fashionable pastime, to dress yourselves as blues or grays and worm your way into the homes of your prospective victims, in order to study them, and see whether they suit your taste and are worth adding to your collection. I have read of that in the Council factory novels. But there was never any romance in it to me. So I appeared to suit you, after my father had taken you into his home so trustingly? You deceived him; but you never deceived me."

I saw her glance turn to the dagger again.

"Elizabeth, you are talking nonsense," I said, with an affectation of brusqueness. "Let us sit down in the next room, and I propose a compact. You shall take the dagger, provided you do not attempt to harm yourself with it till you have heard me. Is that agreed?"

She scrutinized me for half a minute. Then she nodded. I preceded her into the library with an affectation of indifference which I was far from feeling, for I heard her stoop to pick the dagger up, and wondered each instant whether I was about to feel the point between my shoulders. However, my faith appeared to inspire her with a measure of confidence, for she followed me into the middle room and consented to sit down.

But when I faced her, toying with the blade and all aquiver with the reaction from the terrific nerve-tension, I could hardly find words to utter. Whatever purpose Lembken might have in using me, I had the full measure of his mind. He had thought that my three weeks spent in David's house had inspired me with a passion for the girl; and he had brought her here, to leave her helpless in my power, a lure to bind me to his interests beyond the possibility of double-dealing.

Before I could begin, Elizabeth collapsed. She began to weep without restraint. I could only wait till she grew more composed. I stared out through the window, looking down toward the Airscouts' Fortress, whose roof rose perhaps twenty feet beneath me.

I saw the sentry with the swan badge, pacing below. Above him was the luminous wall of the fortress, and over it, floating in the air, was a host of ghostly shapes, airplanes encased in their phosphorescent glow armor, which, as I watched them, rose one by one into the air, circled, and flitted noiselessly away toward the south, like bubbles blown by children.

It could not have been late, for curfew had not come into operation, and London was ablaze with the solar light; but the crowds had gone home and everything was quite still. As I withdrew from the window Elizabeth rose and came timidly toward me.

"Arnold, have I done you a wrong?" she whispered.

"You misunderstood me," I answered. "But you could not have thought otherwise. If we understand each other now we can help each other — isn't that so?"

She seized me by both arms and gazed into my face with an imploring, pitiful appeal that wrung my heart.

"Then I thank God," she said, "for that impulse which held me from self-destruction. Arnold, do you remember that promise I made to you one day?

I remembered it; I remembered it, and it was that
alone which stayed my hand this afternoon, when the
emissary from Lembken came, and there was only
the one barred door between us, and I stood behind it,
with the knife at my breast.   Then I resolved to keep
my promise to you, and to let them bring me here,
and — to kill Lembken — but it was you!   When you
disappeared from the Strangers' House this morning we feared for your safety.   We thought you had
been seized or lured away.   Then my father was
summoned on some pretext back to the Strangers'
Bureau, and the airscout came — Lembken's man.   I
thought I was for Lembken —"

She broke off, and I took her hands in mine.

"Elizabeth," I said, "my dear, I do not understand
anything of what you tell me.   How could they bring
you here against your will?"

She looked at me in amazement.

"No, I see you do not understand," she answered.
"And yet you are dressed as a priest.   I cannot tell
you now.   But the airscout who had been sent for
me was sorry when he saw that I was not willing, like
most women.   He took the knife from me, but afterward he let me keep it; he was kind and promised to
carry the news to Jones, our friend.   The airscouts
are disloyal to Lembken, and hate his cruelty, but he
dared not disobey.   We went by scoutplane from the
roof, and Lembken's women took me and clothed me

in this dress of palms, and carried me here, laughing at me. They did not find the knife. I hid that; I meant to serve the Province and the world by killing Lembken. But then I saw you, Arnold, and— and—"

She burst into a new storm of weeping. I drew her to me and placed her head on my shoulder. I felt a cold, burning fire of resolution in my heart which never disappeared. Something, some spiritual door was opened in me. I became part of the wretchedness of the world and suffered its sorrows; pleasure seemed the worst part of life then. I think, too, I loved Esther the better because of that compassion.

When at last Elizabeth raised her head I was struck by the transformation in her appearance. It seemed the reflection of my own determination. I had put forth my will and conquered, and her own seemed one with mine.

"I am going to save you, Elizabeth," I said. "You are not destined for this earthly hell."

"Arnold, are you yourself in danger here?" she asked.

"Only of hell-fire," I answered.

"You must save yourself and not think of me," she said.

I bade her sit down, and went back to the entrance of the little house. I had half expected that the door

would have been locked, but it stood open, having
become unhasped, and the sickly odor of the pervad-
ing perfume clung to the warm, stale air. I crossed
the close to the gate that led into the garden of palms,
and stood there in hesitation.

The solar lights had been turned off, and all was
dark, except for varicolored lanterns twinkling
among the trees. Yet I was aware of souls peopling
that darkness. I heard the tinkle of stringed instru-
ments; I had the sense of hidden beings in the undergrowth. If hell can wear the mask of beauty, surely
it did that night.

I crossed the lawn and began to skirt the graveled
path that extended before me, working my way
toward the front of the Palace. The squat, white
building glittered against the darkness. Nobody
stirred at the entrance; there were no lights, but
always I had the sense of something watching me.

At last I saw the crystal walls on the west side,
and, beyond them, the phosphorescence of the glow
buildings. I stood in hesitancy. On my right stood
the thickets; on my left the crystal ended in a stone
wall. There was no egress except through the Palace
itself. Lembken left nothing to surprise.

As I turned I heard the rustle of stealthy footsteps near me. A red spark drew my eyes along the
vista of the orange trees, whose perfumed flowers
dispelled the cloying odor of the scented night. I

saw a Mænad's face, framed in a leopard skin, peering at me above a bank of hibiscus. I thought I recognized the girl Amaranth; but it vanished with the dying of the spark, and subdued laughter followed it.

All that was evil in the world seemed to have its focus there. I felt it, breathed it, once more its psychic dominance oppressed me heavily. I saw with sudden intuition why, in a world less stable, witches were burned, how passionately the souls of simple men fought for their heritage of truth and law. This was the negation of life, of all that struggling life that aspired upward, and set its heel upon the serpent's head. Old myths, made real in this new light, flashed into memory.

I hurried back to the close and fastened the gate behind me. The sweat was dripping from my forehead when I regained the safety of the little house. I burst from the first room into the second.

Elizabeth was not there.

I ran into the third room. She was not there, either. Terror gripped me. Had she been lured away during the few minutes of my absence? It seemed impossible. She would have died there.

Then my eyes fell on something that hung outside the window, dangling, as it seemed, from a fixed point above. It was a rope ladder, and moving outward. As I watched, I saw it begin to rise in a succession of short jerks.

I grasped it with my hands. It pulled me from the floor. I clung to it, striving to get my feet upon the rungs. It drew me to the level of the window, but I would not let go. It pulled me through the window-gap, and I swung far out above the Air-scouts' Fortress. Over me I saw the dark outlines of an unshielded scoutplane, high in the air.

I swung by my hands at the rope's end, like the weight of a pendulum, making great transverse sweeps that carried me high above the bridge, from end to end of the fortress roof. I saw the courts revolve beneath me. I swept from the crystal wall out into nothingness, and London was a reeling dance of phosphorescent maze. Then the ladder began to descend. I felt the roof of the fortress touch my feet, wrenched my numbed hands away, and fell. A moment later the airplane dropped beside me as noiselessly as an alighting bird, and two men sprang from it and seized me.

One was the airscout Jones. He caught me by both arms and forced me backward. But the other leaped at my throat. It was David; and he would have strangled me, had not Jones pulled him away.

Then, to my vast relief, Elizabeth ran forward, interposing herself between us. "Arnold is not to blame!" she cried. "He tried to save me!"

David's hands fell to his sides. The airscout caught me by the arms and pulled me toward an ele-

It pulled me through the window-gap, and I swung far out above the Airscouts' Fortress

vator entrance. He forced me into the cage, the others following, and we descended a few feet, emerging into a small, bare room with walls of unsquared stone.

Jones sent the elevator up and pulled the door of the shaft to.

"Now you can speak. You have five minutes to explain yourself," he said. He pulled a Ray rod from his tunic and looked at David, who nodded.

CHAPTER XV

SO I told them my story from the beginning. I
spoke of the days of the Institute and Lazaroff's
experiment, of my awakening within the cylinder
at the end of a century of sleep, my flight from the
cellar and my discovery by Jones. I continued, telling of my first bewilderment in London, of David's
kindness which had saved my reason, described my
summons that morning and the relays of spies who
had led me to the Temple. When I narrated my discovery of the cylinder containing Esther's living
body I raised my eyes to David's and perceived that
I was no longer in the position of a prisoner awaiting
death.

David's aspect had changed; he was trembling
violently and struggling to speak. He looked fearfully at me, and Jones was hardly less moved. Then
Elizabeth slipped her hand into mine.

"We believe you, Arnold," she said.

Three times David attempted to speak while I was
sketching briefly the remainder of my story up to the
point of my encounter with Elizabeth, and each time
his voice failed him.

"Arnold, forgive me," he managed to say at last.

174

"We know that every word you have told us is true.
if only you had told me before! But I see how incredible you must have thought your story. Now
listen to me!

"The horrors of this government will not last
much longer. Plans are well under way to make an
end of democracy and restore liberty to the world.
You have unwittingly placed a wonderful weapon in
our hands. No man can be neutral in such times.
Now, Arnold, you have to make a decision which will
affect not yourself only, but all of us, Britain, the
Federation, and the race of men. You must choose
your party." He turned to Jones. "He must be
told nothing until the time arrives," he continued,
assuming a tone of authority. "You will say nothing — nor you, Elizabeth."

He turned to me again.

"Arnold,'" he said, "you must make your choice
now. Lembken needs you for reasons which are
patent to us, thanks to your statement. If you go
back to him he can give you power and liberty to lord
it over the people until the quick day of reckoning
arrives. If you join us you must become an outlaw
and an associate in the most desperate endeavor, play
a leading part and share our dangers."

"How can you doubt me?" I asked. "I am with
you, now, and at all times."

David held up his hand. "Wait!" he said. "You

must first understand our situation, and why we are here tonight."

"It is not necessary, David," I answered.

"Yes, it is necessary. Because you do not know the depth of our intolerable bondage. I am going to tell you of my own life, that you may judge.

"I begin with my father. As I told you, he was epileptic in youth. He outgrew the attacks, and because the Liberal government never dared to enforce the Defectives' Law which it passed in 1930, he was able to marry, much later, a girl to whom he had been engaged for many years. They had lived quietly in what was then called Wales, in a rural community that had somehow managed to escape the excesses which began in 1945.

"But my father was a marked man, because he was on the secret defectives' list, and a Conservative. A few weeks after his marriage the storm of revolution burst over Dolgelly. The army of clerks and civil officers that followed the troops of the victorious democracy raked the country fine for victims. With his young bride my father fled to the mountains, where I was born, and they existed there, heaven knows how, till an opportunity arrived for flight abroad. When the restoration came he returned, and rebuilt his ruined home.

"My father was a student of history, and he knew

that the peace which had descended over the dis-
tracted country was only a lull in the storm of violence. He resolved to teach me all the old knowledge, which had fallen into decay. He wanted me
to play a leading part in political life, as his forebears
had done. But the second revolution was upon us
when I was a youth of nineteen. Fortunately, my
parents were both dead.

"The mob started burning defectives then. For
many there was the chance of submission to the new
government, nominally under Boss Rose, which Sanson was constructing; but there was none for me,
since epilepsy was then, owing to the ephemeral
theory of some forgotten scientist, regarded as the
unpardonable sin. I managed to escape to Denmark,
and spent the next sixteen years upon the Continent,
wandering from place to place as the Federation
came into being. I married a Swiss lady at Lau-
sanne, where Elizabeth was born. We had to fly
by night, when the child was a week old. My wife
could not survive the journey over the mountain
passes in the middle of winter. She died in what was
called Austria, two days after our arrival there.
With Elizabeth I continued my flight eastward, and
found refuge in Greece.

"I said that the mob had begun to burn defectives.
But the Council changed that. The word 'productivity' was the new fetish, and, seeing that the mur-

der of half the population would decrease the output, the Council resolved to imprison defectives in the workshops for life instead. But even this did not work. In 1999 Boss Rose became alarmed at the depopulation caused by the universal terror. Men denounced their brothers for small rewards, and wives their husbands, when they grew tired of them. Men and women were crossing the North Sea in tiny skiffs, or perishing in the waves, flying into the glens of Scotland, organizing in bands and living a hunted life within the forests that had begun to cover the country. Boss Rose issued an amnesty decree. Defectives who returned and were able to produce a hektone and a quarter monthly were not to be proscribed. I returned to Britain and secured employment in the Strangers' Bureau, which had just been established, a post for which my education and experiences abroad qualified me.

"Ten years ago Boss Rose fell under an assassin's dagger. The Council, under the influence of Sanson, issued a decree that no faith was to be kept with defectives. Sanson, then supreme behind the mask of Lembken, began to harry the people. It was then he introduced his system of mating under Council supervision."

"It is abominable!" I cried.

"Yet, like all our institutions, it has its roots far back in the past," said David, "and only needed the

abandonment of the Christian ethic to spring full-
fledged into existence. The Prophet Wells fore-
shadowed it, as did also Ellen Key; and on this point
the followers of Galton joined the Socialist government in a concerted attack upon monogamy. This, in
fact, has been the crux of the old battle between Socialism and the Church: on the one hand the old ideal
of the family as the unit of society, and marriage an
indissoluble bond; on the other the individual, free
from responsibility and seeking his own fancied freedom. Even in the Prophet's time America had practically abandoned monogamy, while the anti-social
propaganda was being secretly carried on by the
teaching of what was called sex hygiene in the
schools. When the churches compromised with divorce, Protestantism finally collapsed, and flung half
the civilized world back into paganism."

"It was said that the children—" I began.

"The answer was State rearing, Arnold, as had
been urged by many men and some women of liberal
and progressive minds. We tried that in 2002. Elizabeth was torn from me. For six months we had
public crèches in every city. There was much public
dissatisfaction, though the children were not taken
from their mothers till they had been weaned. That
was the time when the Guard was formed, consist-
ing of Janissaries trained from youth by the Council
and pledged to them. However, what caused the

abandonment of the crèche system was a quite unexpected happening. Despite the utmost care, despite a process of automatic feeding in germ-proof incubators, which made it impossible for any of the little inmates to lack the advantages of the latest hygienic theories, the children died.

"This phenomenon was never explained satisfactorily, and the mortality, which ranged from eighty to ninety per cent, shocked the Province profoundly, for it meant an intolerable lessening in the productivity of the next generation. The children were returned to their parents. Elizabeth, who was above the age curve of maximum mortality, came back to me, and, in spite of rigorous inspection by the officials of the Childrens' Bureau, I have managed to keep her.

"But I must be brief, Arnold. I have told you that it was decreed no faith was to be kept with defectives. The net was cast over all who, trusting to the proclamation, had returned from the forests and waste places, and from abroad. Gradually they were sorted out and ascribed. Many records of heredity had disappeared during the Revolution, but they had my father's in the Bureau of Pedigrees and Relationships. Since then I have waited in suspense daily. They know it, and, if I have not been condemned to the workshops, it is through Lembken's favor, for he was head of the Strangers' Bureau before the assassination of Boss Rose, and I worked under him."

"But is there no law?" I cried. "Is there no charter of liberty at all?"

"Why, yes, Arnold. We still have Magna Charta, and Habeas Corpus, and many other documents, and occasionally these are invoked. There is an old man in the paper shops who has appealed against imprisonment and carried his case through twenty or thirty courts since he was shut up as a boy, and if he lives long enough his appeal will come before the Council. But you see, Arnold, one of the first acts of the victorious democracy was to institute the election and the recall of judges.

"They think I fear for my own liberty," he continued, beginning to pace the floor. "They do not know — happily they do not know."

Then he went on to tell me that which concerned the girl's arrest that afternoon.

It appeared that Elizabeth was one of those very few who were physically almost perfect, and, as such, she had been in danger of being placed on the list of those who were to enter the harems of the whites. David's sole hope of saving her lay in the fact that she was penalized six points because her grandfather had had epileptic seizures. But she approximated so closely to the Sanson norm — and the child had been innocent enough to head the district list of those qualifying in mentality by examination upon the Binet board — that there had been little hope for her. This fear had been increased by the fact that Lembken had seen Elizabeth, and had recently summoned her and her father to the Council Hall, under the pretext of wishing to confer some favor upon an old subordinate.

Now I gathered in the last threads of the skein. David had returned from the Strangers' Bureau that afternoon to find the apartment empty. Jones had conveyed the news to him, and had secreted him in the Airscouts' Fortress, pending a plan of rescue, a task which was only rendered possible through the disaffection of Lembken's airscouts. Jones had seen me in my priest's robes, and the two had come to the natural conclusion that I had been a spy, playing one of the romantic parts in fashion among the whites, and approved in the Council's novels, in order to see Elizabeth before selecting her. We had been discovered at the window, the position of the little house had given Jones the opportunity of rescuing the girl with his scoutplane, and, but for my return while the rope still dangled before the aperture, I should never have known the secret of Elizabeth's disappearance. No wonder David had flown at my throat.

"Now, we must act at once," said David. "We are going to seek refuge in the forests where our friends are hiding. Jones will carry us there tonight when he starts in his scoutplane on patrol duty. It is a difficult problem to pass the night patrol. But Jones can get us through. And now, Arnold, what is your decision?"

"I made it long ago," I answered.

"You are with us?"

"Indeed, I am."

David wrung my hand hard. "You have decided wisely," he said, "and by your decision you have taken the only means possible to save the woman you love. For the Sanson régime is crumbling, and your presence means, what you cannot yet imagine, to the cause of liberty. We have five thousand outlaws and fugitives from the defectives' shops, scattered in secret hiding places about London. We have made Ray rods in the shops and have secreted provisions. Tonight the heads of the movement are to assemble —"

"In the cellar where I lay so long!" I exclaimed, with sudden intuition. "And Jones had been there with Ray rods when he found me!"

"Correct," answered Jones, in his laconic manner.

"We remain here until midnight," said David. "Then Jones will take us when he starts to relieve the first patrol."

"Be assured that I am with you to the end," I said. And I swore that I would do all in my power, so long as I had life and liberty, to fight for human freedom. And as I swore I had a vision of the girl, mangled and crushed upon the stones beneath that tropical, aerial hell beneath the noble dome of England's shameful temple.

I think the resolution in my manner must have enkindled David's hopes, for he put out his hand and caught mine again, and wrung and held it.

"You do not know, Arnold, how necessary you are to us," he said. "But tonight you shall be told. I am old, Arnold, and I have little courage. I have lived through too many changes and frustrated hopes. I had grown used and resigned to things that had come to seem unchangeable. The freedom of my youth was only a dream to me. Sometimes I doubted whether men had ever been free. It was your surprise, your ignorance, then the indignation which you thought I did not see that made me begin to understand my own degradation. And it was today's events that gave me heart to work with all my might for the cause to which I had only languidly adhered. I have been one of the revolutionary committee for months, and now I shall fight whole-heartedly, and you with me."

"David," I said with sudden conviction, "you are a Christian."

His eyes suddenly seemed to blaze. "I am!" he cried. "As we all are. I have temporized with evil all these years, but now I cannot do so any more.

The hope of the world can never be crushed out; it is spreading everywhere. All of us are enlisted under that flag that was raised on the Mount two thousand years ago. We see that without Christ, life is intolerable. I knew your faith from the first, Arnold, although I dared not speak, I knew it at the beginning because I thought you were a Russian. That was why I befriended you. We know our own!" he cried triumphantly.

Elizabeth put one arm about her father's neck and extended her free hand to me. I clasped it, and then the airscout's; and so we pledged ourselves.

CHAPTER XVI

JONES left us and came back with some food. Upon his arm he carried a stranger's uniform, which he handed to me.

"You cannot wear those robes," he said. "Take this. It should fit you; it belonged to one of our recruits who was ascribed last week and has not yet returned it to the Wool Stores."

I was glad to see the last of the priest's robes. He carried them away, promising to return for us in an hour. Elizabeth made us eat, but we had little heart to do so. At her insistence, however, we made the best display of appetite that was possible.

The room was only faintly illumined by the reflected solar light that issued up the elevator shaft. With it there mounted the sound of the voices of the airscouts in their barracks below. Sometimes the elevator rushed by, arousing a thrill of fear in each of us.

David drew me toward him and began speaking softly.

"You know nothing of Paul," he said. "His name is Paul Llewellyn — for we observe Sanson's laws no longer. He was to have mated Elizabeth."

"Married?"

"Yes, married, before the Cold Solstice. His grandfather was my father's steward at Dolgelly. Our families remained in touch through all the civil turmoil, and he is the last of his, as Elizabeth is the last of mine. He was given the name Paul, the father retaining the family name, which was to alternate in each generation, as is the custom nowadays. That law of Sanson's must be one of the first to go. It aimed, of course, to destroy the vestiges of the family that remained.

"Paul was a Grade I defective, and we felt sure that Elizabeth would come under the same classification, so that they would be free to mate. They were waiting for the lists to be published, but Elizabeth had not been ascribed when the last list went up, and meanwhile Paul was sent to the defectives' shops. Arnold, did you ever hear of the doctrine called Apostolic Succession?"

"Of course, David."

"That the functions of the priesthood are transmitted by the laying on of hands? The English Church possessed the tradition, and it has never been lost, though most of our people attach, I am afraid, some magical idea to the ancient rite. Our bishop is a poor, illiterate old man, a machinist by trade, but Bonham laid his hands on him before he was burned in Westminster Hall. Bishop Alfred was to have

blessed the union. A week before Fruit Equinox,
Paul was taken in the bishop's home by Sanson's
spies. Both were condemned to life imprisonment
in the defectives' shops as Christians. Both escaped
among the last batch of fugitives. Elizabeth hopes
to meet Paul tonight."

"And I hope so, with all my heart," I answered.

The cage stopped at the door and Jones came in.

"We can go now. The last of the scoutplanes has
gone," he said.

We went up to the roof. Deep night was over
and about us. The phosphorescent fronts of the
glow-painted buildings gave London the aspect of
long lines of parallel and intersecting palisades of
ghostly light; but the glow paint illumined nothing,
and the deep canyons of the streets were of velvety
blackness. The white circle of the fortress wall surrounded us. Outside the region of the glow, London
was an indistinguishable blurred shadow, save where
the searchlights from the departing scoutplanes
illumined it. They hovered in a long line above the
city, their position only discernible from the white
searchrays that emanated from them as they swept
the city below. Slowly they made their way into
the southern distance.

I groped for reality in this succession of bewildering scenes, and hardly found it. Rain began to fall,
spattering on the crystal walls of the adjacent gar-

dens, in which the flickering colored lights still twinkled. My face was wet with it. I was thinking of the old days, when life was free: Sir Spofforth's rain-swept garden, the scent of Esther's tea-roses, and the hum of the ungainly, noisy town of Croydon that last evening. I saw Esther's face vividly upon the velvet screen of the night.

Elizabeth's hand stole into mine.

"You are our hope, Arnold. You can inspire us to victory," she whispered.

Jones had gotten the scoutplane ready, and the vessel now rested on the flat roof, as a bird on its perching place. It was a little craft, even smaller than my memory of it had been, and it carried no Ray shield to betray its presence. Jones drew David aside and held a whispered colloquy with him.

"We are about ready," he said, as they came back to us. "I've shifted the searchlight to the rear socket to balance the extra weight. She'll carry us. I'll have time to take you to your destination and report for scout duty when Hancock comes the round. But if I fly with the searchlight showing, any of the planes may signal me to stop — "

He rubbed his chin, and the old irresolution came upon his face.

"If I fly dark it's a leather vat offense," he added. "And the battleplanes would fire on us."

He paused and rubbed his chin again.

"I'll fly dark," he said, and so settled the matter firmly in his own mind. And, his mind thus made up, I knew nothing would change it.

There was some difficulty in disposing of us. Finally Jones placed us three in the double seat, Elizabeth in the center and David and I on either side of her. He himself squatted upon the chassis before us, the wheel in his hands. He touched the starting lever with his right foot, and the craft rose heavily into the air, straining beneath her burden. In spite of the counterbalance of the searchlight behind, the nose of the plane dipped constantly, so that our flight was a succession of abrupt ascents and declinations.

It was freezing cold up in the air. Gradually we ascended, till I felt the fresh wind from the Thames estuary beat on my face. Presently the south was cleft by flaming serpents, with eyes of fire.

"The food airvans from France," said David, pointing.

Now we soared over the outlying factories and warehouses. A huge, glow-painted building sprang into view out of the shadows below.

"The defectives' workshops for this district," David continued. "Yonder is the Council's art factory."

The darkness in front of us began to be studded with long parallelograms of dazzling glow, set at wide intervals, each capped with the conical Ray guns. From these, extending fanwise toward the ground, appearing pink in contrast with the glow's intensely purple white, the searchlights wavered.

Jones halted the scoutplane. "The battleplanes," he said, pointing. "They are posted nightly around London now. You know the reason, David?"

David started and placed his hand in inquiry upon the airscout's shoulder. Jones's voice sank to a whisper.

"It is the merest rumor among our men," he said. "One reads it in their faces rather than hears it spoken, for we are afraid of one another. One can be sure that Sanson has his spies among us. But the scoutplanes are sufficient to patrol London and detect fugitives, and if the battleplanes are sent out there is hope the rumor may be true. If the Tsar has broken out from Tula—"

"Thank God!" said David in a tense whisper.

"He will overrun Skandogermania in a week, for it is as disaffected as Britain. The airscouts there will go over to him. There is no force to stop him, except our planes and the Guard."

I saw the joy on David's face. Could barbarous Russia indeed bring freedom to the Western World?

"It is only a rumor," continued Jones. "A rumor, you understand, David, backed by the presence of the battleplane squadron around the city nightly, words let fall in the People's House, retailed by gossiping servants, the sudden summons last night of Air-Admiral Hancock — "

"But the Russians have been slaughtered in thousands!" I exclaimed. "I saw the picture upon the screen."

Jones laughed and David smiled.

"Those pictures are for the people," said the air-scout. "They were taken by night inside the fortress here. The Guard dressed for the part."

"Still, how could the Russians win without the Ray?" asked David doubtfully.

"I can answer that," I said. "All history shows that no weapon is strong enough to conquer men who are ready to die for a right idea against an evil one. Ideas are stronger than the deadliest arm man has contrived. That has always been so and always will be so."

Again Elizabeth's hand crept into mine. "You must tell our people that, Arnold," she said. "You know the secret of stirring them."

"But Hancock will stand by Lembken?" inquired David.

"Yap, and will hold at least a quarter of our men to him," said Jones. "He will serve Lembken through Sanson, so long as Sanson remains loyal. If Sanson turns against Lembken to seize the supreme power, Hancock will fight him to the death

Sanson sent the Air-Admiral's son to the Rest Cure
as a moron, years ago, when Hancock was unknown.
Sanson doesn't remember it, but Hancock remembers."

I shuddered. "Why, then, is not Hancock with
us?" I asked.

"There are traditions of loyalty in his family,"
answered Jones. "Hancock is queer. Now we go
up. Hold fast."

The scoutplane creaked and rocked and plunged
like a ship in a gale as, foot by foot, he jerked her
head into the higher air. The gleaming glow parallelograms of the battleplanes seemed to shoot downward as we soared above them. We had passed
them when, like some black air monster, a large, dark
plane glided beneath us. I felt our scoutplane thrill
as she shot upward, so suddenly that she rose almost
to the perpendicular, jerking us back against the
uprights.

Jones was straining madly at the wheel, and I
realized that the dark plane was in pursuit of us. I
saw her swoop out of the night, missing us by a yard.
She disappeared. I heard the divided air hiss as she
approached again, and the next instant the blinding
searchlight enveloped us, and a voice hailed us,
piping thin through the frosty night. Then the light
was astern, and groping impotently beneath us as we
rose to a higher level. Jones strained at the vertical

rudder, pushing the plane's nose up and still upward, battling like a weather-beaten bird against the wind.

Again the searchlight found us, and then, out of the heart of it, turning the keen white glare to a baby pink that fringed it, there hissed a light ten times more brilliant, snapping and crackling, into the void. Jones veered, still mounting. The dazzling light flared out again. The upright that I held snapped in my hand. I slipped in my seat, but David reached out and held me.

Once more the Ray flash came, but under us. The darkness and our pilot's courage had saved us. The searchlight groped far underneath. Our scoutplane dipped, soared, dipped, caught the wind, and we volplaned at furious speed for miles down a gradient of cushiony air.

I felt Elizabeth tremble, and placed my arms around her to hold her. Jones stayed the plane and clapped his numbed hands together, whistling through his teeth. He jerked his head around. The moon was beginning to rise; it was a little lighter, and I saw that his face was dripping wet.

"A thread of an escape!" he said. "If she had struck us fair with the Ray we'd have buckled up like paper. Snapped one upright, didn't it?"

There was a cut of two inches in the steel — a clean cut, and the edges fused as if from fire.

"That was Hancock's dispatchplane," said Jones.

"He carries no light. But — the voice didn't sound like Hancock's."

"Are we safe now?" asked David, looking back to where the shrunken figures of the battleplanes were ranged behind us on the horizon.

"Safe long ago," said Jones. "But it was touch-and-go while I was trying to top that southeaster. He lost us at the summit, though, and he couldn't have caught us on that down-grade."

We started again, traveling more slowly, at a lower altitude, and planing downward until I heard the wind in the tree boughs and saw the glistening snow beneath. We brushed the top-most twigs. The scoutplane flitted backward and forward, seeking the old road.

"I ought to know it in the dark," said Jones. "I don't want to turn on the searchlight if I can help it."

To and fro we went like a fluttering bird, until the cleft of the road appeared among the trees. Then we dropped softly to the ground. I was almost too cramped and cold to move. With difficulty I descended and helped Elizabeth out. David followed, and we three stood chafing our hands and stamping until the circulation was restored.

Jones leaned forward from the airplane. "I'll run her into the trees in case anyone comes along and sees her," he said.

"We shall not see you until — ?" asked David.

"I'm not going back," answered the airscout. "Not after this night's work. You'll see me in ten minutes."

"You are going to join us?" inquired David, joyfully. "Is it — do you mean Hancock knew you?"

"No. That wasn't Hancock, either. I know who it was — at least, I think I know. No, I've had enough of the Twin Bosses, after Elizabeth's adventures. Put me down as the first airscout who went over."

David grasped him by the hand and shook it warmly. Jones whistled again, drew back, and the scoutplane rose to the tops of the trees, beat about, and vanished.

David turned to me. "Arnold, are you prepared for a great and stunning revelation?" he asked.

"Yes, he is prepared," answered Elizabeth for me.

We set off through the trees along a small, well-worn trail, until the crumbling bricks beneath us heaped themselves into a mound, and I saw the ruined foundations of the Institute before me, and the hole in the cellar roof. A sentinel leaped out at us.

"For man?" he asked, leveling a Ray rod.

"And freedom," answered David.

The sentinel called, and in a moment a crowd came rushing up a short ladder, wild-looking men with beards and hanging hair, all dressed in tatters and rags, a woman or two, and a youth who ran forward with a cry and caught Elizabeth in his arms. I saw the happiness they shared.

David led me to a tall old man with bowed shoulders and a ragged white beard that spread fan-wise across his breast. His hands were seared and twisted like those of one who has lived years of hardest toil, and the staff on which he leaned had a crooked handle.

"Bishop Alfred," he said, "this is the Messiah who was to come."

CHAPTER XVII

THE CHAPEL UNDERGROUND

IN THE subterranean chapel, lit by rushlights that sent the shadows scurrying and made fantastically unreal the eager faces and the dissolving groups that clustered now around me, now around David, and again gathered about the tall old bishop with his peasant's face and child's eyes, David told them my tale, and then in turn told me the legend that I had brought so wonderfully to fulfillment.

The more bewildered I appeared, the stronger grew their faith, for the legend foretold that I was to come unknown to myself, and with no expectation of my own mission. They saw the cylinder, and there was none who doubted.

There were some thirty men and women present, of whom a dozen formed an inner council which had already formulated the plans for the new government. Some were delegates from outlaw bands in the recesses of the forests, some, like David, fugitives from the government bureaux, and three or four, Paul among them, those who had most recently escaped from the defectives' shops. There were representatives of various trades, who had come from London at imminent risk, intending to return:

one from the traffic guild I noticed in particular, a
giant of a man with a black beard as crisp as an
Assyrian king's, who said that, at his signal, his
guild would rise and fling themselves, to a man, upon
the Guard.

It was a touching reunion. Two generations had
gone by while men remained in ignorance of all that
we and our ancestors had known: popular freedom,
public rights, liberty to choose their trades, the
sanctity of family life, and, above all, the absence
of the galling inquisition and atrocious tyranny of
Science run mad.

The elder men remembered with horror the period
of the revolutions, in which a man would have given
all that he had for life and bread. They regarded
the epoch that had preceded this as the dark age of
the world, much, I think, as we, in our turn, looked
back upon the freer age before the Reformation.
They had a misty tradition of a century in which
men starved, in which the rich oppressed the poor
and the poor dwelled in foul, sunless tenements and
dressed in rags.

That tradition was true, and of the Moyen Age,
before these things, of course they knew nothing.
Now all had bread to eat, and light and air; but they
lived in a world with neither hope nor joy, resource
nor initiative, nor happiness in labor, in which one
cherished the home ties furtively, while over their

children always hung the menace of the defectives' workshops, or the horrors of the Temple. And on them preyed the privileged caste of whites, taking toll of their daughters, lording it as judges and bureau bosses, in the name of Science emanating from a madman's brain.

I began to gather, to my relief, that only the very ignorant believed that the Messiah would be a supernatural being. There was superstition enough hidden in the hearts of all, for faith, denied, creeps in, in strange guises; but the world awaited, rather, the inevitable leader who must come to set free a people grown over-ripe for freedom. For the horrors of the new civilization had reached the point where men had grown reckless of life. Everywhere was the anticipation of the approaching change, and even Sanson must have seen that neither his Guard nor his great Ray artillery could save his crumbling power. Science had overplayed her part when she had bankrupted human hearts.

Everywhere the deep sense of intolerable wrong was spreading. And although not even the very old remembered the time when Christianity was a living faith, yet the hopes of all hinged on it. There was no other hope for the world but the same Light that lit the darkness in the most shameful days of Rome's high civilization. So they had enrolled themselves beneath that ancient banner of human freedom;

dozens had died under torture rather than disclose the hiding place of their treasured Scriptures — of such parts as had come down to them, rewritten in the new syllabic characters. There was a rich harvest to come from many a martyr's blood.

So, then, there had filtered down through the years the faith that in 2015, or seven and thirty years after the institution of the new era, a Messiah was to arise and restore freedom to man. It had begun with the discovery of the cylinder that contained Esther's body, somewhere about the middle of the preceding century, and after the first revolutionary outbreak.

In some manner unknown the cylinder had made its appearance in the world. At first it was believed that it contained only the embalmed body of a woman, within a case fashioned so cunningly that none could open it. But later the rumor spread that at the end of a certain time the case would open of itself, and the woman awaken and come forth.

I inferred that Sanson, in spite of Lembken's statement to me, had obtained access to Lazaroff's papers, and had shrewdly resolved to turn the popular legend to his own use by placing the date of the fulfillment of the prophecy. He set the cylinder within the Temple and diffused the report that, when Esther awakened, they two would rule the world together and offer immortality to man.

The cylinder had, then, first appeared about 1950.

It had become the symbol of the Revolution—Freedom sleeping. It had been carried before marching armies. It had been a rallying point for the defeated. Men had fought and died over it. It had been struck by unnumbered bullets. It had been lost and regained upon a dozen battlefields. Then it had vanished with the inauguration of the reactionary régime, to appear once more, the inspiration of new hopes, when Sanson sprang to his leadership, like a god, about the year 1980.

And all this while I had been sleeping within the vault, as heedless of the passing years as Esther in her undreamed of journeyings. That I had escaped notice was due, no doubt, to the single fact that the wall of the vault had fallen in and hidden my cylinder from sight, embedded, as it was, in mud up to the neck. Those who had read of me in the papers might not have prosecuted their search hard, thinking that the cylinder had been removed already.

As the years went by an amplification of the legend had spread until it grew to be a rooted popular belief that the Messiah who was to come would issue from a second cylinder. That was the reason why neither David nor Jones, nor any in the cellar doubted me.

Old Bishop Alfred grasped my hands in his. "This is not chance, but a wonderful sign from God," he said. "To think that while we met here you lay within that case a few feet from us! I have doubted and dreaded, as all have, but nothing can daunt me now. We shall win freedom, we shall have our two names again."

David whispered to me that, grown a little childish with age, the poor old man longed for the day when he could assume the ancient episcopal pomp. To sign himself, Alfred London, was his life's dream, and he had vowed that till that day came his family name should never pass his lips.

After I had heard the story we kneeled in prayer, and the Bishop read to us from the syllabic version of the Bible, as it was known. It comprised only a few portions of the Old Testament, chiefly parts of Isaiah which some scribe had thought prophetic and necessary to be saved. Of the Synoptic Gospels there existed only a few fragments, too, but there was the "Sermon on the Mount" from the "Beatitudes" to the end, and the whole of the magnificent "Gospel According to St. John," together with most of "Acts" and "Corinthians," debased to some extent, and containing interpolations that had crept in, but on the whole faithful to the original. Though the entire Bible has, of course, been recovered, I am convinced, and many agree with me, that the world has gained immeasurably by the removal of the scaffolding of the Temple of Truth during more than two generations. Never again will literal interpretation be placed upon Old Testament mythology, the poetic allegory of "Creation and the Fall," or the chronology that offered the life cycles of tribes as the events of one man's life; nor will the warrior god, Jehovah, be considered anything but an incompletely discerned aspect of the divine.

Afterward, at David's urging, I rose to speak. I hardly knew what I should say, but, as I stood in hesitation before the meeting some Pentecostal power seemed to lay hold of me, and a torrent of impassioned words broke from my lips, till I felt all minds and hearts enkindled from the flame in mine. I spoke of the old, free world, of old, illogical, and cherished customs, preserved through centuries, uniting men in a fellowship that logic could not give; of ideals and traditions carried onward from age to age, ennobling faith and strengthening a nation's soul; of pride of family other than that of pedigreed stock; of initiative and resourcefulness, charity and good-will for weak as well as strong; of a ruling class bound by its traditions to public service, and open to all below who had the character and gifts to enter it.

But one thing I could not explain; when Bishop Alfred, rising, incredulous that the weak should have been protected, that they aroused pity instead of wrath, inquired, if we had really had this Christian use, why we had lost it.

When I ended I came back to myself, to find that

I was standing tongue-tied before them. I heard a
sigh ascend from every lip ; and then they were about
me, falling upon their knees, grasping my hands,
imploring me to accept their service and devotion.
Elizabeth was weeping happily.

"I knew, Arnold," she said.

Then the revolutionary committee took their seats
upon the benches and, while the rest gathered about
them, proceeded to consider the reports brought in.
It was an informal meeting, hampered by none of
those rules made by democracy for the restriction
of free speech, and conducted with earnestness and
quiet decorum. Man after man rose up and made
his report, the leaders of the guilds pledging so many,
describing their enthusiasm, stating the number of
Ray rods in his possession, and pledging absolute
obedience to instructions.

Then I was acquainted, as succinctly as possible,
with the progress of the movement. It was known
that during the next few days Sanson meant to
address the people in the Temple, using some anni-
versary celebration as his occasion. He was universally credited with the plan to effect a *coup d'etat,*
deposing Lembken and assuming the rulership of the
Federation. He had attached the Guard to him with
favors and gifts, so that intense hatred existed
between it and Lembken's airscouts. There was thus
a triangular contest between Sanson, Lembken, and

the revolutionaries; and the fear was that, if the air-scouts were split by faction, the Guard would overwhelm them and establish Sanson in Lembken's place, making a greater tyranny still.

It was, therefore, debated whether it might be possible, as unhappily it seemed necessary, to make some terms with Lembken that should ensure Sanson's overthrow.

"We have gained one piece of priceless information from you, Arnold," said David. "We know now that Sanson's plans relate to the awakening of Esther. Five days is almost too short a period for our plans to mature; yet we know that Sanson's coup must synchronize with the opening of the cylinder. It is believed that he has actually made some discovery, not, of course, of immortality, but for prolonging life, which he intends to offer the populace, should any champion, posing as the Messiah, come forth to challenge him. That will be a test such as has never yet been made in the world's history, the choice between liberty and immortality, so-called. And it will be difficult for the multitude to choose the former and to reject the latter."

"If the people have the choice they will choose wisely," said Elizabeth, from within Paul's arm. "Have no doubt as to that."

"How do you know?" asked David.

"Because they want the love that is their birthright," she answered boldly, "and love knows it is immortal and does not fear death."

I saw the committee leader smile, and there came upon his face a very affecting look. An elderly man, a member of the privileged caste, he had voluntarily laid aside the white robes of his order and taken to the forests, to organize the beginnings of the Revolution. As he spoke, the detailed scheme began to be clear to me, and I understood that the rulers of the world were matched by no mean antagonists.

First he alluded to the belief, already current among all the revolutionary bands, that the Federation's troops had been overwhelmed before Tula, and that the Tsar's forces were already pouring through Skandogermania to seize the battleplanes from the disaffected airscouts in Hamburg and Stockholm and launch them against London. It was believed that the Council must be in desperate straits to have had recourse to the moving picture lie, as worthless as the falsehood that the escaped defectives had been retaken.

What seemed to me a psychological confirmation of this report was the circumstance asserted by him, that the torture of heretics, the activities of the vivisectionists, and the weeding out of morons were proceeding with unexampled rigor. For tyranny always becomes most cruel when it approaches its downfall, by inspiring terror, to create submission.

"You have heard," continued the old man, "how Lembken lured Arnold to the People's House. Lembken knows who he is. Then he must be aware of Sanson's plans and is plotting to use Arnold in a counterstroke.

"He is old and obese and pleasure-loving. But you must not forget that he rose to power by the most cunning craft, inspiring, as he undoubtedly did, the murder of Boss Rose, and buying over the air-scouts. Sanson underrates the old fox, but Lembken has his ear to the ground all the while he is supposed to be roystering in his devil's palace. Now, friends, we can despise no weapon that will aid our cause. If we have to use Lembken, as the lesser evil, in order to unite the airscouts under Hancock against Sanson——"

"Never!" shouted the black-bearded leader of the traffic guild. "He has taken—taken—taken——"

The giant broke down and covered his face with his hands.

"My daughter," he raved, raising his face with the tears streaming down his cheeks, and clenching his enormous hands. "Only today—today—I would not desert the cause, or I should have forced my way into the People's House and killed him——"

I thanked God, the father did not know that I had seen her in the Council Hall.

The old leader got up and put his arm about the giant's shoulder.

"But for the sake of freedom you will consent," he said.

The other threw back his head. "Yes — for the cause, yes," he answered quietly, and moved away. He stood with head drooping upon his breast, like some huge statue. I understood then the strength of the enmity to the government. No Ray artillery could withstand such a wild passion as the deviltries of Science had awakened.

"I can only offer the outlines of my plan," resumed the old man, returning to his place, "because, at such a time, we must trust as much to the spontaneous instincts of our people as to a detailed scheme which may go wrong. But it seems to me that it is essential first to enter into communication with Lembken. We will offer him his palace, perhaps, and an untroubled life hereafter. It is a hard compromise, but there seems no other way, for Sanson must be destroyed, and everything depends on Hancock.

"Five days hence, when Sanson summons the people into the Temple, as many as possible of our men will assemble there, with Ray rods beneath their tunics. Arnold will advance and challenge Sanson. We shall spring forward, seize him, possess ourselves of the cylinder, assume possession of the

Temple buildings, and set up our government. Meanwhile the airscouts will take possession of the barracks and Ray artillery.

Here I interposed. "Is this the only way?" I asked. "Are there not annual elections? Would it not be possible — "

I was unprepared for the outburst of bitter laughter that answered me.

"Do you really believe, Arnold," asked David, "that anything can be done like that? Even in your other life, history — the history that is not taught — informs me that the election of popular representatives had become farcical, especially in the home of democracy, America, through the refusal to permit unauthorized candidacies, through the demand for large sums of money to be deposited as a preliminary, by ballots drowned with names of unknown men, representing nobody knew whom, and fifteen to twenty feet in length; by ruffians at the polls — a device much used in Rome when she started on the democratic down-grade that led to tyranny; by stuffed ballots and lying counts, and voting machines . . . . in short, Arnold, we have so far improved upon those crude devices that the ballot is now the strongest weapon in our masters' hands. And when freedom has been restored it will never be seen again. We shall never count heads, except among small bodies of committees, and the days of so-called representative government will never recur so long as men remain free."

It was evident that his words had touched their imaginations in some way unknown to me, for they sprang to their feet and cheered him wildly. I learned afterward that all the laws, the most subversive of human rights, all the most fearful promulgations of Sanson were put to the farcical test of public approbation. The democratic State had killed itself, as it always does, but the shell remained to protect the tyranny that followed, as it always does, too.

Before the noise had quite subsided, Jones, who had come in quietly, stood up in the midst of the assembly.

"The plan to seize the Ray artillery is impossible," he said bluntly.

"Why?" demanded a dozen voices.

"Because the small Ray guns upon the battleplanes are useless against the glow paint on the Guards' fortress, and the Guards' great Ray artillery will pick off our battleplanes one by one as they expose their unprotected parts while evolving in the air. It is impossible to protect the parts of a plane around the solar storage batteries, because the glow rays disturb their action. Then, again, when each of our men has discharged his Ray rod, where is he to replenish it without access to the solar storage within the Guards' fortress? Even our airplanes, with their week's supply, have to be replenished there."

"Hold a battleplane where we can gain access to it, so that the rods can be recharged from its supply."

"Not practicable," said Jones.

"If each man has three Ray rods, he can kill three of Sanson's men."

"But unless you take the fortress the Ray artillery can make a desert of London."

"What would you do, then?" asked the committee leader.

"Cut the solar supply cables."

"Twelve feet underground, in steel and concrete?"

"No. At the heart of the world's power system," said the airscout. "In the Vosges. It is not impossible. The Ray artillery there is not carefully guarded; the early nights are dark. Make Sanson's Ray guns useless at a stroke, and then storm the fortress in the old way, man against man."

I saw the face of the black-bearded leader redden with blood. "Yes!" he cried, "that is the way."

"And then we shall have two names again and life will be free," said Bishop Alfred, musing. "Two names, as our fathers had."

All caught the enthusiasm. The committee leader held up his hand for silence. "Wait! Who will go?" he demanded.

"I can.   I will," replied Jones, boldly.   "I was born there.   My father was a Frenchman, removed to England because he cherished national aspirations.   I will succeed or die there."

"Where will you get the airplane?"

"I have it here," said Jones, as simply as if he could produce it from his pocket.

Again the mad clamor burst forth.   Jones, as the first airscout to come over, filled all with enthusiasm, and belief in our success.

"And who will go to Lembken as our emissary?" asked the committee leader presently.

"I will," I answered.

David started toward me.   "No!   The risk is too great," he cried.   "We need you in the Temple on the appointed day.   We need your leadership for the sake of the cause.   If Lembken refuses, or tricks you, all will be lost."

I answered rather sadly.   "You forget," I said, "that I, too, have all I hold dear at stake.   For this cause, too, I shall succeed or die."

CHAPTER XVIII

FOR a long time I could not persuade them to let me go. But I pleaded so hard and set out the arguments so forcibly that at last I persuaded them. For it was clear that if Lembken, realizing that his power was waning, should accept our offer, then my plan was the wisest; and, if he refused, our desperate chance would lose but little by my death.

It was even possible that the rôle for which he had cast me was the same that I was to play for the Cause. He had meant to use me against Sanson; and the more I thought of it the stronger grew my conviction that he had meant to have me challenge Sanson in the Temple.

So, one by one, the opposing arguments ended, and the committee leader gave me my instructions.

"You must evade the battleplanes and enter London afoot," he said. "You will proceed to the People's House, demand admission, and offer Lembken our terms: his palace, honors, wealth and pleasures. If he accepts you will return to us bearing his acceptance in the form of writing, that we may have a hold on him to use with Sanson, should he betray us afterward. If you are detected by the search-

214

lights before you reach London, you will be taken
before Hancock, to whom you will make your
demand for an interview with his chief. A mes-
senger will remain posted near this meeting place
in order to convey you to us on your return, wher-
ever we may be. Now, God be with you, Arnold!"

I think they understood the turmoil in my heart,
for they were very considerate, and troubled me with
no more suggestions than these. For myself, I confess that the thought of Esther's peril obliterated
from my mind nearly all other considerations, and,
in truth, I cared more for her safety than for the
Cause. I could do nothing till the time of her
awakening came; but, when she awakened, I meant
to be at her side.

The rushlights were blown out, and we bade each
other adieu at the cellar entrance, and separated.
Many of those who were present had traveled miles
through the forests in order to attend the meeting.
It had been arranged that David and Elizabeth
should make their quarters with the band com-
manded by the leader, to which the bishop and Paul
belonged. I was to accompany them as far as the
old road, where our paths divided.

When we reached it, Elizabeth turned and, putting
her hands upon my shoulders, looked very earnestly
at me.

"Arnold," she said, "the day is near when we four

shall be friends in a happier world. God bless you and protect the woman you love."

I pressed her hands. Then David grasped my own in his.

"Good-bye, Arnold," he said. "The Providence that brought you to me will act to save us all."

And he, too, was gone. I waited at the edge of the old road, watching them disappear among the trees. The last thing that I saw was the bishop's white beard, a spot in the darkness. Then I was alone, with the London road before me, and a mission as desperate as any that was ever undertaken, and as pregnant with possibilities.

I do not know how long I had been traveling, whether five minutes or twenty, nor whether I walked or ran. I became conscious of a soft whistling in the air, and, glancing up, saw a dark airplane, black against the risen moon.

I sprang from the road and hid myself in the underbrush.

The airplane dipped, passed me, and dipped again, with the purpose, evidently, of alighting in the road. It passed beyond my sight, flying low, and veering from side to side as its occupant examined the ground for a resting place.

As I rose to continue my journey I heard a low hail among the trees. I started around, to see the old bishop approaching me at a jog-trot. He came up panting, and stood before me, holding his pastoral staff against his breast.

"Did you see the airplane?" he asked, following the road with his eyes.

"What are you doing here, Bishop Alfred?" I asked in astonishment, for there was an expression of supreme, benignant happiness upon his face. "Are you alone?"

"Yes, alone," he answered, smiling. "I left them quietly. They would not have let me go. I followed you until I saw the airplane. I am going to Lembken in your place."

"But you will be put to death!" I cried. "Surely, you know —"

"Yes, but that is all right," he answered. "It is three years now since any priest was burned for the faith. I have been thinking about it for a long time. Now I am ready. I am going into the People's House to preach the Gospel. I — I ran away from David," he added, chuckling at the success of his maneuver.

I threatened and pleaded in vain, for the old man's face had the joyousness of a child's.

"It's no use talking, Arnold," he said, patting my arm affectionately. "I am a stubborn man when my mind is made up, and it is made up now. I have thought about it a long time. You see, I am the last bishop in England. I am not a learned man, but the Lord Bishop of London" — how happily he said that!—"laid hands on me an hour before they burned him in Westminster Hall. Now it is right that I should follow him and take on martyrdom. It will give inspiration to the people. It will be a wonderful encouragement to them to see me among the fagots. I have prayed the Lord to give me strength, because I am a cowardly old man, and He has done so. I should like to consecrate my successor before I die. But the Russians will take care of that, and it is fitter that they should renew the line in England. They will be here in a few days to save the world, and then we shall all be one."

"How do you know?" I cried.

"It is given to me to know," he answered, wagging his white head. "So there is no longer any reason why I should not go into the People's House and bear testimony to the truth. You can go back now. I will carry your message to Lembken before I die."

Before I could restrain him he had started off along the road, and his quick jog-trot gave him almost as much speed as my scrambling, wild pursuit. I caught him, however, a hundred yards away.

"Bishop Alfred, you must go back to your friends," I said. "Your idea is nonsense. There is no need to sacrifice yourself."

He shook his head and detached himself. I

stumbled over a projecting root, and when I was on my feet again I saw the old man another fifty yards away. Once more I was approaching him. And then I halted suddenly and drew back among the trees, for just beyond the bend in the road lay the dark airplane, and the old man had stopped beside it, evidently waiting to be taken in.

However, since he continued to wait there, I advanced noiselessly toward it, with the hope of rescuing him, until I realized that the dark airplane was empty.

The occupant had left it, but for what reason, or where he had gone, I could not surmise.

I was just where the old road joined with a small, twisting path that struck back among the trees. Some instinct cautioned me to silence. If I had spoken . . . . but I did not speak, and then, among the trees, following the crooked trail not fifty paces away, I saw the aviator, walking with head bent downward, evidently unconscious of human proximity.

I held my breath in terror lest the old man should speak. But he stood motionless as a statue beside the dark airplane; he seemed wrapt in a reverie. The hope arose of saving him. That was Hancock's airplane; his fate, then, lay with Hancock, and Lembken had told me that the Air-Admiral was a Christian. Surely he would take pity on the old, childish man. He knew me. I might appeal to him . . . .

The twisting track, which had hidden him from my eyes, brought him into view once more, clear against the low moon that made the moving figure a silhouette against its circle. I crept up, until suddenly I reeled and nearly fell, overcome by the magnitude of my discovery. For this was not Air-Admiral Hancock, but Hugo Sanson, the madman who ruled the Federation!

For a few moments I was powerless to stir. A raiding beast of night went rustling through the trees behind me. I heard an owl hoot. I lurked like some savage in the underbrush, and everything went from my memory, save Esther in peril, and Sanson, the evil genius of humanity, powerless in my hands if I could spring on him and strangle him before he had time to draw his Ray rod.

Then the tracking instinct awoke in me. I began stalking him as stealthily as any moccasined redskin followed his quarry. He was now only twenty paces away, and his walk showed that he suspected no danger.

It was a trail unknown to me, and I could only follow in patience. It wound to right and then to left, until at last it blended in a wider trail. And then I knew where I was. We were on the road that led to the cellar.

The scattered bricks became the heaping piles. I crouched low. Almost upon this site Sir Spofforth's house had stood. There, where the beeches waved their leafless arms had been Esther's tea-roses. And here were briers, sprung, perhaps, from those. It did not need these remembrances to make my resolution firm.

Sanson was going down. If he had gone there an hour earlier he would have walked alone into the presence of men who had a thousand deaths laid up against him. But Fate had saved him for me!

For an instant the thought occurred to me that possibly Sanson, acquainted with the details of the popular conspiracy, had come to offer terms against Lembken. But I dismissed that thought as impossible. Sanson would hardly have come there for such a purpose; at least, he would have come with the Guard.

The short ladder had been removed and hidden among the trees, but Sanson seemed to know the way intimately. Lying upon my face among the bricks, I saw Sanson enter the cellar, holding in one hand a little solar light. He passed through the gap in the wall into the vault.

I made my own descent with infinite care, taking pains to dislodge no stone that might betray my presence. Now I was in the cellar on hands and knees, watching Sanson as he moved to and fro inside the inner chamber. My brain was working like a mill — and yet I did not know wholly what I should do. If I killed Sanson, could I be sure that his death would set Esther free? Could I seize him and exact terms from him? Then there was a certain difficulty in springing upon the man quickly enough to prevent him from drawing his Ray rod; and there was the innate revulsion against choking a man to death.

As I deliberated, Fate seemed to solve my problem, for my fingers touched and closed about a smooth object that lay on the ground. For a moment I thought it was the branch of a tree. But no branch grew so smooth. A polished stave? It had been fashioned and grooved . . . . It was a Ray rod.

If I had doubted my mission I ceased to do so in that moment. I felt along the weapon in the darkness, from the brass guard, which stood up, leaving the button unprotected, to the little glass bulb near the head, through which the destroying Ray would stream. I raised the Ray rod and aimed it.

The solar light moved in the vault, and the shadow cast by the wall went back and forth as Sanson tramped to and fro. He was muttering to himself. He passed across the gap, and the little light shone on me. But he did not look toward me, and then he was behind the wall again and the light vanished.

Next time he passed I would fire. Yet I did not fire, and back and forth, and forth and back he tramped, talking to himself as any lesser man might have done. I had no compunction at all; I would have killed him as I would have killed a deadly snake; and yet, so diabolical was the fascination he exercised over me, I could not press the button.

I gathered my resolution together. I would fire when he passed the gap again. No, the next time. Well, the next, then. My fingers tightened on the handle. I saw Sanson emerge, the spark of light in his hand. The tight, white tunic was in the center of the gap. Now! I pressed the button, aiming at his heart.

The glass of the Ray rod grew fiery red. The button seared my hand, and a smell of charred wood filled my nostrils. I dropped the weapon, and it fell clattering to the ground. Sanson was standing in the gap, unharmed.

My Ray rod was the one that I had unwittingly discharged on the occasion when I scrambled for the cellar roof. It had given me life then; it seemed now to have brought me death. Of course it was useless till it had been recharged; now it emitted only the red-mull rays: heat, not cold combustion.

Sanson had halted as I aimed. Now, at the sound of the falling Ray rod he sprang forward and turned his solar light on me. His poise was a crouching leopard's. In his left hand he held the light, and in his right was his own Ray rod, covering me.

I looked at him, I stared at him, I rose upon my feet and staggered to him. Something in his poise, the whitening hair, brushed back, something in the man's soul that the years could not conceal reminded me . . . . I stood looking into the face of Herman Lazaroff!

CHAPTER XIX

THE STORY OF THE CYLINDERS

"SO IT was you, Arnold," said Sanson quietly. "Well . . . . what do you think of Sir Spofforth's theories now?"

All my hatred and fear of him had died in that blinding revelation. Bewilderment so intense that it made all which had occurred since my awakening dim, a sense of pathos and futility at once deprived me of my fears and robbed him of his power; and we might have been the fellow-workers of the old days again, discussing the problem of consciousness.

He seated himself on the mud mound, and his voice was as casual as if we had just returned to the laboratory after escorting Esther home. And indeed I could with great difficulty only convince myself that I had not fallen asleep and dreamed this nightmare.

"You see, it has all come to pass, Arnold," said Sanson, twirling the Ray rod idly between his fingers. "A world such as I foretold — a world set free. Enlightenment where there was ignorance; the soul delusion banished from the minds of all but the most foolish; the menace of the defective still with us, but greatly shrunken; the logical State so wonderfully conceived by Wells, with Science supreme, and almost a world citizenship. It is a glorious free world, Arnold, to which humanity has fallen heir, and the fight for it has been a stupendous one. And it is a world of my creation! I have done what Caesar, Charlemagne, and Napoleon failed to do; I have brought humanity under one sway, out of the darkness into light, out of ignorance to knowledge. I have set man, poor plantigrade, on his feet firmly. He looks up to the skies, not in the blind and foolish hope of bodiless immortality, but knowing himself the free heir of the ages. Wasn't it worth the battle, Arnold?"

My sense of pity deepened. Surely there can be no worse fate for any man than to accomplish his desires! I thought of all the unknown idealists who had given their lives to the accomplishment of great projects and failed, achieving nothing — inventors, dreamers, a gray, fantasmal legion whose lost hopes ranged back from age to age; and I saw how their works were blessed and their failures glorified in contrast.

"Yes, I thought that it must be you as soon as I examined the sheets from the Strangers' Bureau," continued Sanson, in his matter-of-fact manner. But it seemed so incredible that the cylinder had erred that I allowed my pressing duties to let me forget my impulse to take immediate action. Unfortunately, while we were fellow-workers I did not take your finger-prints, but I had, of course, observed your characteristic indexes, and also, if you remember, you were kind enough to my fad to permit me to take your cranial measurements. I did not think that there could exist two heads like yours, combined with those indexes, within a single century. For your occipital region is excellent, approximating my norm, while your frontal area is that of a moron. In short, you are a typical Grade 2 defective, Arnold — essentially so; and I have no doubt that, thanks to your five centimeters of asymmetrical frontal development, you have emerged into this universe of reality still clinging fondly and affectionately to your dualistic soul theory.

"But never mind!" he continued, smiling rather grimly. "I have no intention of handing you over to Lembken's ridiculous priests to be tried for heresy. There will be no more priests after a little while. The public mind is now ripe enough for the abolition of this stupid compromise of the transition period from God to Matter. One more animist will do little harm in a world in which they are still far from uncommon. And then, I am not a man of cruel impulses, Arnold, and I do not want to penalize you for having come into a world in which you are an anachronism. So you have spent three weeks in London?" he ended, scrutinizing me sharply.

"Yes."

"And came back by night to see your birthplace, I suppose," he said maliciously. "I don't know how you escaped the battleplanes. Unless they are growing slack . . . . I found one scoutplane without its searchlight working, and shall send its commander to the leather vats if I discover him . . . . well, Arnold," he resumed, "I could not believe that you had come out of your cylinder before your time. You came within an ace of disrupting my work, my world, if you only knew it — you with your missing five centimeters! I put implicit faith in Jurgensen's mechanism, and, as it proves, I was to blame. I came here tonight to see if you could really be gone."

"You knew that I was here?"

Why not, Arnold, since I put you here?" he returned, looking at me in a quizzical manner. "I have paid you periodical visits during the last five and thirty years. You looked charming in your sleep, Arnold! The fact is, it was a difficult situation. There was no way of destroying you, even if I had been so minded. I might have buried you ten feet underground, or thrown you into the sea, I suppose, but the men who moved you would have betrayed me unless I murdered them — in short, it was a problem how to dispose of you without violating my naturally humane impulses. So I did the best thing — covered the cylinder with mud and let you lie here.

"That Jurgensen timepiece was splendidly contrived, Arnold," he continued. "Too splendidly, in fact, for in the haste of sealing you I left the pointer six months ahead of time, as well as with Esther. It has perhaps occurred to you that you went to sleep in June and awoke in December?"

It had not occurred to me, but I made no answer to his sneering question.

"In fact, Jurgensen gave me a six months' leeway on his hundred-years clock, and the complication of figures prevented me from discovering it. I moved the pointer to the end of the dial, assuming that the last point was a hundred, and not a hundred and a half. And then, Arnold, there was another most regrettable mistake. You remember that you were sealed up quickly, and rather impulsively, so to say? I found that, in hurriedly capping you down, I forgot entirely to add twenty-four days upon the smaller dial for the leap-years; and so you returned that much ahead of Esther. It was a very bungled arrangement excusable in you, but not in me."

"Lazaroff!" I began, and then corrected myself with an apology as I saw his brows contract. "Sanson—"

"Thank you," he replied ironically.

"You will at least answer two or three questions, will you not?" I pleaded. "How did you induce Esther to enter the second cylinder? Why did you trick me? And how have you contrived to outlive the century without appearing more than half your age? I think my questions pardonable."

"I shall answer them all," said Sanson. "I may tell you that it was never my plan to send our monkeys ahead of us into this world. I meant to go, Arnold. But unexpectedly there came into my life something against which I had made no provision. In other words, absurd as it sounds, I fell in love. Then I planned to take Esther with me. But this plan, too, was changed, for, to be quite frank, I gathered that she preferred you to me. I then conceived the entertaining idea of taking you both with me, so that our rivalry might be renewed in a world where your advantages of personality would be counterbalanced by my power. Arnold, I never for an instant doubted that I should stand where I stand today. So, having persuaded you to enter the cylinder — and how I laughed at your imbecile complaisance — I invited Esther to follow you. There was no difficulty. On the contrary, she could hardly be convinced that I was in earnest. However, I speedily convinced her by the simple process of putting on the cap. Then, since the cylinders can be manipulated from within, I myself entered the third."

"You, Sanson!" I gasped. "You, too, have slept a hundred years?"

His look became envenomed, and the quick gust

of passion that came upon him was, to my mind, evidence of a mentality unbalanced by unrestrained authority.

"Arnold," he cried, "would you believe that an end so carefully planned, so mastered in each detail, could be thwarted by an instant's lack of balance? You remember that, of the three cylinders, one was already set a century ahead? That, save for the six months' leeway that existed on all the dials, and was, therefore, immaterial — that one, calculated to the utmost nicety, leap-years and all, was the one I had selected for myself already. That was the one Esther entered. The dial upon the second cylinder I set in your presence, but omitted the four and twenty days. That was your cylinder. And the third — mine — do you remember? — was set to sixty-five.

"I removed this cylinder to a second vault of which you do not know. I awoke in 1980. Arnold, I entered it and forgot the dial! When I recovered strength — and I had supplied some food products to last me during that brief period of recovery — I hurried to this vault. I found only your cylinder, behind the fallen bricks. When I saw that you still slept I thought your mechanism had gone wrong. Then, going back to examine my cylinder, I realized the truth. I, who had loved Esther with all my power, and vowed with all my will to win her, I, a young man of twenty-five, must wait for five and thirty years before she awakened. When my time came to claim her I would be old. O, Esther, what I have endured during these years!"

The baffled love of half a life-span overcame him. I watched him, almost as shaken. The tyrant of half the world, greater than any man had been since the days when the Caesars reigned, he had bound himself to a more awful law than any he could contrive. It wrung my heart even then, the man's grim hopes and long enduring love, checked by so slight a chance.

"I found Esther was gone," continued Sanson presently, rising and beginning to pace the vault. "I might have re-entered my cylinder, but I did not know whether she survived in hers. I knew my ambitions claimed me, and my duty to save humanity and raise it up from the ape. Even she had to yield to that sacred and pitiful impulse. I learned soon that the cylinder which contained her had been discovered and adopted as a symbol of freedom. I found the world aflame and flung myself into the heart of the revolution. By will I made myself the master of men. In six months my dominance was unquestioned. I could have become supreme, but I chose to work through others, that I might have the leisure to devote myself to my plans for the regeneration of man. I have succeeded; I have made the world better, Arnold, and I have made it free. But now, when at last the reward of my long toil approaches, when at last I can show Esther what I have achieved for her, and lay the world at her feet, I am an old man, and the prize has turned to ashes."

His grief conquered him again, and he paced the vault like a madman, weeping with all the abandonment of one who is above the need of conventional repressions. I remembered the antics of the crowd that followed me to the court. Sanson's grief was as unrestrained as their malice. But I was brought back from pity by the realization of this new and dreadful complication. Sanson loved Esther still. And he had worked for her. I recalled her immature feminist views. He had believed her youthful impatience of authority rested upon as firm a conviction as his beliefs! He thought he had freed humanity. And all the uncountable wrongs of earth had been heaped up by him as a love-offering to lay at Esther's feet.

I flung my prudence away. I clasped him by the hands.

"Sanson," I pleaded, "don't you see, don't you understand what the world is today? Each age has its own cruelties and wrongs; but, if poverty has been abolished, have you not set a heavier yoke upon men's necks? Their children torn from them, the death-house for the old, the vivisection table —"

"That is all true, Arnold," he answered, "and sometimes, even now, that old, inherited weakness that men termed conscience stirs in me. That fatal atavistic folly!—for what is death, after all? A painless end, a placid journey into nothingness, a resolution of the material atoms into new forms, which shall, in turn, create that consciousness men used to term a soul. Their children? Bah! Arnold, through suffering we win upward. In the world-nation that is to come, the narrow, selfish instinct called parental love—a trick of Nature to ensure the rearing of the race—will not exist. It will have served its purpose. All I have done is nothing in comparison with the great secret now almost within my grasp. That is the meaning of the vivisection table—the research work that will enable me to offer man immortality!"

I recoiled in horror at the sight of the fearful fanaticism upon his face.

"Yes, it is that, Arnold, which I am almost ready to bestow upon the world!" he cried triumphantly. "The old problem of consciousness and tissue life on which we worked so long has practically been solved by means at my disposal in a civilized world. Then we shall live indeed. There will be no requirement that knowledge should progress painfully through the inheritance of our fathers' labors. We ourselves shall climb the ladder of omniscience. The fit shall live forever, and we shall weed out the moron and defective without scruple, preserving a race of mortal slaves to labor for us in the factories and in the fields, holding them subdued by the threatened loss of that life which we shall control and permit to them so long as they are obedient. That is the noble climax of man's aspirations. Immortal life, in these bodies of ours, and Esther mine, not for a span, but for eternity!"

I believed him — I could not help but believe. Can anything be impossible, so long as man is gifted with free will for good and evil? Must he not have the ladder to scale Olympus, and thereby learn of heights beyond? I flung myself upon my knees before Sanson, like some poor father pleading for his son's life, and implored him to draw back. As he stood watching me I babbled about the terror in the world, the boon of death, the long-linked chain of humanity, bound all together as a spiritual unit, which he would sever. I reminded him of the old days under Sir Spofforth, of the old, free world we had lost. How had he bettered it? I think I moved him, too, though, when I ended, he was regarding me with a cold smile of negation.

"You want me to turn back, Arnold," he said. "Once there was a time when I hesitated. But . . . . can even that God of yours turn back? Come with me, Arnold, and for the sake of the old friendship to which you have appealed I will give you power. Defective as you are, you shall live your life to the full capacity of your talent. You shall not suffer because you came so unkindly into this world of ours. If your mind turns toward pleasures such as that foul defective Lembken enjoys, they shall be yours. If not, then you shall work with me as you used to do. When I and Esther rule the world together, immortal as the fabled gods, you shall sit at our feet and be our confidant."

That I hoped still to win Esther had never entered the man's mind. The sublimity of his egotism was the measure of his blindness. Just as he had entered the cellar, so self-absorbed that he had failed to see the benches and the crucifix, nor dreamed that here, where his evil dreams began, their end was planned, so, now, he did not see. The devilish will that had carried him thus far would bring him to destruction.

At my hands, if I played the part shrewdly. But I lost all self-command.

"Though you have all the world at your feet, Sanson," I cried, "you can never hold me to obedience, nor Esther either. I love her, and we shall both die before we yield!"

For an instant I saw his face before me, twisted with all the passions of his thwarted will; then I saw the blinding white light leap from his Ray rod as he fired at me.

CHAPTER XX

"I AM not at all afraid," I retorted, nettled at Lazaroff's sneer, "but how do I get in?"

A dog was yelping somewhere outside the Institute, and all the dogs in Croydon seemed to have taken up its challenge. It was difficult for me to make my voice audible above the uproar.

"I am not at all afraid," I repeated, "but —"

I was back in the cellar with Esther and Lazaroff, and we were examining the cylinders. As I looked about me, I seemed to be in the cylinder still, but gradually it expanded, until it became a vast hall, dark, save for a little window near the ceiling, through whose half-opaque crystal a little light filtered in dimly.

Lazaroff seemed to have aged. He wore a white beard, and his touch was very gentle as he bathed my face with water. As I stared at him he became . . . . somebody whom I had once known . . . . Bishop Alfred!

"Now you are better," said the old man, with his child-like smile.

I put my hand up to my aching head. There was a scarred groove along the top of the scalp, where the glow ray had plowed its passage. I began to remember now.

The howling of the dogs broke out afresh. The din was terrific, and the mournful tones of the poor animals' cries made the place a pandemonium.

"Arnold!" whispered a soft voice at my side.

Elizabeth was kneeling there, and David stood behind her. Next to David stood the little woman who had been our neighbor in the Strangers' House, and a multitude of men and women, and children, too, watched me through the gloom.

"Where am I? Who are all these?" I asked. Then, lighting upon a more momentous question, "How long have I been here?"

"Three days, Arnold," whispered Elizabeth.

"Then in two days — two days —" I gasped.

"No, Arnold, tomorrow is the day," interposed David, coming up to me softly. "Sanson has proclaimed a meeting in the Temple at sunrise, and it is now late afternoon. We are all in his trap. He must have found you, taken you unaware, and fired at you, but afterward he changed his mind and brought you here in his dispatchplane, where he found Bishop Alfred awaiting him, and Elizabeth and myself, who had gone back to find him. I bought a few days' respite by surrender, and there was even pleasure in the thought that my daughter will not meet her fate in Lembken's palace."

"Where, then?" I asked, struggling painfully up.

"In the Vivisection Bureau — with these," he answered, indicating the assemblage.

"Where are we, David?" I cried in anguish.

"Beneath it. In the vaults where Sanson keeps his morons, Christians, criminals, and dogs, to await the table."

I was upon my feet raving like a madman, making my way round the vault, striking my fists against the damp stone walls, crazed with the thought of Esther. They followed me, and some laid their hands on me in restraint, but I thrust them away. They thought I could not bear to share their wretched fate. But the nearness of the crisis, the thought of Esther in Sanson's power deprived me of my senses.

The vault was an enormous one, the only access being at the far end, by means of an oak gate, heavily barred. In this further portion were chained, all along the walls, the dogs destined for the experimental work above. As I drew near the gate the howling broke forth afresh. It steadied me; I came back to my senses; somebody was at my side, clasping my arm and speaking a few timid words in my ear.

I swung around and caught at the little woman who had been our neighbor. She had her children with her, and the three held each other closely, as if their last hour had begun.

"What are you doing here?" I asked.

I did not know David was near, but at the words he clasped me in his arms.

"She is here, Arnold," he answered, "because the last act of terrorism has brought her. Sanson's reason has left him, and he has flung his net wide over London for victims. He has gathered everyone: morons, Christians, criminals, suspects. She taught her children fairy stories. The inspectors had long suspected it, and they terrified the little girl into admission by threatening to kill the mother. They were then adjudged morons. The mother pleaded to be allowed to accompany them to the table, alleging that her father had been color-blind. Her prayer was granted; she is going, Arnold; we all are going—"

"No," said the old bishop in a regretful tone, "not one of us is going. You see," he added in explanation, "the Russians are in Stockholm, and it will not be long before they arrive in London to free the world. That is why Sanson lost his self-control. He knows. He wants to finish his enemies at home before they come."

"How do you know?" demanded David, while everyone grew still and listened.

"It is given to me to know," said Bishop Alfred simply, beaming and rubbing his hands. "I should like to have followed my dear master, the Lord

Bishop of London, to the fagots, but none of us will go to the tables now, and we shall all have our two names again."

David drew me aside. "Arnold," he said, "this situation would have robbed stronger men of their wits. I am afraid that our case is hopeless. One of the Guard, who knows me, has told me that Sanson is preparing for a holocaust of victims tomorrow, to celebrate his coup. He will stop at nothing to appease his blood thirst. Arnold, all our people know who you are. For their sake you must lead and show them how to die, as the first Christians died. It is hard, my dear boy—"

I knew he was not thinking of death, but of my tragedy.

"Your capture has rendered our plans abortive," he went on. "But still there may be some hope unguessed by us. Unto the last we will not impugn God's power. Now, my friends," he added, turning toward the crowd, which circulated in the vault slowly, always following me, "let us show the Guard where our strength lies."

In the gloom of the vast vault, above the howling of the dogs, the hymn was raised, old Bishop Alfred leading, in a voice singularly sweet, although in speech the tones were broken. All kneeled.

Afterward David spoke briefly. He reminded us of the brave traditions of martyrdom and its happy,

expectancy. We were going to face our fate together, strengthened by our companionship and in
the knowledge that our death would create a revulsion of sentiment that would sweep Sanson from
power and restore Christianity to the world. They
cried out their approval, and there was no face but
reflected David's dauntless resolution. Then it was
as if some soul of merriment swept over us all. I
saw strangers embracing, there was clapping of
hands, and the concluding hymn was shouted so
joyously that a slit in the little window overhead
was thrust back, and I saw the face of a sentinel stare
in on us with something of superstitious awe.

The glass must have been soundproof, like that
which enclosed Lembken's gardens, for, as the slit
was pushed back, I heard the cries of the multitude
in the courts above:

"Sanson! Sanson! Sanson!" they howled. "Out
with the Christian morons! To the Rest Cure! The
Rest Cure!"

The slit was pushed into place, cutting off all
sound. Darkness was falling. The little light within
the vault faded. Gradually the voices died away.
Sometimes a hymn would be started, but mostly we
sat silent now, and even the dogs ceased howling,
and only stirred and whined at intervals. I heard
the little woman's children whimper, and fancied
her motherly face bent over them as she quieted their

A man near me leaped up and craned his neck, looking into
the gloom

fears. I only felt Elizabeth's presence, and that of David, good, fatherly man, on whom I leaned more than he knew. At last the only sounds were the bishop's mumbling voice, as he talked to himself, and the staccato tapping of his stick on the stone floors.

"They are coming," I heard him say. "They are gathering up the Stockholm fleets. They will be here—"

"Who?" I burst out.

"The Russians," he answered gently. "See them coming; big men, with bloody crosses on their breasts."

A man near me leaped up and craned his neck, looking into the gloom. One or two cried out at the old bishop's words, and some listened and whispered eagerly. Time passed. Most of the prisoners slept. I was still too sick and dizzy from my wound; I waited in a sort of apathy, and I seemed to see Esther within the opening cylinder, and Sanson, creeping like a foul beast of prey toward her.

I had been dozing. I started up at the sound of bolts being withdrawn, the heavy door at the far end of the vault was opened, and flashing lights shone in on us. The dogs, awakened, began to howl again. There was the stamping of heavy boots upon the stones, and a detachment of the Guard appeared before us.

They numbered seven. Six of them were privates, carrying solar torches and Ray rods; and in their midst stood a tall man with a black beard and a curved sword sheath that clanked on the stones. I recognized in him Mehemet, the Turkish commander.

Some, who had slept and mercifully forgotten all, sat up in bewilderment, others leaped up, thinking the hour had come. As we stood blinking at the lights, Mehemet spoke a few words, and the soldiers flashed their torches into our faces until they lighted on mine. Then Mehemet stepped forward and laid his hand on my shoulder, and drew me toward him; and the soldiers closed about us.

David sprang toward them.

"You shall not take him alone!" he cried. "Let us go with him, every one of us. We shall go to death together."

And others sprang forward too, clamoring, beseeching. "Take us all!" they cried. "Take us together!"

Mehemet shrugged his shoulders and turned away. The captives flung themselves before the soldiers, who hesitated.

It was then that the old bishop, who had never ceased to mumble, I think, came quietly up to us.

"It is all right. Let him go," he said gently. "He will come to no harm."

A tall man with a black beard and
I recognized in hi

ord sheath that clanked on the stones.
Turkish commander

"It is my orders," said Mehemet, looking with respect at Bishop Alfred. "I have come for him alone."

Half quieted by the bishop's intervention, my fellow-prisoners ceased to offer forcible resistance. But they wept and prayed, and David grasped me by the hand.

"We shall be together in spirit, Arnold!" he cried. "God be with you. God be with you." He flung his arms about me, and the guards, touched by the scene, permitted him to accompany me as far as the door. They picked their way carefully by the light of their torches, to avoid treading on the dogs, which crept to their feet or strained, yelping, upon their chains. At the door I found Elizabeth.

"We shall be with you in your hour, Arnold!" she said, embracing me and fighting back her sobs valiantly. "We shall all think of you tomorrow."

The crowd dispersed. The last thing that I saw was the white, terrified, maternal face of the little woman, as she clutched her children to her breast, and, over her, the bishop's pastoral staff, held up as if to shield her.

The door was closed behind me, and the soldiers shot the bolts home. In front of me was a flight of winding concrete stairs, dividing at a central space into two portions that ran right and left respectively. We took the left. I expected to emerge into the Vivisection Bureau, to see the eager students of the medical school, and Sanson, the presiding devil, there. But instead I saw a gate above me; a guard unlocked it. Then I found myself standing alone beside Mehemet, in the interior court between the Temple and the Airscouts' Fortress, between the Science Wing and the Council Building.

High above me the bridges crossed, spanning the gulf in whose recess we stood. I saw once more the palms against the upreared crystal walls.

As I watched I saw the battleplanes take their flight once more, one by one, from the roof of the 'Airscouts' Fortress, rising into the dark night like luminous balloons. In the distance London glowed like day.

Behind us, in the outer courts, a multitude was shrieking curses upon the Christians; and, for the first time, I heard threats against Lembken, and realized that Sanson's plans were made for that coup which I was never to see.

"We are going to Sanson?" I asked Mehemet, nerving myself for his affirmative reply.

He spat. "The jackal!" he said. "Sooner would I become a Christian than serve such spawn. We are going to the People's House."

Evidently Sanson did not know that the main prop of his new house had fallen.

CHAPTER XXI

AMARANTH

I STEPPED out of the elevator into a part of the Palace that I had not seen before. The room into which the waiting negro ushered me was completely dark, though a thin line of light at the further end showed me that there was a lighted room beyond.

I strained my eyes, striving to penetrate the gloom. I took a few steps forward, stretching out my hands to feel if any obstacle were in the way. Looking back, I could not even discern the heavy curtain that had dropped soundlessly behind me.

I knew that there was someone in the room, and that it was not Lembken. I waited; I heard the rustle of a woman's garment. Then swiftly the room was flooded with the soft solar light.

It was bare, except for the rugs and a low divan pushed against one wall, with a little table beside it. Everything was of the color of gold: the walls, the ceiling, the rugs upon the floor. And before me, clothed from head to foot in a sheer, trailing garment of dull gold, stood the girl Amaranth.

Her dark hair was bound back in a loose Grecian knot, her sandaled feet gleamed white on the gold fabric under them; she stretched out her white arms to me and, taking me by the hand, led me to the divan and placed me at her side.

"Poor Arnold!" she began in a caressing tone, "you have suffered so much in your ignorance and your desire to help your friends. But all your troubles are ended now, and your friends shall not be harmed. Do you think you can love me, Arnold?"

She looked at me with neither boldness nor hesitation, and then, folding her arms, drummed her sandal heels against the foot of the divan.

"Are you not lucky, Arnold, to have won my love!" she continued. "I gave my love to you from the moment when I first saw you enter the room in which I sat with Lembken, looking so stern, so resolute, like one of those adventurous heroes of the twentieth century of whom we read in our romances. That is why I made Lembken tell Mehemet to bring you here. He was so hurt by your departure that I think he would have let his plans go to ruin rather than himself plead with you. He is very sensitive and kind.

"You are not afraid to love me, Arnold?" she continued, looking at me with curious scrutiny. "You need not be afraid. Lembken has grown tired of me, so I must find another. He has taken a fancy to Coral, my blue, an absurd little yellow-haired thing. You shall see her."

She clapped her hands twice, and a door opened,

apparently a part of the wall. A fair-haired girl, dressed in a loose blue tunic and Zouave trousers, entered, carrying a tray on which were two golden winecups.

Amaranth took the nearest cup in her hands, touched the rim with her lips, and held it out to me.

"Drink with me, Arnold," she said.

But I would not drink, lest the corruption of the wine should dull me and disarm my strength in the spell of that enervating hell. I handed back the cup to her.

Amaranth looked at me for an instant with quivering lips. Then she burst into tears and hurled the cup at the maid. She flung the other also. The first missed its mark and fell against the base of the wall, where it shed its ruby contents in a widening stain. The second cup struck the maid's cheek and cut it, and the wine drenched the blue tunic.

The maid smiled, biting her lips, stooped down, picked up both cups, and, placing them on the tray, departed silently. Amaranth sobbed as if her heart was broken. Then suddenly she turned and flung her arms about me.

"Arnold, I love you!" she cried. "You saw her? She is Lembken's favorite now, that yellow-haired fool with the blue eyes like saucers. Lembken means us for each other. Can you not love me?"

I sat in silence, trying to pick my path cautiously

through the mists of bewildering doubt. Amaranth unclasped her arms from about my neck, and her face assumed a look of mockery.

"Oh, I know!" she said, "it is that Elizabeth of yours whom you think you love. And you think you can only love one at a time, in your romantic twentieth-century way. Well, I will match myself against her. You shall bring her here, Arnold, and I will fight her for you, and I will be your blue and she shall be your white, and I will serve you obediently till I have won your heart. Look on me, Arnold! See how beautiful I am! For I was born here; I am Boss Rose's daughter, and I have never left the People's House. Look at the whiteness of my skin! The sun has never shone on it. Look at my lips, Arnold! Put your mouth to my cheek — it is as soft as the bloom upon a nectarine. Do you think, then, I am afraid to match myself against your Elizabeth?"

She smiled contemptuously, and tilted back her head, and clasped her hands behind it, and watched me through her lashes. Yet I detected a resource of feverish resolve in her; and I knew that she and I, Mehemet, Sanson, were that night weaving the threads in a fabric upon the loom of destiny, and that each word we spoke flashed like the thread-bearing shuttle over it.

So, piecing my words together with infinite care,

because the lives of Esther and all those who were
dear to me hung on them, I answered her:

"Forgive my sullen mood. You have promised
that my friends shall go free; yet they expect to die
at sunrise, and it is hard to be at ease. How can I
save them?"

Amaranth unclasped her hands and turned to me
with a quick gesture of penitence.

"Ah, it was wrong of me to speak of love first,
when you have such a burden of sorrow, Arnold!"
she answered. "I had forgotten that men's minds
are troubled in the world below. Here we are free
and have no cares, except how we shall take our
pleasures. And to think that you left us to help
your friends, when Lembken would have done everything you wished!

"Now I will set your mind at rest. Lembken has
already given the command that your friends shall
live until Sanson has spoken in the Temple, and when
he has spoken he will no longer have power — if you
obey Lembken. But he was deeply hurt by your
leaving him, for he is very sensitive to unkindness,
and so he asked me to speak to you on his behalf.
Now, if you act loyally, you may save your friends
and the world. Tomorrow there will be an end to all
of Sanson's mad schemes of tyranny. Mehemet and
his guards have abandoned him. Lembken knows
everything; he knows all the desperate plans his

poor people have made, and his heart is wrung for them."

She paused, and placing her hand on mine, looked very earnestly at me.

"Arnold, you know that Sanson has been poisoning the people's minds against Lembken, in pursuance of his plan to depose him," she continued. "So your part, which will be detailed to you later, will be to enter the Temple tomorrow among the priests. You will defend Lembken against Sanson. You will remind the people how they elected him from year to year, because he was their friend. Tell them he has not changed. And in return liberty shall be established and the hated Guard disbanded. Lembken asks only for his dignity and wealth, and his friends in the People's House. He is growing old, Arnold, and desires power no more."

She watched me with that centuries-old look, and in my heart I knew I had not fathomed hers. This was what I had meant to propose. Yet — yet I doubted her.

"It is agreed, then," she cried gaily, "and now you will be one of us. It is past midnight, Arnold, and in a few short hours you shall be hidden in the priests' room to be coached for your part. Till then —"

She ceased suddenly, as the sound of voices came

from the room beyond the further door. She slipped
from the divan.

"Sanson has been with Lembken," she whispered.
"He is coming this way. Arnold, do you want to see
your enemy broken? That will be a glorious beginning to this first night of ours, and afterwards we
shall go to the revels in the garden. I shall be proud
of you, Arnold, for now the girls are taunting me
because Lembken is tired of me. How I shall be
envied! But come here quickly!"

She took me to the door in the wall through which
the girl Coral had come. At a distance of a few
paces it was invisible. I wondered how many
more such doors were set in the walls of Lembken's
palace.

"You shall listen here," she said, "I trust you
Arnold. You will not lose your self-control and
enter, no matter what you hear? Ah, I shall test
your love for that Elizabeth! But I trust you, and
the beginning of this night's masque shall be the
humbling of your enemy. Stay here until I call
you!"

She thrust me behind the door and withdrew,
closing it. I heard the rustle of her garment as she
crossed the room — then nothing.

I found myself standing in a dim corridor that
ran as far as I could see in either direction. The
nameless horror of the Palace overcame me, and it

was with a strong effort that I controlled my wild impulse of flight.

As I stood there I heard the sound of stealthy footsteps, and, looking up, saw the maid Coral coming softly toward me. She was carrying the tray, with two full winecups, and she stopped beside me and set it down on the carpet.

She stood looking at me. Her eyes were blazing with anger, and her slim body shook under the blue tunic. But on her mouth was the same set smile that I had seen when she picked up the cups.

She said nothing, but, placing her hand against the door, opened it an inch or two without the slightest sound. At that moment I heard a door opened, the rustle of Amaranth's robe, and a lithe tread on the floor.

Sanson spoke. "I have said all that there is to say," he answered. "Why do you plead with me? Do you think a woman can plead with me where Lembken failed? He shall have his honors and residence here — no more."

"But spare your prisoners, Sanson," said Amaranth softly. "Spare Arnold. For my sake," she said, pleading.

Sanson spoke curtly. "All Christians and all morons must be tomorrow's sacrifice to the new era," he answered.

"Do not go, Sanson," Amaranth besought him,

as he moved away from her. "Listen to me! You, who are so merciless and cruel, why do you not take all?"

"I have all that I need," he said impatiently. "What more?"

"Why have you spared Lembken? Why do you not slay him and rule with us? We hate him. He is a tyrant, and you know the fate of his women when they have ceased to please. You who have made yourself the master of the world, for whose sight we throng the sides of the crystal walls as you cross the courts below — why have you refused the pleasures that are for the world's masters?"

He stood still; I fancied that he was looking at her, trying to measure his problem in the balances once more. Coral cast a glance at me. The smile was still on her face, but she nodded her head thoughtfully, as if she, too, had her problem.

"Listen, Sanson," continued Amaranth fiercely, "when Boss Rose climbed to power he built the People's House and made it a pleasure-palace for the world's elect. Then he died under a murderer's dagger, and Lembken, who had long envied him, came to rule in his place. He, too, has lived his time. Now he is broken. You, the next ruler of the world — why do you not do as he did? We are tired of him. We want another lord, Sanson."

I knew that she was clinging to him as she had

clung to me. I did not look at Coral, but I knew that she was still smiling.

"You can set us free, Sanson," continued Amaranth gently. "You can rid us of our tyrant."

The murmuring voice went on and on, and Sanson made no answer.

"You have not entered the People's House for seven years until tonight. Do you think we have forgotten that you exist? Do you think we have not wondered why the master of the world has left us to the whims of that fat old man? Sit by me, Sanson. Do you not see how you have toiled while Lembken has taken his ease? You have waited so long for one woman. Oh, yes, I know; all a great man's secrets are known everywhere, though he thinks them in sanctuary, securely guarded. You can take her — but take us too. Live your life, Sanson! Save us and reign over us! Take me, Sanson — "

I heard the man breathe as if in a trance. That strange pity which he inspired in me awoke again. All the long tragedy of his life, the vigil of five and thirty years, the love that must prove vain — I realized it all. For this vain love he had ensnared the world, and now the world leaped at him to ensnare him. Devil as he was, in will his life had been, in one respect, a hero's.

"Drink with me, Sanson," I heard Amaranth mur-

mur. "You do not know the taste of wine. A pledge
to our love. A pledge to our lives!"

She was conquering. The tyrant of the world was
almost prostrate at the feet of this girl of twenty
years. Attila's fate was to be his. I heard him
groan in bitterness of conflict.

Amaranth clapped twice. Instantly the girl Coral
stooped down, pushing me fiercely from the door,
and, taking up the tray, went in. Amaranth took
the brimming winecup and touched it with her lips.

"Drink, Sanson!" she murmured.

I was watching them now. I saw Sanson rise and
raise the cup in his hand. He did not drink, neither
did he reject it, but stood like one in a daze, all movement inhibited by the fierceness of that inner struggle. Amaranth seized the second cup from the tray,
leaped from the couch, and raised it on high.

"To our love, Sanson!" she cried, and drained it.

At that moment the jagged cut on the girl Coral's
face grew red with blood again.

Coral stood holding the tray, and she looked at
Amaranth and smiled. She stood like a tinted statue.

Sanson was still standing in front of the divan.
He had not drunk; he held the cup in his hand and
was himself as immobile as a statue.

"Will you not drink the pledge that I have drunk?"
asked Amaranth, laying her fingers lightly on his
arm and leaning toward him.

And I had underestimated Sanson after all. Now, at the moment of surrender, his indomitable will flamed out, seeming to possess his body and mold each feature, every muscle to its unconquerable resolve.

"I will not drink!" he cried, and flung the cup to the floor.

He turned and strode from the room like the conqueror he was. He passed the curtain, which fell behind him. He had won his hardest battle, taken unaware, fighting against a cunning ambush; and I knew now that hardly an earthly enemy could conquer him.

I was in the room now, for there was no need to hide myself any longer. I watched Amaranth, who, as statuesque as Sanson had been, stood looking after him. A minute passed.

Suddenly she wheeled about and clapped her hands to her side. She staggered; a spasm of pain crossed her face, and she looked searchingly at Coral. The maid in the blue tunic looked back at her, smiling.

Their eyes did not waver until Amaranth swayed backward and fell on the divan. A scream broke from her lips, and then another; a third; she wrung her hands and moaned.

I kneeled before her. "What is it, Amaranth?" I cried.

She raised herself and looked wildly at me. Her

Sanson's indomitable will flamed out. "I will not drink!" he
cried, and flung the cup to the floor

face was ashen pale, the features pinched; dark rings had crept beneath her eyes.

"She gave me the—wrong cup," she whispered.

I tried to go for aid, but Amaranth clung to me. "There is no hope," she sobbed. "I must die. Stay with me, Arnold!"

Her head fell back and she breathed heavily. I turned and saw Coral beside me, a smiling, waxen doll, the new queen of the harem by the dying one.

"Go!" I thundered at her.

She shrugged her shoulders daintily and went, leaving the winecups on the floor.

Amaranth's hand trembled upon my sleeve. I bent over her. Her eyes fixed themselves on mine.

"Put your hand under me," she muttered; "raise me. All is lost now. Sanson has beaten Lembken, and everything is ended. Save your Elizabeth if you can."

She drew my face toward hers and spoke in panting accents:

"It was Lembken's plot. He learned that Sanson held you in the vaults. His case was desperate. He asked Mehemet's aid. Mehemet said he—his men would not desert Sanson while he lived, but if he died they would follow him for Lembken. I was to poison Sanson and thus win over the Guard. I was to drug you only, and keep you out of the way. Lembken liked you; he would not let you be killed.

He has been communicating with the American bosses. The plan — the plan —"

She gathered her strength with a last effort of will.

"The plan was of long standing. Events hastened it. Mehemet knew it. Britain was to have a God again, Mehemet's God, and the American Mormons were to unite with us, for their faith is nearly the same. The people would have a god, and this would unite all nations against the Christian Russians. They are in Stockholm. The American battleplanes are on their way to help us against them. When Sanson was dead the guards were to join the airscouts. Now you must go. Save your Elizabeth. Kill Sanson. I can say no more. Escape —"

She muttered something that I could not hear, and then her eyes, which had closed, reopened and wavered on mine again.

"I loved you, Arnold," she said in a weak, clear voice. "I'm glad I died before I lost you. I used to wish I had been born in other days . . . . the twentieth-century days, when . . . . women were different . . . . all different . . . . men mated one only . . . . give the people those days again if you beat Sanson, Arnold."

She tried to stretch out her hands to me. Her eyelids quivered, and she sighed very deeply.

I saw a crimson stain upon my hands. It was the wine from Sanson's winecup.

CHAPTER XXII

ESTHER

I LEFT the dead girl on the divan and went into the hall. My head ached, and I was still dizzy from my wound, but I had grown suddenly composed, and all my perplexities had vanished in the face of Esther's imminent need of me.

There was nobody in the hall. The negroes were gone, and the palm gardens were dark and seemed deserted. Silence had descended everywhere. Withal it was the silence of hushed voices, I knew, and not of emptiness. Within those walls, in hidden rooms, lurked those who waited yet for the death agony of the man who had already escaped the baited trap.

I wondered whether Sanson had bought the attendants, if he had come alone, whether the fear of him forbade an ambush in case Amaranth's plot should fail. He had evidently gone down in the elevator, for it was not in the cage, but it came up to me when I pressed the button, and I descended, stopping at the first door I saw, which must, I knew, give access to the Temple.

The corridor into which I stepped was as empty as the palace hall above. The airscouts who should have been on duty here were gone. I did not realize that I had formed no plans and felt no fear until I found my way unopposed. Before me was a door, leading into one of the numerous small rooms through which one entered the Temple, and at my side was a little window, through which the cries of the mob beneath were borne to me fitfully on the gusty air.

I stopped and looked out. The sky was thick with battleplanes. No longer at their stations about the city, they cruised hither and thither, approaching one another and retiring in a manner seemingly confused and aimless. Sometimes a group would gather as if conferring, forming a polygon of light with changing sides as they maneuvered; and presently a single impulse seemed to animate them all, for, like a flock of wheeling birds, they swung around and sailed off together, till they were only pin-points of light in the southwest.

Beneath me the courts were packed with a vast multitude that had assembled for the morrow's ceremonies. Looking down on them, I saw that they were held back by two lines of the guards, armed with Ray rods, drawn up before the Temple.

They jostled and swayed and howled fearlessly, as if they knew the imminence of change; yet their cries were not all against the Christians and the morons, nor yet against Lembken, nor all for

Sanson. I tried to fancy that among them were groups of our few thousand, gathered out of the forests to play their rôle at dawn.

Yet for the moment Sanson had triumphed. I thought upon how little hung the fate of the world. A palace women's intrigue, the jealousy of a girl, a cup of wine, and Lembken's schemes were broken.

Then it came to me that the conical, glow-painted Ray guns on the encircling wall were trained no longer outward but inward, dominating the Temple courts and all the multitude within them. And in a flash of comprehension I saw the scheme of Sanson. If the people rejected him on the morrow he meant to kill all those within the walls, all human beings inside the circle of the fortress, confident that thereby he would destroy all his enemies. He meant to level the Temple and the palace above, the Council Hall, the Airscouts' Fortress, involving everything in one colossal ruin which he would bestride — the unchallenged master of the Federation.

This done, the Russian fleet would be attacked and destroyed, and with it the last obstacle to world dominion.

I saw this with one flash of intuition. Perhaps I lingered in all for forty seconds beside the window. It was hardly longer, for the thought of Esther drove me through the doorway in front of me. I found myself within the dark, enormous area of the Temple.

I was in a circular gallery surrounded by a brass railing, which ran high up around the interior. The only light was the faint reflection from a single solar bulb that shone across the gulf. Beneath it I could discern the shining, golden surface of the Ant.

I felt my way around the gallery, working toward the light, which seemed to descend as I approached it, until, standing immediately above it, I looked down and saw it shining an unknown distance beneath. It showed now the uplifted antenna of the idol, the edge of the stone altar in the center of the bridge that spanned the Temple, and the round body of the cylinder, which seemed to hang in space above it.

I had entered the Temple upon a floor one stage too high, and there was no way down from the gallery; it would be necessary to go back to the elevator and descend to a lower level, that of the bridges that spanned the interior court.

But that was too dangerous, and I could wait no longer. I estimated that the light was five and twenty feet below. I swung from the brass rail and dropped into space. It was a mad plunge in the dark toward that slender bridge a hundred feet above the Temple floor. But fortune was with me, for I struck the golden grille around the altar-stone and tumbled inside, rising upon my feet with only a bruise or two.

The grille was about four feet high, and the ends formed gates which, when opened, made the altar-stone one with the two bridge spans that extended to meet it from either side of the building. It formed thus a sort of keystone in aspect, though not architecturally, since it did not support the spans, which seemed to be on the principle of the cantilever. I saw now that the stone was suspended by steel chains from the roof, and over it, hung by two finer ones, was the cylinder.

Presently I could grasp the meaning of the mechanism. Cylinder and stone altar were in counterpoise, so that, when the first was drawn up, the second would descend from between the spans to the level of the Ant's pedestal, forming, as it were, a sacrificial stone immediately before the idol, disrupting the continuity of the bridges also, and leaving a gap between them.

But I spared no thoughts on this. I looked through the cylinder's face of glass, and, though I saw but the dimmest outlines there, I knew that I had found Esther again, and that there were to be no more partings, so long as we both lived.

I do not know what follies I committed there, for I forgot everything but her. Forgotten was the imminent danger, remembered only our reunion. I flung my arms about the iron case and called to her, telling her of my love, as if she heard me. I came back to sanity at length to find myself kneeling before the case upon the stone, with the tears raining down my cheeks.

It was a mad wooing of a sleeping woman upon that giant slab, swung by its chains from the vault above, and vibrant under me. Each movement set the heavy mass to trembling as the chains quivered, and the cylinder, too, danced before me, like some steel marionette.

I stretched my hands up, feeling for the cylinder cap. It was still on the neck, but it had almost reached the end of the thread and moved under my fingers. I could not see the figures upon the dial, but I knew that Esther's awakening was not many hours away.

I twisted the cap between my fingers. I could dislodge it. If I did so . . . . Lazaroff had told me that would bring death, but surely not when there remained only a few short hours before the awakening. Air must have been entering in measurable quantities during some days. And, even if Esther died — better that than to awaken in Sanson's arms!

It was a terrific choice. I hesitated only a few moments, but they were a century of agony to me. Then I set my fingers to the cap, wrenched it free, and flung it from me. It tinkled upon the stones beneath. And, hardly venturing to breathe, I clung to the cylinder and waited.

No sound came from within. I clung and tried to place my ear against the opening.

At last, in maddened resolution, I swung the cylinder toward me by the chains, tilting it downward until I got purchase upon it. I bore with my full weight upon the metal edge. I plunged my arms within. I felt the heavy coils of Esther's hair, her eyelids, cheek, and chin; I placed my hands beneath her arms and drew her forth. How I contrived it I do not know, for platform and cylinder rocked fearfully as they swung; but in a moment, it seemed, I held her light and wasted body against my own. And we were on the rocking altar-stone together, while the cylinder swung rhythmically above, passing our heads in steady, sweeping flights as I crouched with Esther in my arms behind the golden grille.

I pressed my lips to hers, I chafed her hands and pleaded with her to awake. And presently, as if in answer to my prayer, I heard a sigh so faint that I could scarcely dare believe I heard it.

A deeper sigh, a sobbing breath — she lived; and with amazed, awed happiness I felt her thin arms grope instinctively toward my neck. She knew!

I kneeled beside her on the altar-stone, listening with choked sobs and wildly beating heart to the words that came from her lips in faltering whispers:

"Herman! What have you done? You have killed him! Then kill me, too! I don't want to live! Murderer! Kill me! O Arnold, my love, to think that neither of us knew!"

Then:

"Yes, I love him, Herman, and I have told him so. You were too late to prevent that. I saw your heart tonight. Kill me, I say! Yes, I am ready a thousand times to go where Arnold has gone. Be sure that I shall follow him, through any hell of your devising!"

So Esther whispered, living over again those minutes of dreadful anguish that she must have passed in the cellar after Lazaroff had put the cap on my cylinder and driven me on that strange voyage of mine. The little solar light shone on Esther's brown gown, turning it golden. And I remembered — with how strange a pang — the night when she had worn that gown in the drawing-room of Sir Spofforth's house.

"Esther," I whispered, bending over her, "it is I. It is Arnold."

I saw her eyelids quiver half open, but I knew that she could not see me. She moaned. I interposed my body between her and the light.

"You have been ill, dearest Esther," I said. "But now everything is well. You know me, Esther?"

"Arnold," she whispered, "I have been with you

all the time. I dreamed . . . . Herman had sent
you . . . . a hundred years away."

She became unconscious the next moment. I knew
the mighty grip of that first sleep. It was in truth
twin brother to death, for, with my head against her
breast, I could discern hardly the slightest stirring.
But she lived; all was well. And now the need of
saving her came over me. I caught her into my
arms — she weighed no more than a small child —
and hurried across the bridge. I believed that the
outer door upon this lower level communicated with
the bridge over the interior court that led to the Airscouts' Fortress.

I traversed the little room and pushed the swing
door open. Before me was an elevator shaft, evidently that up which I had made my first journey to
Lembken's palace. But as I emerged into the corridor I saw, not ten paces away, their backs toward
me, two of the Guard.

I was too late. The Guard had occupied the posts
vacated by the airscouts. The Temple and all the
approaches to Lembken's palace were in Sanson's
hands.

They had not seen or heard me, and in a moment
I had withdrawn within the little room. There still
remained one chance. By crossing the bridge again
and passing through the priests' robing-room on the
other side of the Temple, I could reach all parts of

the buildings. Perhaps there were no sentries in the gallery above the auditorium. I knew how vain the hope was, but there was none other.

I carried Esther upon the bridge again. As I was about to set foot upon the altar-stone, which still rocked slightly, I fancied that the bridges themselves were moving. I leaped on the stone, stumbling against the grille. One moment I hesitated, to assure myself that Esther still breathed. A piece of her brown dress had come away and broke like burned paper in my hand. I raised her higher in my arms, so that her head rested against my shoulder, and opened the grille gate to step upon the farther span.

That moment of delay had ended all my hopes. There was no second span. For swiftly, noiselessly, the span was swinging away from me, pivoting upon its further end. It was already too far away for me to make the leap, encumbered as I was with Esther. I glanced backward in horror. The span that I had crossed was moving also, acting in unison. They vanished in the gloom at the sides of the Temple.

I stood with Esther in my arms upon the altar-slab, poised on that unsteady resting place high in the Temple void. There was no refuge anywhere. Over me was the vault; far underneath the Ant with its gleaming, upraised tentacle.

As I stood there the little solar light went out.

CHAPTER XXIII

THE HEART OF THE PEOPLE

THE Temple was profoundly dark. Crouched on the swinging stone, helpless in Sanson's power, I was not conscious of fear. Rather, a melancholy regret possessed me that this was the end, as it inevitably must be. A hundred years of separation, the knowledge of each other's love — no more; and all had gone for nothing. Yet, there was cause for happiness that this much had been granted me, to die with Esther; and the loss of all hope brought calmness to my spirit and acceptance of the inevitable.

It may have been two hours later when I heard the cries of the mob once more. I heard the tramp of feet upon stone; and then, through every swinging door below, invisible forms came trooping in until they covered the whole of the vast floor. They shouted against the Christians in an unceasing pandemonium, and the walls and hollow roof re-echoed that infernal din until another spirit that underlay the mob fury, something of awed expectancy, swept over the concourse, and the last shout died down, and a new and dreadful silence arose.

It lasted minutes, perhaps, broken only by the stir

of feet on the floor, the rustle of robes, the sighs that whispered through the darkness; then, out of that silence a low chant began. It was that dreadful chant that I had heard before, crooned first by a few and then by many, tossed back and forth from side to side of the Temple floor, until all caught it up and made the walls echo with it:

"We are immortal in the germ-plasm; make us immortal in the body before we die."

There was a dreadful melody, one of those tunes that seem to rise spontaneously to a people's lips as the outpouring of its aspirations. Again and again that dreadful, hopeless chant rose from below, swelled into a din, and died.

Then shouts broke out again as the mob spirit seized upon some who had assembled there:

"Make us immortal in these bodies of ours!"

"Make us immortal, Sanson!"

"Give me eternal life!" raved the cracked voice of an aged man; and that blasphemy against Nature seemed to shock the mob into silence, until once more the low chant swelled and echoed and died away in wailing overtones of helplessness.

Suddenly a single solar light flashed at one side of the Temple, and, high above the multitude, where the end of the bridge span rested against the curve of the wall, I perceived Sanson. He was standing alone upon the drawn-back span, which, shadowy and vague, gave him the aspect of a figure poised in the air.

He was a master of stage-craft. It even awed me, that calculated effect of the dark Temple and the crowd, invisible each to his neighbor; and the hypnotic *mise en scène* of the solitary figure aloft beneath the single light. I, too, felt the contagion of the universal expectation.

Sanson uttered no word, but stretched one arm out and pointed across the Temple. Then I heard the tramp of men coming from the direction of the elevator shafts; and suddenly a second light burned across the vast void of the dark.

Upon the second span, now dimly visible, drawn back against the wall opposite Sanson, I saw the prisoners from the vaults, marshaled under the charge of the Guard. There, at the extreme edge, Elizabeth stood, a slender, virginal figure, her hands clasped over her bosom; at her side David, behind them the patriarchal figure of Bishop Alfred. Behind him were ranged the other victims of Sanson's rage. They, too, under that single light, seemed to be poised in air.

At the sight of them, hysteria swept the minds of the mob into frenzy.

"The Christians!" they screamed. "Kill them! Kill them! Out with the dogs who hold their bodies cheap! To the Rest Cure! Ah—h!"

The groaning end was drawn out as the vibration of a G-string. The air was heavy and foul with hate; I felt it as something ponderable.

A woman's voice rang shrill through the Temple, and the devil that goaded her had raised his head now after two thousand years of stupor. He returned into a world that had forgotten him since the first shapings of Europe's peoples began, out of the deepest place in hell.

"Sacrifice them!" she shrieked. "A human sacrifice upon the altar-stone!"

The whistling, strident voices of the mob answered her: "Sacrifice them! A human sacrifice!"

Surely Sanson's stage-craft was working well. He stood there, facing his victims across the void. He raised his hand, and every voice was stilled.

"I have called you together, citizens, upon this day," he said, "because, as you once chose freedom in place of bondage, so, now, the time has come to choose again. I have given you liberty, I have given you peace, I have enlightened you and raised you to man's true dignity. The Christians used to say that man was half ape and half that mythical vertebrate known as the angel. I have driven the ape out of you and made you all angel. That is to say, all man, standing on his own feet, not leaning against imaginary gods to prop him. It has been a difficult battle, for all the vested evils in the world have fought against me. But I have won: your God, your Christ, the superstitious, stubborn heart of man have yielded. Now the old order is ripe to perish everlastingly. There remains one more enemy—"

"Death!" screamed the shrill woman's voice. "Make us immortal in our beautiful bodies, Sanson! Give us life, everlasting life!"

"The Ant," pursued the speaker patiently.

It was an unexpected anticlimax. The crowd groaned in disappointment, and the silence that followed was of unutterable grief. That Sanson would bestow his boon upon them, all had believed. Nor had they anticipated Sanson's declaration. For the idolatrous symbol, which was all they knew of worship, had possessed itself of their imaginations, their aspirations had cleaved to it, and, as must be, what had begun as a symbol had ended as a god.

Sanson was too shrewd not to see immediately that he had struck the wrong note. He swung himself about, facing the captives on the opposite span, and his voice reverberated through the Temple.

"You have demanded sacrifices, human sacrifices," he cried, "and you shall have them, but not in honor of the Ant. There is no Ant, no God. But there is Freedom, hidden within the cylinder where she has lain since the beginnings of time, waiting for this day to dawn, now ready to emerge into a world set free. To her we sacrifice!"

He stood there, a dramatic figure, the incarnation of rebellious pride, Lucifer defying God, or some old Titan in revolt against Olympus. But, as he paused, the cracked voice of the old bishop piped through the Temple.

"But I can give you eternal life, my people," he cried clearly. "I have the Word that alone can set you free. It is the same that Bonham spoke to you in Westminster Hall while he was burning. You heard him and went home, and some were afraid, some wondered, and some forgot; but that Word never dies, and it will be told soon in a million homes, because, by God's mercy, the Russians are at hand to set you free."

The deep-breathed "Ah!" that followed was not of hate but of fear. Something was stirring in the hearts of the multitude, molding them against knowledge and will. I felt it, too: a mighty spiritual power, a Light that clove the darkness. I saw the old bishop stand out at the end of the span and shake his clenched hand at Sanson, silent, opposite.

"You cannot raise one finger save by the will of Him whom you deny, Sanson!" he said. "You are not going to make any sacrifices. You, who have raised your will against heaven, this night your soul will be required of you!"

The sense of something imminent and mighty shook my limbs. I stood up, clinging against the grille. There was no sound in all the Temple. Protagonists in the eternal drama, the bishop and Sanson faced each other.

Suddenly I perceived that the solar light above the bishop had moved. It had moved outward; and now it was approaching me. And the light above Sanson was moving, too. I understood what was happening. Sanson had quietly given the command for the bridges to be swung together.

An instant later the little lights that crossed the gloom were dissipated as ten thousand more flashed out, illumining the vast interior of the Temple. I saw the packed multitudes below, thousands on thousands, their faces upturned, each with the same stamp of fear on it, as if the same workman had carved the features. I saw the groins and arches, the gallery above me, filled with the Guard; Sanson upon one nearing bridge, his Guard about him, too; upon the other, David, Elizabeth of the slender figure and the clasped hands, and Bishop Alfred and the rest of the prisoners. I waited, my arms about Esther.

Once more I heard a single sigh float upward. Then the woman's voice that had shrieked before cried piercingly:

"The Messiah has come, who is to make us free!"

I saw Sanson stiffen and catch at the rail of the nearing bridge. I saw David, now only an arm's length from me, staring incredulous; Elizabeth with wide-open eyes, the bishop's calm face, the Guard like carven effigies.

Then, as if the power that held the populace in unison were suddenly dissolved, they broke from their places. They sprang with frantic, exultant cries toward the Ant; they formed a dozen human chains that reared themselves above the pedestal, dissolved, and poured over the golden idol. Among them I saw clusters of men — our men — with Ray rods in their hands. They poured out into the rooms that lined the passages. They swarmed up pillars and reached out hands to the captives. They howled at Sanson, whose bodyguard, closing about him, formed an impenetrable defense. The conspiracy had not miscarried.

But all were shouting at me, and the fanatic spirit of hate that Sanson had evoked seemed to have recoiled and turned on him to his destruction.

Suddenly the approaching spans stood still. They remained motionless, each end some three feet from me. Then, slowly, they began to recede.

"Jump, Arnold!" I heard David scream above the uproar.

I saw the plan to isolate me there, where none could reach me, helpless in the mid-Temple. I gath-- ered Esther high in my arms, stepped back, and sprang; I felt myself falling. Still clutching Esther with one hand, I groped in blindness with the other.

I struck the edge of the span. Hands held me; hands pulled Esther free; I stood among our friends, and behind us already the Guard was beaten backward.

I saw the tattered outlaws' figures everywhere. Only around Sanson were the Guard still potent. He saw the situation; he knew his power was crumbling as Lembken's had crumbled; and, pushing his body-guard aside, strode forward and held up his hand for silence. Even then — so great was his power — at the gesture, all motion in the Temple ceased; I saw arrested Ray rods, not yet discharged, held stiffly, limbs halted in air, necks craned toward the speaker and immobile.

"Choose, then!" Sanson called in words that rang like a trumpet's blast. "It is your supreme moment. Will you have your Messiah or will you have my gift — immortality?"

"Give us God!" screamed the woman's voice; and then a thousand and ten thousand answered him:

"Give us God!"

"The God of Bonham!"

"Our fathers' God, Whom we denied."

The people had answered truly in the supreme moment, as they must always, that the world may not cease. For, in the words of Renan, "the heart of the common people is the great reservoir of the self-devotion and resignation by which alone the world can be saved."

CHAPTER XXIV

THE maneuvers of our party had been so skilfully planned and carried out so surely that the Temple fell into our hands almost immediately. Entering upon that side which faced the Airscouts' Fortress, our men had surprised and overpowered the guards posted about the elevators, and driven them in flight toward the Science Wing, into which Sanson withdrew to rally them about him.

The Council Hall and offices beneath it were occupied as quickly. Including the Airscouts' Fortress, we had thus three-fourths of the quadrilateral in our possession; but the Guard held the Science Wing in strength, and, of course, the surrounding wall, armed with the Ray artillery and commanding everything within it.

The change of fortune was so swift that I could hardly grasp its significance immediately. Carrying Esther, and surrounded by a frenzied mob, I was dragged from the bridge to the corridor of the elevators, between Elizabeth and David, pent up among five hundred men, some carrying Ray rods and trying to force their way through the Temple in the direction of the Science Wing, others returning, realizing the impossibility of pushing through the crowds, and others, merely spectators, unarmed, who had gone mad with delirious joy. The confusion was indescribable, and, to make it worse, these people seemed to look to me for leadership, while I was caught in the throng and helpless. Precious moments were passing.

Into the mob burst a man heading a little group of revolutionists.

"Follow me!" he shouted. "To the Science Wing! Capture the bridges! Follow me!"

As he spoke the Temple lights went out. I was not yet clear of the bridge. Inch by inch I struggled onward, but in the darkness the confusion was still more undisciplined; and while the oncoming party still fought for a foothold I heard a rending, straining sound behind me, a crash of wood, and a mighty fall that set the whole building echoing. Shouts, oaths, and groans came from below; the span on which we stood shook from the concussion.

There was no need to ask what had occurred. Sanson had cut down the farther half of the bridge, securing himself against attack from the upper floor of the Temple.

Then a voice, bellowing with rage and ferocity, arose:

"Follow me! Seize the elevators! To Lembken! To the People's House!"

The mob broke and dissolved, carrying me with it into the corridor. I saw the leader with the Assyrian beard heading the rush for the elevator shafts. He carried all with him. But the shafts were empty; the elevators had been drawn up. There followed howls of fury.

"Lembken!" shrieked the mob. "Out with him! Out with the defective!"

It was queer, that word; but one impulse animated all. They plunged after their leader, scrambling up the ironwork of the interior, and clinging there like flies as they worked their way upward. The little band of disciplined men alone stood still, and their chief turned to me with a wry look.

"We are too late," he said. "Sanson has got his men together. We shall have to storm the Wing from below. Half our men have joined in that mad attack on Lembken, who is helpless, whereas Sanson—"

He shrugged his shoulders in despair. Then David turned to me.

"You must bring them back, Arnold," he said. "They will obey and follow you. Leave Esther—"

He saw the look on my face, and began to plead with me. "It is your duty, Arnold." he cried. "All will be lost unless you can draw off our men from the Palace. I will protect her with my life." He bent down and looked into Esther's face, and an

expression of amazement came upon his own. It
occurred to me afterward that he had never believed
that Esther really lived. But at the time only the
thought of this flickered through my brain, and it
yielded to more urgent ones.

"They will follow you!" cried David.

I hesitated no longer. I placed Esther's unconscious body in Elizabeth's arms, and, without stopping to glance at her, lest it sap my resolution,
I plunged into the shaft and began to scramble
upward.

Somehow I reached the summit. I fell upon my
hands within the Palace. The mob was swarming
everywhere, in every room, it seemed, and through
the gardens. I ran out under the dome. The winter
sun shone through a gray fog, a blood-red ball of
fire.

The yelling mob swept through the groves. Its
fury was unleashed, and the remembered wrongs of
years impelled it to universal destruction. I saw at
the first glance that these men were beyond the power
of argument. With their bare hands they tore up
palms and tossed them down into the courts through
jagged holes in the transparent walls. They tore the
panes out of their settings, twisting the thin, un-
splintering glass until it writhed everywhere, coiled,
crystal snakes among the uprooted flowers. They
spared nothing. The yellow orange spheres gleamed

in the rank grass.   The scent of orange flowers was choking.

I ran among them, calling on them to follow me back, for the sake of our cause, to join their comrades, hard pressed by Sanson.   Most of them did not seem to hear me; some raised their heads from their work, stared at me for a moment, and resumed their wild task of ruin.   It came to me then that I was unknown to them.   Not one in a hundred of these men had seen my face more than a moment or two upon the altar platform.

I turned and ran through the Palace rooms, still calling, and still unheeded.   The mob was sweeping onward like an avalanche.   They had torn the costly hangings from the walls.   From the blue rooms, mull rooms, red rooms, purple rooms, all the baroque, fantastic, and depraved trappings of Lembken's gleaning were heaped into great rolls at which the furious army hacked and tore.   In one place it was venting its rage upon a heap of masquerade clothing. Pieces were flung from man to man, and some, tearing great rents in garments, thrust their heads through them and continued in the pursuit, with skirts about their shoulders and leopard skins about their bodies.   A tun of wine had overturned and spilled, and the contents crept like a rivulet along the floor, seeping from room to room.   The conduit that fed the artificial brooks, being slashed, poured out a muddy stream that dogged our heels, befouling the slashed rugs and tattered coverlets. And ever the cries became more furious.

The mob was yelling with one universal voice. Palm trees were hurled from man to man, clods of earth clung to walls, mud spattered everything. I followed, breathless, imploring, pleading in vain. No one paid me the least attention. Some, indeed, scowled at me, but the spirit of destruction, seizing them before the words were framed on their lips, hurled them along. They swept me with them. At the head was the giant, bellowing in frantic wrath. The mob followed him, hypnotized; and he, armed with a spiked stanchion which he must have wrenched from some portion of the wall supports, dashed the weapon in furious assault against each door, and shattered it, leading the chase down every corridor of the bewildering place, returning, hot on the scent, dog-like, and the great arms thrashing the club from side to side.

The Palace was enormous. We had not covered half of it, and we had seen no one. But, as we ran, shouts came from another party behind us, roars mingled with shrieks, and, keening above all clamor, I heard that bloodhound cry that breaks from human throats when the death hunt draws near to its finale.

With an answering roar our mob turned and

sprang toward its victims, smashing down doors and wrenching weapons from legs of tables and woodwork of the walls. The quarry was found. Like bolting hares they turned and scuttled into the small, hidden room, where they cowered, women and negro eunuchs, still dressed in the masquerade of the revels that Lembken had held that night even while his empire was breaking from his hand. Horned women, women in dominoes, in striped and spotted hides, Elizabethans wearing hooped skirts and huge, starched neck frills, Victorian girls with parasols and corseted bodies, a motley, cowering crew, less abject only than the cringing blacks, eyed their pursuers with terror-stricken looks that sought their eyes for pity and found only hatred.

The giant leaped out before his followers and whirled his spiked club. "Where is Lembken?" he roared. "Where are his men?" All the while his eyes searched the women's faces; but he did not find her whom he sought.

"There are no men," a frightened woman gasped. "There were never any but Lembken. We have never seen any others in our lives."

He had lied to me, then, when he spoke of his friends. How long would he have endured me there before the poisoned cup came to me? I felt my own hate and wrath become implacable as that of the mob.

The giant clutched at a cringing negro boy and

The giant leaped out before his fo

"re is Lembken?" he roared. "Where
"

pulled him from his knees. "Where is he?" he shouted.

The boy was tongue-tied with fear. But a girl stepped forth bravely. "That way!" she said, pointing toward a door.

The mob whirled through in a torrent, following the Assyrian-bearded giant. I heard their shouts grow fainter. The women bolted, scattering through the dismantled rooms, seeking some other refuge. But one of them stopped and then came toward me quickly.

"She lied! He is there," she whispered, pointing toward a wall. "Kill him, but whisper my name in his ear before he dies."

I looked at the girl and recognized Coral, the maid who had supplanted Amaranth. I turned quickly toward the wall, and my eyes discovered the hidden door, flush with the wall. I burst it open and ran through.

I raced along a winding passage, hearing the mob's cries far away as they ran on the false scent they had taken up. I emerged suddenly upon a little platform fronting a part of the crystal wall that was still standing in the rear of the Palace. The mob had not yet found the approaches to this secret refuge.

A glass gateway within the wall stood open, and outside, at rest in the air, I saw the dark airplane, with Hancock at the wheel. And at the gate, hesitating to set his feet upon the narrow plank that led to safety, was Lembken. His arms were filled with bundles, and on his shoulder a monkey perched, mouthing and gibbering. At his side kneeled a young girl, with hands clasped, urging Lembken to flight.

The old man heard me and turned around. I saw Hancock start forward, raise a Ray rod, and aim it at me. But Lembken stood in the way, and he could not fire.

The girl leaped at me, clutching me by the arms with surprising strength, and crying to Lembken to fly. But the obese old man only stared into my face. Fear seemed to have paralyzed him. He did not remember me, but my presence seemed to awaken some association in his mind, and, as I watched, I saw it flash into consciousness.

"Jacquette!" he screamed in a tremulous falsetto. "I have forgotten her. I must go back for her."

He scrambled past me, and the girl, releasing me, ran after him. I followed. On we ran, till Lembken turned into a tiny room, once meant to be a hiding place, no doubt, but now doorless and bare. Again I heard the shouting. The mob was drawing near.

On a perch beside the entrance sat the gaudy macaw, head on one side, preening her plumage.

"The people's friend!" she cackled. "The peo-

ple's friend! Friend — friend — friend —friend —
frien —"

With a cry of delight Lembken snatched at her.
She fluttered to his shoulder. He turned, and, with
monkey and bird against his sagging cheeks, he began
to make his way along the passage. As he ran I saw
another corridor at right angles to this, and, at the
end, daylight and the waste of uprooted palms. The
mob was sweeping past. They saw him; they
howled and dashed to cut off his flight.

Lembken saw them, doubled back, dashing in panic
from room to room. The mob was everywhere about
him, searching for him, blocking all exits; their
howls were a continuous sound.

They were upon him. Lembken fell on his knees
and pulled a Ray rod from his robes. With shaking,
nerveless fingers he forced up the guard. He held
it to his breast; but it fell from his hand.

"Kill me!" he muttered to the girl.

She flung her arms about him; and thus the mob
found them.

The giant leaped at them. His bellowings shook
the walls. He sprang for Lembken, caught him by
the throat, and forced his head upward. I saw the
loose spike in his hand. The monkey chattered, the
parrot stretched out her neck and snapped, shrieking
her phrases. Between the men the frail girl wrestled,
dashing her weak fists into the giant's face.

The roaring mob choked the narrow corridor on either side. "Death to him!" they shrieked. "Death! Death!"

The old man caught the words upon his tongue and screamed.

"Not death!" he yelped. "I'm Lembken. I can't die. I never thought of death — dying — going nowhere — nowhere — nothing — I want to live — "

He cowered behind the girl, thrusting her between himself and his enemy. So furious were her struggles that she forced the giant away. She dashed her fists into his eyes again and again, until he turned on her and gripped her by the wrists, twisting her backward. He looked into her face for the first time.

"Let him go!" she screamed. "Don't hurt him. He is old — he is old — he has done no harm — he is the people's friend — he has told me so — I love him —"

The giant dropped her wrists and staggered back. His horror-painted face became a tragic mask. He moaned, and his hands groped impotently in the air for something that he failed to find. It was not the blood in his eyes that blinded him. For this was she whom he had sought, torn from his home, the last to share Lembken's favor, the child whom I had seen dragged from the Council Hall, her innocent child's heart loyal in his last hour to the only lover she knew.

It wrung my heart, the pity of it: this blossom of love that sprang from that festering, rank soil of human baseness.

The next instant the mob swept over us. They seized their prey and stamped out the life beneath their feet. I saw the quivering body tossed high in the air and dashed from wall to wall, trampled on, hacked, and torn. I saw it poised against the crystal walls, saw the dark airplane swoop to safety amid a hail of Ray fire; and then the air was filled with zig-zag flashes of blinding light.

CHAPTER XXV

THE COMING OF THE CROSS

I STOOD with a small group of our men beneath the dome, where Lembken's gardens had been. The havoc that had been wrought is almost indescribable. The beauty molded by the most cunning hands in Europe had been obliterated in one short hour. The gardens were a waste of uprooted trees and trampled earth, while from the broken conduit a dozen muddy streams were pouring like high waterfalls upon the courts below. The Palace was a mass of wreckage, in which the mob still moved, shouting for fire to finish the work of destruction.

I had been recognized at last, and we were searching for our men among the rabble, gathering the nucleus of a force to render aid to our party, hard-pressed, below. I had managed to achieve something at last: I had detailed a dozen men with Ray rods to guard the women. That was all I could accomplish.

The ground about the Temple was already strewn with blackened, twisted figures. From the conical Ray guns on the enclosing walls swept sheets of blinding flame, a soundless cannonade that pecked at the interstices in the walls of the Temple and of the

Airscouts' Fortress, seeking for some unpainted spot between the blocks of stone, some small, abraded surface where the cold Rays might find lodgment. I heard the crumbling of disintegrating mortar and saw fragments of stone flying from cornice and pediment. Soon gaps would open and the whole splendid pile tumble into a heap of shapeless ruins.

The Rays flashed to and fro like brilliant lightning. I was half blinded; all I could discern was that Sanson still held the Science Wing, from whose windows the Guard were picking off our men beneath them. I surmised from the shouting that we were attacking the Wing from the ground floor of the Temple.

We had gathered most of our men together, and we plunged for the elevator shafts and scrambled down. My pulses hammered with fear as I entered the corridor below. But there stood David, and Elizabeth kneeled beside him, with Esther's head in her lap. She looked at me and smiled with so brave an effort that I realized her own anxiety. Somewhere in the deadly tumult Paul was fighting, unless, indeed, he lay among those shapeless masses that strewed the courts.

Our men swept by me and poured along the corridor toward the bridge.

"I have fulfilled my promise, Arnold," said David. "Now I must take Elizabeth within the shelter of

the Airscouts' Fortress, and you will follow with
Esther. Then each of us must do his best to rally
parties to the assault. All is not going well, Arnold.
Our Ray rods are emptying fast, and the storage
batteries within the Airscouts' Fortress have been
destroyed, so that we cannot recharge them; the
attack upon the lower level of the Wing has failed.
Sanson has placed a Ray gun there. All hangs upon
the battleplanes, and they have not returned."

He put his arm about his daughter and hurried
her toward the bridge, while I picked up Esther, still
plunged in that first sleep, and followed him. I saw
him lead Elizabeth to safety, but as I was about to
follow, a sheet of purple light swept past me, tearing
a stanchion from the bridge and knocking down a
part of the brick house on the wall above, where
Lembken had taken me that night of our first
meeting.

A gun was playing on the bridge. It was impossible to cross at present. I drew back, waiting.

Then a babel of cries broke out on the opposite
side, so fierce and wild that, grasping Esther more
tightly, I rushed to a window at the further end of
the corridor, commanding a view of the exterior
courts. The long bridges were packed with our men,
making a mad sortie to scale the enclosing walls.
Streaks of light, pitiably thin, flashed from their
Ray rods, and, with exultant shouts, the Guard

sprang forward to meet them. They were dragging lighter Ray guns behind them. For an instant it seemed as if the revolutionists would scale the walls before the heavy Ray artillery could be reaimed at them. The foremost files of the opposing forces clashed and surged and swayed in a rain of meteor flashes. The blackened corpses heaped the bridges, hung, toppled over, and went to swell the heaps below. Then, with a renewed outburst of shouting, the Guard drove back the attack and placed their guns.

The blinding flashes swept the bridges, playing like ribands of silvery blue along the course of their discharge. Everywhere along the bridges swarmed the stampede of flight, checked where the Rays caught the fugitives and twisted them into charred lumps, sweeping away the superstructure also, and the bridge rails. I saw one bridge go down, as a deflected Ray wrenched it from its piers. It spewed its burden upon the stones below, and from among the dead, little figures leaped up and began to run for refuge toward the Council Wing; and there a blast from a Ray gun found them, and the heavy doors crumbled upon them, and wood and men were ground into the same pulpy blackness. The Ray had found the weak spots of the great buildings, and from the Temple top huge stones came crashing down, rebounding along the courts and splintering into fragments. Clouds of dust rose up like smoke from conflagrations.

The flowing tide of the Guard's victory rolled on unchecked. Their shouts were frightful. They held the courts, now piled with debris from the buildings above them. I ran with Esther back toward the bridge, crossed it, and gained the shelter of the Air-scouts' Fortress. Before me was a flight of stone steps; I ran up, shouting. Nobody answered me. I gained the summit and found myself alone there.

Looking down from the roof I saw that the Guard were swarming in the Temple. They had regained that; they had driven our men from the Airscouts' Fortress, on which I stood, trapped, since it was impossible to cross the courts. Where were our forces? I saw the locust cloud of attack break against the doors of the offices beneath the Council Hall. That was our last stronghold. The Ray flashes played on the walls, but they held fast.

Then out of the south a flock of giant birds came wheeling. They swooped toward us and resolved themselves into the airplane fleet. They dipped their luminous wings and circled around us, and a mazy pattern of light shot downward upon the ranks of the Guard.

The battleplanes had settled their differences, and three-fourths of them had returned to fight for us.

I saw the Guard race back for their sheltering

walls. The Ray artillery shot upward to meet the challenge of the battleplanes. To and fro overhead wheeled the great shining birds in soundless duel. The conflict appeared the more frightful because of this silence. Only those at the guns knew what was happening.

But presently, as the flock wheeled, I saw one tower like a shot pheasant and then tumble. It plunged into the court and lay, a shapeless mass, upon the stones. The Ray gun had found its defenseless parts as it maneuvered. A second battleplane came hurtling down. It struck the Temple wall, seemed to cling there like a bat, and, fluttering like a dying thing, plunged to the stones beside its shattered mate.

The Guard was winning. The enclosing walls stood fast. Our last hope seemed to be gone. The sun was dipping into the west.

I dared not carry Esther through that fire-swept zone. It was my plan, should Sanson's men reoccupy the Airscouts' Fortress, to seek refuge within the little, half-secret room where Jones had hidden us. Meanwhile I waited on the roof, behind the glow-painted shield of a single empty airplane that was resting there. Twilight fell, and the soundless fight went on. The battleplanes were circling higher, and their fire was utterly ineffective. I judged, from its growing infrequency, that their solar batteries were becoming emptied. Meanwhile our men, pent in the council offices, waited for the finale.

Hourly our situation grew more desperate. Another battleplane went down. The game was in Sanson's hands after all. Our only chance had been in the surprise, and the mad rush to the People's House and the confusion in the Temple had spoiled all plans and allowed our enemy to concentrate his men. Where was he, I wondered.

Suddenly shouts broke out again from the walls, and were caught up and echoed back from the Council Hall. Southward, high in the sky, pin-points of light appeared, like vagrant stars, which became larger, wheeled, extended.

The Guard cheered frantically. I heard the cry "America!"

If this was the Mormon fleet, come to aid Lembken, there was no doubt with which side it would join. Perhaps the Guard knew already that Sanson had outwitted Lembken and outbid him for its support.

The airfleet snot upward, drew together, and a single light, detaching itself, flew like a rocket upward, moving in the direction of the oncoming battleplanes, which seemed to hang poised above, like a new group of Pleiades. The rocket's apparent speed dwindled, until it seemed to move as slowly as any star. I saw a second light shoot downward, detaching itself from those clustered orbs, to meet it. I held my breath, as all must have done, for not a Ray was fired, nor was there any sound as the fate of the world hung upon those nearing points. They circled about each other, a binary star; they moved together; and suddenly they plunged downward, the whole oncoming fleet following them, and the roar of a thousand throats rang from the Council Hall:

"The Russians! The Russians! The Tsar! The Tsar!"

The lights grew larger and resolved themselves into the glow parallelograms again, and the great fleet of battleplanes descended toward the wall. Again the pattern of light interplayed with the answering fire from the Ray artillery of the Guard.

The new squadron was armed with Rays almost as strong, taken in Stockholm, and worked by Swedish gunners. Searchlights and glow rays blended in heliotrope and pink and blue, playing about the walls, carrying the most murderous death that man had ever devised. And it appeared incredible that death lay hidden within that warp and woof of color that intercrossed through space, blending and twisting, and forming a thousand patterns upon the night. Once a battleplane, caught as she wheeled, came crashing down; but the next moment the persistent Ray found an unprotected place in the walls at last, and hammered at it, dislodging mortar and stones, till, with a mighty roar, a tower fell toppling into the court, leaving a great breach in the Guard's fortress.

Instantly two battleplanes lit like great birds, and behind their shields a score of men swarmed out, carrying swords and Ray shields, interlocked. The line swept onward, to encounter the Ray rods of the defense. I saw it crumple and twist. But other battleplanes had alighted along the breach, and everywhere small groups were forming between the Ray guns, which could not be aimed before they were attacked, the gunners sabered, and the great conical machines made useless. The valor which had overthrown the Federation's troops before Tula was not helpless here.

But from each wing a blast of fire caught the downward swooping battleplanes and crumpled them. No attack could live before that devastating crossfire. I saw the groups of swordsmen wither, fall back, until the bodies heaped before them, on which they planted their glow shields, formed an impregnable rampart. But the artillery was retaken, the battleplanes, surprised and broken in the ebb-tide of defeat, were piled in indistinguishable heaps within the courts. The Guard turned the artillery upon the stubborn line that mounted the breach. Once more the fortune of the day was turning.

I saw the ragged figures of our men run from the

Upon the walls the Guard were swa
R

the defenders. Out of their midst the
hed

Council Hall across the courts. Then the Guard about Sanson in the Science Wing streamed forth to meet them. The Ray rods flashed, and the ghastly murder began once more.

Upon the walls the Guard were swarming toward the defenders. Out of their midst the Ray artillery belched. It found the chinks among the shields, and a sheet òf white flame swept through the Russians' ranks. Their wall of interlocked shields had carried them into death's jaws, but now the jaws were closing. I closed my eyes in anguish.

I opened them in darkness.

There was no flash from the conical guns, which glittered in impotence upon the walls. For an instant I did not understand. The next I knew. Jones had cut the supply cables in the Vosges Mountains. He had kept his promise, and in the moment of defeat.

The same mad exultation seized all. I heard the new note of victory as our men from the Council Hall bore back the defeated remnants of Sanson's army. I saw the Russians leap from behind their shields and swarm into the fortress; saw the flash of their swords against the spurting fire of the Ray rods; saw the defeated Guard fly through the courts, to meet death there.

Then I stood face to face with Sanson.

CHAPTER XXVI

THE ADMIRAL OF THE AIR

I SAW defeat written upon his face, but there was no sign of fear. He stood alone, unarmed, confronting me, and if he had fled when he saw that his cause was lost I do him the justice to believe it was his undaunted will which drove him to flight, that he might plan new havoc for the world.

No chance remained for him. By the glare of the searchlights I saw the last vestige of rout end at the Temple doors. Trapped and surrounded, the Guard begged for quarter. This was accorded them; but instantly the prisoners were lost to sight in the presence of the enormous multitudes that came from London, swarming into the courts.

Sanson's gaze shifted from my face to Esther's, and, as if she felt the man's presence, she stirred, and her eyelids unclosed.

"Arnold!" she whispered.

"Yes, dear," I answered, bending over her.

"I dreamed that—they had run up the annex thirty stories, Arnold, and painted it shining white."

"You must sleep and dream no more," I told her. She murmured and her eyelids closed. Again the kindly unconsciousness of sleep held her.

I placed her against the anchored airplane and turned to Sanson. He was facing me with that strange and half-quizzical look that I remembered so well. It had in it more of humanity than the expression of any other of his moods.

"Arnold," he said softly, "if I were an ignorant man I might be tempted to believe that there is a God, sometimes."

And that was his way also, to speak of other things in moments of imminent alarm.

"Why?" I inquired.

"Because He is so merciful to His defectives, Arnold. To think that you, with your missing five centimeters, should have defeated me!

"Come," he continued, clapping his hand on my shoulder. "A truce for a few minutes. A truce, for the sake of our old friendship. You are not to blame for your share in this night's ruin of civilization. You were the victim of circumstances. And then— you are a defective and could not understand. Arnold, I have never had any friend but you. And sometimes I feel the need of one. Even the gods felt that, and I am far from a god, though, later, perhaps . . . ."

He broke off and resumed, after a short pause:

"Join me. Here is my frank proposal: join me, and, since indeed I would not hold any woman against her will, if Esther chooses you she shall be

yours. This night has undone the labor of many
years, but those that are past are but as a drop of
water in an ocean to those which are to come. I
have the secret of immortal life at last—not ghostly
life in some gold-decorated heaven, but life in the
flesh. I will bestow the gift on you—"

"Let it die with you," I answered passionately.

He laughed.

"This night's work, which seems so wonderful
tó you, is but an episode," he said. "Come with me
to America, Arnold. In six months I can build up
my world anew. I shall be less scrupulous and
humane in the future with this miserable mob. No
moron shall live, no defective go free. I have resolved that. Man can rise only by crushing out
weakness and setting himself upon the necks of those
who were born to serve. In six months America
will be mine; in twelve, the world. From this time
onward it is a battle to the death against all that
retards the human race."

His features flushed with the energy of his voice.
I looked at him, almost in admiration. I was dum-
founded at the audacity of his designs. Trapped
here, a prisoner upon the fortress roof, his life
already gone when he was found, this man of sixty
years planned his universal empire. He was mad,
beyond doubt, mad enough to dream impossible
things and make them his in his brain's fertile king-

dom; and it was such madness as moves mountains.

"Sanson, I will do this much for you," I said. "I will hide you from the mob's fury in a little room near this roof, so that you may not be torn in pieces. I will assure you a fair trial at the hands of the new government. That is all I can promise."

Would this dream vanish in the realization of fact? I saw his face fall, as if he had come to understand his position at last.

"Where is it?" he said presently. He spoke slowly, and in a bewildered manner, as if he were still struggling with his dreams.

I took him by the arm and led him to the elevator entrance. "It is a little room under the roof," I said. "The elevator passes it, but it is hardly more than a hole in the wall. One would not look for you there."

I pressed the button, but of course the elevator did not ascend, since the solar power was cut off.

Sanson withdrew his arm from mine. I saw him assume a listening attitude. "Arnold!" he cried weakly, "they are coming! Listen!"

As I relaxed my guard, he dealt me a buffet that sent me flying down the empty shaft.

I had a confused consciousness of falling through space, of clutching at the shaft walls; and then I was upon my knees, bruised and staring up at the light overhead.

Fortunately the elevator had stopped a few feet from the top. Still dazed, I sprang to my feet and began scrambling up the ironwork. At last I staggered out upon the roof once more. I saw a dozen Sansons, each of whom carried Esther in his arms.

I tried to force reality into these visions, to snatch the living Sanson from among that crowd of ghosts. But they had sprung into the dozen airplanes that lay upon the swaying roof top. A touch of the starting lever, a half turn of the wheel, and as my power of vision came back to me I saw Sanson rise with Esther into the air. He held her on the seat against him, the arm that encircled her controlling the wheel, and he was gone into the heart of the giant moon that was just rising in the east, blood-red behind her veil of clouds.

I stared after him. The airplane was rapidly diminishing in size. He had outwitted me at the last, by one of those clumsy tricks he loved, such as a schoolboy plays.

I staggered toward the edge. I was minded to fling myself down on the stones below. One more victim of the day's work would mean nothing, and doubtless David and Elizabeth believed that I had died long ago. I tottered upon the brink; but then a shadow glided toward me, and a small airplane stopped at my side. It was unshielded, and at the prow was a pair of the elongated jaws. Air-Admiral Hancock leaned out of it toward me.

"Where is Sanson?" he asked quietly. "He was here. He was seen here."

I pointed into the west, where the parallelogram of light was diminishing to an irregular star. I leaped into the plane beside him. "Take me with you!" I cried. "He has stolen Esther — the goddess of the cylinder."

Hancock said nothing but touched the lever. Instantly we shot upward and raced like a swallow across the void, skimming and dipping as the wind caught us and the heavy prow plunged through the unequal air-banks.

The buildings drew together beneath us. The shouts of the multitude grew faint and died. The luminous point in the west grew larger, and against the sky, now whitened by the rising moon, I saw the dark body between the glow lines, as one sees a ship at sea from a mountain top. Sanson was heading southward, perhaps with the intent of reaching France and rallying the forces of the Federation there. We mounted higher. The forests stretched beneath us. Always we mounted. I cast a glance at Hancock's face. There was a look on it that boded ill for Sanson. I was trying to remember something that Jones had told me about him, but my own anxious thoughts beat down the elusive memory. I, too, felt that there would be no mercy for Sanson when the accounts were squared.

Would anyone have mercy? I saw the answer to that question swiftly, for, looking back, I saw two lanes of airships, strung out behind, like flying geese, converging toward our leadership. Battleplanes, scoutplanes, dark against the brightening heaven, came hot on the chase. They were in pursuit of the common enemy of the human race, and there was none among them, no man in London but had some outrage to avenge.

We mounted higher through the bitter cold. My hands were numb, but Hancock kept his wheel, seated there, a grim, immovable, resolute figure. Now we burst into the heart of a fierce, rocking snowstorm, which blotted out the fugitive; but by some instinct Hancock seemed to know his course, and he held it surely till we rose above the storm and saw the glow parallelogram nearer.

Sanson rose too. He must have sighted us and resolved to test his endurance against ours. We were in air so rarefied that I was choking for breath. The moon rode high; dawn was not far away. We were rushing toward the sea, which lay, a blur of inky blackness, underneath, edged by the white line of the chalk cliffs of the south shore. We were gaining steadily.

But Sanson did not mean to cross the Channel.

The giant jaws upon our aircraft gaped. I saw steel teeth
within them

I do not know what new scheme he had conceived; perhaps he meant to turn and seek some English city where he could defy the new order and reorganize the old. He wheeled; and the long line of the pursuing planes, struggling upward, wheeled together, trying to cut off his flight. He mounted still and struck out eastward. But, with a furious downward swoop Hancock drove in toward him. I could see Sanson sitting at the wheel, his arm still clasping Esther. He stopped in the air and waited for our approach.

"What do you want?" he shouted.

The tone of Hancock's voice was implacable. "My son, Sanson," he answered.

He wheeled away, and, as he turned placed his hand on a lever. The giant jaws upon our aircraft gaped. I saw steel teeth within them. We dashed for Sanson with terrific force. I shouted in horror, laying my fingers upon Hancock's sleeve and pointing to Esther. But Hancock did not seem to hear or feel me, perhaps he·had never known that I was there; all his mind seemed intent on the accomplishment of his deadly purpose. He drove home before his enemy could evade his course, and like a hawk we plunged, struck Sanson's vessel amidships, and smashed through steel and glow shield.

One instant, in the dead interval of the stopped momentum, we rested motionless together, the gaping jaws choked with their meal and fast within the heart of Sanson's plane. I flung myself across the side, grasped Esther, held her in my arms, and dragged her across our bows. Then Hancock leaped at Sanson's throat.

Our airplane tipped, righted herself, and drifted away. I did not know how to steer or guide, but Hancock must automatically have locked the mechanism to the halt, for we drifted idly, balancing upon the wind. Watching, I saw the two struggling in Sanson's plane.

She shuddered as she hung poised there, mortally gashed, yet fighting still for her dominion of the air. She quivered from prow to stern, and then, of her own accord, shot upward. Up she went till she was but a dark blot in the sky. Then from above something came falling toward the earth, plunged like a projectile, and disappeared.

I saw a tiny figure standing on the doomed airplane alone, and, infinitely small though it appeared, I knew that it was Sanson. I fancied I could see the man's proud bearing; I thought his arms were folded across his breast. The moonlight gilded him, and others have told me that he seemed to ride through the air resplendent, as if transfigured by some demoniac power.

He stood like Lucifer, high above all the world, over his wrecked dominion. I picture his disdain, and the contempt for man with which he shrouded himself in that last moment. The world had broken him in the end, but his colossal spirit could never be quenched.

Then the air vessel plunged into the moon's heart and vanished.

CHAPTER XXVII

THE NEW ORDER

THREE months have passed. It is Easter Day, and we have only begun to struggle with the difficulties before us.

But we are working with a faith that will overcome all obstacles. All the world is at work, for the same impulse was felt simultaneously in every land. The Mormon airplanes never arrived, because, practically at the same hour, America rose in revolt against her masters. And the Sanson régime has been swept away forever.

We were rescued from our airplane by the airscouts who had followed us, and brought back to London. Our friends, who had thought us dead, were overjoyed at our return. It was a wonderful reunion, with not a shadow to mar it, for Paul had passed uninjured through the fighting and was there to welcome us. And gradually, when she awoke, we broke the news of everything to Esther.

The amazing thing about it was that she was much more calm in learning the truth than we were in telling it. She accepted our statements almost as commonplaces of history.

I call to mind the second huge public gathering

312

on the day after the Revolution, when the dread of massacre had proved unfounded. The populace had been taught to believe that the Russians were blood-thirsty savages, instead of which we discovered child-like enthusiasts. It was a shock to most of us to discover that they considered themselves Crusaders, upon a mission to restore Christ to the world. I recall vividly the great red crosses on the breasts of their white uniforms, the icon banners that are still flapping everywhere; then the people's wonder and terror at the horses; lastly the young Tsar's entrance into the capital, to attend the reconsecration of the Temple, and the amazing influence of kingship upon a crowd that had never known reverence or loyalty, except through fear.

Then the universal joy at the release of all the inmates of the defectives and moron shops, the tears and shouts that accompanied the restoration to their families, of those who had been believed lost forever; husbands and wives, parents and children, brothers and sisters, friends and friends. No one was afraid to be glad. It was as if a dark cloud had rolled away and disclosed the sun.

And the astonishment and enthusiasm as the people listened to the teachings of Christianity. After three months there are still crowds at all the street corners, hearing the doctrines and the story of Christ from priests and missionaries.

And Bishop Alfred: at the consecration, when, stepping forward to declare himself, he found, to his surprise and dismay, that the secret of his surname, which he had vowed never to reveal until that day, had passed forever from his own memory. And how proudly he redeemed himself with his ancient title, Alfred London.

There is so much to do, and only a tithe of it has been begun. Indeed, it would have been impossible, but for the agreement that the old national boundaries should be restored, and each State work out its problems independently. Then there was the question as to the composition of the new government, and it was resolved that the committee should avail themselves to the utmost of the established order, eliminating all cruelties. Thus, for the present, because no better scheme can come forth, readymade, from human brains, the socialized State will continue. It would be impossible to go back to the old days of competition, and we shall never return to those days of squalor, poverty, and destitution, recognizing that, if ever revolution was justified, our fathers' was against the commercial greed of a materialistic world.

The hardest part of this problem will be to steer a course between the corruption of Social Democracy and the tyranny of Social Autocracy. But we have an ideal in the separation of wealth from power,

the latter to be the attribute of the few who are born
and fit to rule, the former the possession of the
bulk of the nation. Whatever our judges, their
office will be for life, and they will be appointed and
not elected.

In time custom will crystallize into laws again;
but, since the existing laws were too cruel to survive, and the old are too arbitrary and antiquated
to be renewed, we choose to exist law-free rather
than live by paper schemes.

But if we are tolerant and lax, so that we resemble
more a benevolent anarchy than an organized State,
we have set our faces like flint against two things.
First of these comes divorce. It will be recognized
under no circumstances whatever; and so far is this
from being considered tyrannous that the vast bulk
of the people never desired it. In the old days it
was the shameful privilege of a small caste alone —
that same caste that, by abandoning its duties and
responsibilities and cutting free from the Catholic.
conception of civilization, brought down the old
order. We are convinced that the permanence of
the marriage bond is the foundation of every society
of free people.

The second is eugenics. Looking back, we see
how this madness over-ran the world until, within a
century from the time of its inception, it had enslaved
humanity. The theory of Galton, that because the

university-trained son of a distinguished man became distinguished, while the illiterate son of a burglar died unknown, ability is inherited, may have appealed powerfully to our ancestors, but to us it is symptomatic of that inability to reason which we think characterized the twentieth century. Eugenics was the natural product of a time which, steeped in materialism, laughed at the belief in a human soul, or its concomitant, that each soul needed to work out its earthly pilgrimage in a body adapted to its abilities. But even from the material viewpoint we see that the movement was fallacious. We know that the proportion of those afflicted with inherited maladaptations has remained constant through history; moreover, since there was no human norm, the demands of the eugenists increased continually, till they had bound nine-tenths of the world to their hideous Juggernaut car.

So the first act after our victory was to burn the Bureaux of Prints and Indexes and Pedigrees and Relationships. That was our only vandalism.

But more than everything we hold to Christianity as the foundation of our State. We see now that the nineteenth and twentieth centuries were the worst since pagan times. Our ancestors read, without qualms, of negroes burned at the stake, of equatorial nations massacred, not in excess of misplaced zeal, as heretics, but only for — rubber! We know that without Christian ethics human nature is back in the days of Rome, Bagdad, and Carthage. We hope that there will be established, as in the olden days, Christian orders of young men, who shall serve three years in them before they come of age, bound by the triple vow, to fight these renascent wrongs where-ever they can be found.

Having found truth once more, we are not greatly troubled by doctrines. The critical investigation which destroyed the Protestant theory of the Bible's literal inspiration has only strengthened the older claim of the universal Church to be herself the re-pository of truth. Not rejecting the claims of criti-cism, we feel the living truth of Christianity so far to transcend its theological garb that, if the formula has been misstated, many would revise it. The con-sensus of opinion is, however, that the minds which drew up the Apostles' and Nicene creeds arrived as nearly as possible at a correct formula.

But the Visible Church is humble in her hour of success. She feels no triumph. Reverently, peni-tently, at the huge consecration meeting in the Temple her leaders asked for guidance and inspira-tion. At present sectarianism inspires in us the same horror that schism inspired centuries ago. The first act was to reunite the ancient Greek and English churches by omitting from the Creed that clause beginning "proceeding from," which had, it was felt, no significance that was essential. The next will be to negotiate with the Vatican for union. But the stupendous difficulties of this reconciliation are acknowledged.

The Age of Faith is coming back to the world, and, as in that splendid twelfth century, when it was in its zenith, there is a sense of youth in us. We feel that we are upon the threshold of a new epoch, uniting the triumphs of every preceding age. It is an age of joy, and will be vitalized by that art which, since the Reformation, has been sundered from human life. Its first achievement will be the magnificent cathedral that is to rise upon the site of the old Ant Temple. It will be a new world indeed. We know each age has its own cruelties and wrongs: the Inquisition of the sixteenth century; religious massacres in the seventeenth; in the nineteenth factory slavery and the prisons with their silent cells. We do not hope greatly to lessen this sum of suffering. There will be injustice always, new wrongs will arise, new evils that must be fought; but we believe the Christian norm will always remain with us as a corrective.

Tomorrow bands of axemen are to leave London to settle Kent and Surrey. Paul and Elizabeth are to go, and later Esther and I intend to follow them. David will join us when he can be spared from his work in the government.

It is Easter Day, and in the consecrated Temple I hear the anthem rise:

"Christ our Passover is sacrificed for us; therefore let us keep the feast:

"Not with the old leaven, nor with the leaven of malice and wickedness: but with the unleavened bread of sincerity and truth.

"Christ being raised from the dead dieth no more: death hath no more dominion over him."

The crowds in the great courts are kneeling. I kneel with Esther among them. We know that the sacrifice has leavened the world with truth that shall never pass away.